Y0-BYZ-849

----------- ★ -----------

He was still in the resting room ten minutes later when I emerged from the pool area: a mountain of blubber lying beneath a white cotton sheet that rose and fell with his wheezing breath. The table next to his was empty and I lay down on it.

I lay there, wrapped up and steaming like an enchilada. Sweat poured off my skin. I drifted off for a while.

I suddenly realized something was missing. The room was silent.

Quarry's wheezing had stopped.

I hadn't heard him leave. I pushed myself up from the table and turned to him.

He lay there. He was absolutely still. In the center of his chest, surrounded by an irregular stain of bright scarlet, a transparent rectangular chunk of plastic jutted up at an angle from the sheet, like an electric switch set to Off.

----------- ★ -----------

"Satterthwait has a sharp eye for the absurdities of Santa Fe culture." —*El Paso Times*

"...there are plenty of surprises, bizarre characters..." —*New Mexican*

"...neither a nuance of eccentricity nor a ray of regional color gets past the observant author..." —*New York Times*

Also available from Worldwide Mystery by
WALTER SATTERTHWAIT

A FLOWER IN THE DESERT
AT EASE WITH THE DEAD
WALL OF GLASS

Walter Satterthwait

The Hanged Man

WORLDWIDE.®

TORONTO • NEW YORK • LONDON
AMSTERDAM • PARIS • SYDNEY • HAMBURG
STOCKHOLM • ATHENS • TOKYO • MILAN
MADRID • WARSAW • BUDAPEST • AUCKLAND

THE HANGED MAN

A Worldwide Mystery/August 1995

First published by St. Martin's Press, Incorporated.

ISBN 0-373-26173-X

Copyright © 1993 by Walter Satterthwait.

ACKNOWLEDGMENTS

In Amsterdam, thanks to Anne Coffee,
Ali DeBenis, James Weir and Elzo Wind.
In St. Moritz, thanks to Heidi Reich.
In the States, thanks to Ernie Bulow,
Gaye Browne, Caroline Gordon,
Gigi Guthrie and J. W. Satterthwait.

Special thanks to Reagan Arthur at St. Martin's.

THE FOOL.

MUDLUSCIOUS AND puddlewonderful.

So e. e. cummings once described the thaw of spring. But this was a midwinter thaw, an early February thaw following a blizzard that had piled a foot of snow on the ground. For a week now the snow had been melting during the day and freezing up again at night, so it could melt some more again tomorrow. The mud had become a lot less luscious and the puddles considerably less wonderful.

When it's not buried beneath the drifts, wintertime Santa Fe is primarily a study in brown, and—to be fair—the thaw had added variety and texture to the portrait. In addition to the pale brown of leaf-stripped trees, the paler brown of adobe, and the tan of hillside beyond the green puffs of piñon and juniper, we now had the cinnamon provided by the roadway grit, the milk and bittersweet chocolates provided by the mud, the café au lait provided by the runnels of meltwater.

Sally Durrell's driveway, however, wasn't nearly so appetizing that Tuesday morning. Lying on Buena Vista, a narrow street south of the Capitol Building, it was a small semicircle of rutted black gelatinous muck winding through some barren lilac trees. When I entered it, I could feel the tires slipping beneath the Subaru, and I flipped the lever that transformed the little station wagon into a four-wheel-drive daredevil. The engine coughed—something was seriously wrong in there, had been wrong since the block had taken a couple of nine-millimeter slugs a few months ago—and the car leaped forward and breezed through the ooze.

I braked it, put it in Park, opened the door. I looked down and frowned thoughtfully, the way I always frown. Unless Sir Walter Raleigh was lurking behind one of the lilac trees, to reach the flagstone walkway I would have to breeze through a broad patch of ooze myself. In a pair of ostrich-skin Lucheses that had cost me a couple of weeks' pay.

Sir Walter didn't leap to my assistance. I climbed out of the Subaru and the boots immediately sank up to their ankles, and mine, in mud. Gingerly, the way real men do it, and frowning thoughtfully, and muttering only a very little, I squished and slurped across the bog.

Maybe the mud wouldn't have seemed such an affront if the sun hadn't been so brightly shining that morning, or the sky hadn't been such a cloudless powder blue. And maybe I would've felt better about the whole thing if I could've fooled myself into believing that Sally was going to offer the agency a big chunk of cash. But I knew that I owed Sally a favor, and I was fairly certain that she was going to call it in.

Or maybe, unconsciously, I had a premonition that I was about to get myself into something even more unpleasant than what I was walking through at the moment.

Unconscious premonitions are the best kind. You can always claim, after the fact, that you remember them.

Sally's house was perched on a rise, above a steeply sloped lawn of matted brown grasses humped here and there with patches of snow. It was a wide, two-story white frame building with wooden steps leading up to the covered porch. It faced north, and more snow lay slumped in its shadow and in the shadows of the tall pine trees that flanked it, standing tall and straight like palace guards.

A wooden house meant an old house, older than the city zoning laws that required houses to look as though they were built of adobe, even when they were built, as many of the new ones were, of papier-mâché. But Sally's house appeared new, the siding crisp and unmarred, the paint bright and unsullied. It was perhaps a bit out of place in a town that favored houses made of mud and straw, but it looked comfortable and sedate and respectable. And prosperous. Which wasn't really a surprise. If they were good, lawyers usually did well in Santa Fe, where litigation was as popular as Navajo jewelry. And Sally was very good.

I climbed along the flagstones and then tried to scrape the mud from my boots, using the overhang of the first wooden step. I wasn't spectacularly successful. Well, it was *her* driveway, after all. And *her* mud. I clomped up the steps and knocked on the front door.

After a few moments, Sally opened it. "Joshua," she smiled, drying her small hands on a red plaid dishtowel. "It's good to see you again," she said.

Sally was short. Since I'm on the tallish side myself, Rita tells me that I tend to accuse everyone around me of shortness. With Sally, however, there really wasn't much doubt. I don't know exactly where the official cutoff point for midget might lie, but Sally certainly came close: in her high-heeled shoes she was just a sliver over five feet tall.

She was also beautiful. Her hair was blond and it fell to her shoulders, sweeping in a sleek curve along the right side of her face, like Veronica Lake's. Her eyes were blue and her mouth was red and her features were perfect—all of them, from head to toe. Sometimes her legal opponents—those who hadn't bothered to check out her record, and occasionally even those who had—took a look at this petite, perfectly proportioned woman and they began to treat her like a Barbie doll in court, with that overly solicitous chivalry that only barely disguises masculine desire, or masculine contempt. And Sally would smile sweetly and bat her eyes and, with a cool dispassionate competence, she would proceed to remove their jugular veins. And frequently, as they saw it, their testicles.

'Hi,'' I said. 'You're looking good, counselor.''

And so she was, in a gray wool skirt and a white lace blouse opened at the throat to display a narrow gold-link necklace.

She smiled, ''So are you. Come on in. I'm just finishing up the breakfast stuff.'' She glanced down. ''What *is* that all over your boots?''

''Most of your driveway.''

She looked up. ''Oh Joshua, I'm sorry. I was going to get it graded last fall, but I never had the time.'' She grinned, suddenly impish. ''You wear it well, though.''

''Thanks, Sally. I'll take off the boots.''

''Don't bother, really, I'll get you a rag or something—or here, take this.'' She held out the dishtowel.

''That's okay.'' With the toe of my left boot against the heel of my right, I levered my right foot free. I sat down on the doorstep, wrenched off the left boot, set it beside the other. And now my hands, like the boots, were covered with mud. I looked up at Sally, who wasn't very far up. Grinning, she held out the dishtowel.

I took it. ''Thanks.''

''It's only mud, Joshua.''

''That we know of.''

She laughed. ''Come on. I'll get you some coffee.'' She held out her hand for the towel.

I gave it to her, stood, closed the door, and in stocking feet I followed her. Past a living room on the left—Early American furniture, some watercolor landscapes on the stucco walls, a Navajo carpet atop the shiny hardwood floor—and past a library on the right: another hardwood floor, another Navajo carpet, tall mahogany bookcases filled with books, a mahogany desk supporting a Macintosh computer and a laser printer. Through a formal dining room and around a polished mahogany table and its eight high-backed chairs. Into the kitchen, where sunlight spilled between the lace curtains at the white double-hung windows. Oak cabinets and countertops, a commercial gas stove, a white double oven beside a large white refrigerator. Red Mexican tiles on the floor; off-white linen paper, pinstriped with red, on the walls. In the center of the room stood a circular oak table surrounded by four oak chairs. On the table, beside a wicker basket that held a potted plant, lay a leather briefcase, opened.

"Very nice," I said.

Sally turned to me, cocked her head. "That's right. You haven't been here before, have you?"

"No. Back then, you were living on Alto Street." The floor was warm beneath my feet. Radiant heating.

She smiled. "A long time ago." The smile changed slightly; something entered it: speculation, reflection, perhaps a shadow of regret. I don't know; still don't. She said, "If you hadn't been carrying that torch for Rita, we might've had a whole brood of no-necked monsters by now."

"Grouchy little boys in trench coats."

She laughed. "Lovable little girls carrying legal briefs."

I smiled. "I didn't know that was what you wanted, Sally."

"No," she said. "I wanted the brass ring." Her smile changed again, became crisp, businesslike. "I forget—how do you like your coffee?"

"Very much."

She laughed. "Cream? Sugar?"

"Sugar."

"Sugar. Take off your coat and sit down. Stop looming."

I unzipped the leather jacket, shrugged it off, hung it on the back of the nearest chair, and sat down. Hanging from the back of the chair opposite me was a small wool suit jacket that matched Sally's skirt.

Sally poured coffee from a Melitta pot into a delicate china cup, set the cup on a saucer, and carried them over to the table, holding the saucer in her left hand and supporting the cup with her right. She put them in front of me, I thanked her, and she sat down on the opposite side of the table, hands atop the wood, fingers interlocked, her shoulders tilted slightly forward. It was the way she sat in court.

I remembered it well; she had sat next to me in exactly that way when I was on trial.

She said, "Have you read anything about the murder in La Cienega three nights ago?"

"Enough chitchat, eh?"

She smiled. "Do you know about it?"

I shook my head. I'd been down in Socorro over the weekend, on business.

"I'm representing the accused," Sally said. "Giacomo Bernardi. He's innocent."

I sipped at the coffee. "Uh-huh," I said. "Nice coffee."

"I'm working on this, pro bono, for the public defender's office. You do know that the P.D.'s office provides funds for me to pay an investigator?"

"Not many funds," I said.

Another smile. "Fifteen dollars an hour."

"That many, huh?"

"Are you working on anything right now?"

I sipped my coffee, sat back. "Well..."

"I need help with this, Joshua."

"Okay," I said.

She smiled. "Good. Thank you. I can sweeten the fifteen." She meant using her own money.

I shook my head. "Like Pete Peterson used to say, Money is only something you need in case you don't die."

She smiled. "Who's Pete Peterson?"

"A pilot. Borderhopper. One of the first. Used to smuggle grass from Mexico to Ruidoso."

"Used to?"

"Last I heard, he was a guest of the federal government."

"You know such interesting people."

"One of the perks of the business. So tell me about Giacomo."

"You know, Joshua, I'm not asking you to get involved because I think you owe me something. You don't owe me a thing. I'm asking you because you're one of the best investigators I know."

"Landsakes, Miss Sally. You'll turn my head."

She smiled briefly. "And I'm going to need someone good on this. The state has a tight case. Circumstantial, but tight."

I nodded. "Tell me about it."

Giacomo Bernardi, Sally told me, was a Tarot reader. Four nights ago, on the evening of Saturday, the eighth, Bernardi was attending a congregation of New Age healers in La Cienega, at the home of a couple called Brad Freefall and Sylvia Morningstar.

"Freefall?" I said. "Morningstar?"

Sally smiled wryly. "They're New Age healers, Joshua. They've transcended their original commonplace identities."

"Uh-huh."

Among the others present, with his wife, Justine, was a man named Quentin Bouvier. Bouvier, according to Sally, was not well liked. He had, said Sally, a reputation as a Satanist.

"Come on, Sally. This is Alice in Wonderland stuff. Satanists. People named Morningstar and Freefall. Tarot readers. Are you sure it's a private detective you want? Not a soothsayer?"

She smiled again. "Welcome to Santa Fe, land of the free, home of the occult. It gets even better."

"I doubt that."

Quentin Bouvier, Sally told me, was not well liked in particular by Giacomo Bernardi, primarily because he had just purchased, from a woman named Eliza Remington, an antique Tarot card.

I asked Sally, "Who's Eliza Remington?"

"An astrologer. She was there that night, too."

"Sounds like a pretty nifty soiree. How come I didn't get an invitation?"

Sally smiled. "Actually, she's an amazing little old lady. I've met her. You'll like her."

"Uh-huh. So what was the deal with the card?"

"It's from an old Italian deck, apparently. It was painted in the fifteenth century. One of a kind, and very valuable.

Bernardi felt that Bouvier—'' She smiled. ''This is where it gets better. Bernardi felt that Bouvier would be using the card for evil purposes.''

''Three-card monte?''

''Summoning spirits.'' She smiled again, and shrugged, almost apologetically. ''What can I say, Joshua. He believes in all that. Spiritualism. The occult.''

''Great.'' I nodded. ''Okay. Bernardi didn't much like Bouvier.''

''As I said, no one much liked Bouvier. But Bernardi had an argument with him that night, a very vocal argument that nearly became a fistfight. He threatened the man. And in the morning, Bouvier was found dead in his bedroom. Strangled. The Tarot card was missing and so was Bernardi. The state police picked him up on the interstate, trying to hitchhike to Albuquerque.''

''What do the state police have?''

''The argument the night before. Bernardi's leaving the scene. And his scarf. It was his scarf that was used to strangle Bouvier.''

''Strangle him how?''

''Preliminary report from the medical examiner says that Bouvier was clubbed first, then the scarf was tied around his neck, slung over a beam, and Bouvier was hoisted up off the floor. The scarf was pulled down and knotted to itself.''

''A long scarf.''

''Over six feet long.''

''Very dashing. And Bouvier was hoisted off the ground. Is Bernardi big enough to do that?''

''Bouvier wasn't a very large man. I could've done it myself.''

''He was an elf?''

''He was five foot two. He weighed a hundred and thirty pounds.''

''You said that Bouvier was there with his wife. Justine, is that right? Where was she while hubby was getting hanged?''

''They slept in separate rooms.''

''Not a happy marriage?''

"An open marriage. She was sleeping with a man named Peter Jones in his room. Jones had been involved with Mrs. Bouvier for some time, and evidently with Bouvier's blessing."

"You know such interesting people."

She smiled. "One of the perks of the business."

"And who or what is Peter Jones?"

She grinned. "A spiritual alchemist."

"Am I supposed to ask what that is?"

"Only if you want to."

"Later maybe. Jones and Mrs. Bouvier alibi each other."

"Both of them say they were asleep for most of the night. They heard nothing."

"What was Bouvier clubbed with?"

"A large piece of quartz. It belonged to Sylvia Morningstar, and it was there in Bouvier's room."

"But the blow didn't kill him."

"No. He was still alive when the scarf was tied around his neck."

"Blood?"

"Some. In his hair, on the bedsheets. Some on the floor."

"Would it have gotten on the murderer?"

"Perhaps. Perhaps not. There was none found on Bernardi."

"Prints on the quartz?"

"Wiped clean."

"Bernardi wipes the quartz clean but he leaves his scarf wrapped around Bouvier's neck."

Sally nodded. "I pointed that out to the state police. In the heat of the moment, according to them, Bernardi simply forgot his scarf."

"What about the Tarot card?"

"It hasn't been found."

"So it wasn't on Bernardi."

She shook her head. "But he would've had time to hide it. So, at any rate, says the investigator for the state police, an Agent Hernandez."

"Robert Hernandez?"

"Yes. You know him?"

I nodded. "Yeah. But we're not exactly the best of friends." A few months ago, Hernandez had come close to arresting me for murder. "What does Bernardi say about all this?"

"To the cops and the D.A.'s people, nothing."

"Nothing?"

"Apparently the state troopers who picked him up were a bit rough. Bernardi refuses to talk to the authorities. Any of them."

"A bit rough."

"They beat him. Bernardi was resisting arrest, they say."

I nodded. It was rough work, being a cop, and sometimes it didn't bring out the best in the people who did it. And sometimes, with a few of them, their best wasn't any good at all.

I asked Sally, "What does Bernardi say to you?"

"That he didn't do it. I believe him."

"You always believe them."

"Not always. But certainly in this case. I think he's being railroaded."

I nodded. "Okay. Standard deal. I find out what I can. If it's in your client's favor, then you and the cops get it. If it's not in your client's favor, then you and the cops get that."

She smiled again. "You don't have to tell me, Joshua."

I shrugged. "Just so you know."

"I already knew."

"When do I see Bernardi?"

I SAW Giacomo Bernardi at ten-thirty that morning, at the Sante Fe Detention Center on Airport Road. We talked in the interview room off the medium-security wing. A neon light overhead, cement block walls, linoleum floors, a Formica table, three plastic chairs. Penal Moderne. The Center was run by a private company, Corrections Corporation of America, and it was as clean and humane as a place like that could possibly be. No rats scurrying off into dark corners, no far-off wails and moans. No leering cons rattling tin cups along the bars. From the outside, it could've been one of those drab commercial buildings that optimistic realtors like to call an executive office park. And yet I've never walked into it without feeling sweat trickle down my sides. You left it, even as a casual visitor, only when someone said you could.

Wearing baggy, standard-issue C.C.A. orange cotton pants, a sagging T-shirt, white socks, and a battered pair of running shoes, Bernardi was a man of medium height, overweight, with thick, tousled black hair and a day's worth of thick black stubble salted with white. He was thirty-six years old, according to his arrest report, but he looked closer to forty. His jowls were fleshy, his lips were thick and sensual, his dark brown eyes were half hidden behind sleepy lids. The right lid was puffy, and there was a bruise, turning from blue to yellow, just beneath his right cheekbone. He sat slumped in the chair with his hands in his pockets, looking surly and morose. But, guilty or innocent, if I'd been beaten up and tossed into a cell, I'd probably look surly and morose myself.

"You understand," I told him, "that I'm working for Sally Durrell, your lawyer."

"Si," he said. "Yeah. I unnerstand." His flat, phlegmatic voice was gravelly, and his accent suggested that he'd been born in Italy or that he'd spent many hours watching the collected works of Francis Ford Coppola.

"And you understand," I said, "that the police have a pretty good case against you."

He nodded. "You think I kill him, huh?" His voice was still flat, unmodulated, as though he didn't especially care what I thought.

"I don't think anything, Mr. Bernardi. But Miss Durrell believes that you didn't do it, and she's hired me to learn what I can."

"How much I got to pay you?" With the same dull lack of interest.

"You don't pay me anything. The public defender's office takes care of that."

"How much they pay you, huh? The public defender's office?"

"Fifteen dollars an hour."

He grunted. Few grunts express contempt more effectively than an Italian grunt. "I make more with the cards," he said.

"I don't have your special skills. So do we talk or do I go back to Miss Durrell and tell her to find someone else?"

He eyed me for a moment from beneath his hooded lids. Then, slowly, he sat up. He pulled his right hand from his pocket. In it, he held a small sheaf of papers, maybe twenty or so, soiled along the edges and slightly crumpled. They had been cut, or carefully torn, from larger sheets of lined notebook paper, and each was about the size of a playing card. Without a word, Bernardi laid them out along the tabletop in the shape of a horseshoe, the open end at my side of the table. The sheets—or cards, which is what I assumed they were intended to be—were blank, at least on the sides that faced upward.

Bernardi sat back. "They take away my cards. I make these."

"Very enterprising."

He said, "You pick one now."

"Why?"

"'Cause I got to know." As though that were an answer. I leaned forward and reached out my left hand.

"Right hand," said Bernardi.

"Right hand," I said. I selected one of the homemade cards. "Now what?" I said. "You guess what it is?"

"Put it down on the table. The face up."

I turned over the card and set it on the table. It was a line drawing in pencil, very well executed, of a man about to step off a cliff. He wore boots and a long tunic, belted at the waist, and, like a hobo, he carried over his shoulder a staff with a bundle dangling from its end. Some small unidentifiable animal—a dog or a cat or, for all I know, a wombat—was nipping at his heels. For no discernible reason, the man was smiling.

Bernardi was nodding. "Good," he said. "That's good."

"Yeah?"

He leaned forward. Looking at me, he tapped the card with his fingernail. I noticed that his fingernail had been bitten to the quick. Maybe he wasn't as phlegmatic as he seemed. "This card, he stand for you. He represent you. He's a good card."

"And which card is he?"

He tapped again at the card. "This card, he's the Fool."

THE HIGH PRIESTESS

"HE SOUNDS TO ME," said Rita, smiling, "like an admirable judge of character."

"Very amusing, Rita. Next time, you can be the one who goes over to the Detention Center and plays Groucho to his Chico."

"Don't let the Knights of Columbus hear you say that. Or the Mafia."

"The Mafia wouldn't let this guy in. He wouldn't know a sharkskin suit if it swam up and ripped his leg off."

We were sitting in Rita's office, Rita behind the desk and me in one of the client chairs. For almost three years the office had been empty, and even now, after a month, I still felt a gratifying mixture of surprise and pleasure whenever I looked across the desk and saw her sitting there, saw her hair, black as raven wings, outlined against the pale blue sky beyond the window. I felt other things, as well, but Rita preferred that we didn't discuss those in the office.

Rita said, "You're sounding a bit provincial, Joshua. But I imagine that's because, unlike Bernardi's English, your Italian is absolutely fluent."

"Well," I said. "I admit that it's not up to my Urdu. But then, few things are."

"You're not happy with this case." She was wearing a black bolero vest over a blue silk blouse, and her hair was swept back over her ears and gathered into a chignon. She had an extremely good neck, and her neck was far from being her best feature. I've never been able to decide just what, exactly, her best feature is. Her large dark eyes? The regal Hispanic nose, the arch of Indian cheekbones? The wry parentheses at the corners of her wide red mouth?

"Are you kidding?" I said. "I love it. Astrologers, Satanists, Tarot readers, spiritual alchemists. My culture heroes, all of them. I can't wait to sit down with these honchos and shoot the shit. I can get my aura polished. I can get my chakras looked into. I've been worried about my chakras lately. I think they need recharging."

"I love it when you whine," she said. "You know you're going to take the case. Sally asked you to."

Three years ago, a man named Martinez had shot Rita and her husband, killing him and wounding her so badly that her doctors had been convinced she would never walk again. She was walking now, but she'd been in a wheelchair for a very long time. Three years ago, I had gone looking for Martinez. I had found him, and things had happened, and shortly afterward I had found myself in court, accused of attempted murder. Sally had defended me, successfully, and she had refused to accept any payment.

"Yeah," I said. "But that doesn't mean I have to like it."

"What else did Bernardi tell you?"

"That he didn't kill Bouvier."

"You believe him."

"I'm inclined to. Doesn't make sense to me that he'd wipe prints off the chunk of quartz and then leave his scarf hanging there."

"How did the scarf manage to wrap itself around Bouvier's neck?"

"He doesn't know."

"What did he say?"

What Giacomo Bernardi had said was that after the argument with Bouvier, he had gone off to brood in the library, taking with him a bottle of sambuca—the Freefall-
Morningstar household, New Age or not, evidently kept a
well-stocked bar. He had sat in the library, alone, watching
a soccer match on cable TV and hitting the sambuca vigorously. I'd gotten the feeling, talking to him, that hitting
sambuca vigorously was an activity with which he was not
entirely unfamiliar.

Eventually, he said, he fell asleep, still sitting in his armchair. He was awakened by what he described as a noise.

"What kind of noise?" Rita asked me.

"He doesn't know. A noise. Whatever it was, it woke him
up. And then, he says, he heard someone running in the
hallway. He said it sounded like someone running bare-
foot."

Still groggy from the aftereffects of half a bottle of vigorously hit sambuca, Bernardi had stumbled out of the library and into the hallway. Looking down the hall, he saw
that one of the bedroom doors was open—Bouvier's.
Without thinking much about it, probably without thinking at all, he shambled down the hall and looked into the
room. Hanging immobile at its center, attached to a beam
by a scarf that Bernardi recognized as his own, a long red
silk scarf trimmed with gold, was a very dead Quentin
Bouvier.

Rita said, "Where had the scarf been before this?"

"In Bernardi's bedroom closet."

"He panicked?"

"He panicked."

Bernardi had told me, "I got afraid." Some of the flatness had left his voice. He had sat forward, his hands on the
Formica table. "I see my muffler, you know. My scarf. And
I see his face, that man's face, all black and swollen up. And
his eyes, you know, they are like this"—he showed me with
his hands—"wide open, you know, and sticking out.
Looking at me. And I got afraid the people would think I
done this. And so I left."

"What did he take with him?" Rita asked me.

"Only his coat. A navy pea coat. I don't think he had much else."

"Not the Tarot card?"

"He says not. He says he didn't even think about the card until after he'd left La Cienega."

"How did he leave?"

"He walked. He doesn't have a car, he'd gotten a ride there from one of the other guests, a woman named Veronica Chang. Anyway, he walked. This was about five o'clock in the morning, still dark. He walked down to the entrance to the interstate and hitchhiked until he got a ride. He was standing there, he says, for over an hour before someone stopped. The sun was beginning to come up."

"Did he get the driver's name?"

"No. And he doesn't know what kind of car it was, either. American, he says. An older model."

"The state police will locate it, if they haven't already. At that time of the morning, anyone leaving La Cienega probably lives there."

"Probably. The ride took him as far as Bernalillo. He had some coffee and doughnuts at a diner and then walked over to the next interstate entrance. He was trying to make Albuquerque, where he knows some people. The state police picked him up there, at the Bernalillo entrance, at seven-thirty."

Rita asked, "Do you know who found Bouvier's body, and when?"

"Bouvier's wife, Justine. Six o'clock. I got that from Sally. The state cops were there, at the house, by six-thirty."

"What was the time of death?"

"He hadn't been dead long. Couple of hours, max. Sometime between four-thirty and five-thirty."

"If Bernardi's telling the truth, he came on the scene almost immediately afterward."

"Yeah."

"Did he shut Bouvier's door when he left the room?"

"He says he didn't. But according to the wife's statement, it was shut when she arrived at six."

"Presumably, then, the murderer shut it *after* Bernardi left the house."

"Probably the murderer, yeah. No one admits to seeing it open. No one admits to being out in the hallway all night. And if anyone *had* seen the door open, probably he would've looked inside to see if everything was all right. And he would've seen Bouvier hanging there."

"Assuming there was enough light."

"Right. Assuming that."

"Do you have the names and addresses of the rest of the people who were present in the house that night?"

"Yeah. Got those from Sally, too."

"Put them into the computer and, when I can, I'll run them through the databases."

"When you can?"

She smiled. "When I can. I know you'll find this difficult to believe, Joshua, but I do have one or two things on my plate besides your Mr. Bernardi. I'm doing some asset searches for Kevin Lehrmer, up in Denver. I'm doing a due vigilance for Ed Norman. And I already told you that I'm trying to locate that man from Scottsdale, Frederick Pressman."

"Yeah. The guy who disappeared with two million dollars. How you doing?"

"I've learned his new name—Ralph Bonner."

"How'd you get it? Girlfriend? Relative?"

"An old girlfriend. I got her off the phone records. She's in Phoenix, and I asked Steve Chapman down there to check her out. He made a garbage run, found a letter with Bonner's name and a return address. He was staying at the Hilton in Houston at the time. A week ago."

Once you put your garbage out on the curb, it loses all of its right to privacy, and so do you. The highest court in the land, the Supreme, has determined that anyone who wants the stuff can just zip up to the bag, toss it into the backseat, take it home, and peruse its contents at leisure. Be careful what you throw away.

Rita said, "Bonner's description matches Pressman's. The real Ralph Bonner is buried in a cemetery in Syracuse, New York."

"So Pressman has papers."

"Birth certificate, Social Security, Texas driver's license, passport. He booked a flight from Houston to Mexico City for last Friday. He wouldn't need the passport for Mexico—not immediately, anyway—so I suspect he's headed for somewhere below the border."

"Brazil?"

"I don't think so. According to his college transcripts, he's got three years of Spanish. No Portuguese. And he could've flown to Brazil directly. I think he'll be aiming for one of the smaller countries, possibly one with a sizable contingent of American expatriots. Costa Rica. Guatemala."

"He could've flown directly to either one of them."

"He's being cute, I think."

"But you're cuter, Rita."

"I'll find him," she said. "In the meantime, you put those names into the computer—"

"Well, see," I said. "What I was hoping, see, was that *you'd* put them in the computer, see, and then I could take off and—"

"Joshua, you're perfectly capable of typing some names into the computer. I know that you like to pretend that computers are some sort of black magic—"

"Spiritual alchemy."

"What *is* spiritual alchemy?"

"Beats me."

"Well, spiritually or otherwise, put the names and addresses into the computer."

"Yes, dear," I said. "You know what this is? This case? Aside from being a major pain in the ass, I mean."

She sat back, put her arms along the arms of her swivel chair. "What?"

"It's unreal. All these space cadets. It's like one of those English mystery novels of the thirties. An isolated manor house filled with eccentrics. A nighttime murder. One of the eccentrics, probably innocent, has been arrested by the local constabulary."

She smiled. "But then you show up, the debonair amateur sleuth, and you begin your careful investigation. And finally, in the last chapter, through your incredible powers of observation and your supreme skill at ratiocination, you identify the real murderer."

"Well, to tell you the truth, what I was planning to do was keep beating up on people until someone confessed. I'll try to be debonair about it, though."

"The difference here," she said, "is that this *is* a real house. With a real corpse in it, a person who was once very much alive. And who died in a very messy way."

"Yeah. There's that."

"Tell me about this Tarot card."

"Yeah," I said. "I think the card's important."

She nodded. "It's missing. Someone's dead. Until we learn otherwise, I think it's safe to assume that it's important."

I took out my notebook, flipped it open. "Okay. From what Sally and Bernardi tell me, the card is from a deck originally hand-painted in Italy in 1494. The deck was commissioned by Pope Alexander the Sixth. Rodrigo Borgia. You're familiar with Rodrigo?"

"Lucrezia's father."

I smiled. "One way to put it. According to Bernardi, it was short of a full deck. Which makes sense because that's what most of these people in La Cienega would be playing with."

"Joshua." Mildly reproving.

"You know that a Tarot deck has twenty-two major trumps? Major Arcana, they're called."

She nodded.

"Well, those twenty-two cards, the Major Arcana, they were all that were painted. And then, over the years, the deck got split up. Right now, eleven of the cards are in the Louvre, in Paris, and ten others are in a private museum in Catania, Italy. This card's been missing for a long time, at least since the eighteenth century. But according to Bernardi, there are stories, legends, that it's turned up from time to time in the possession of different occultists. A guy named Court de Gebelin, in Switzerland, sometime around 1776. Later, around 1886, with a French guy named Eliphas Levi. The last person who claimed to have seen it was Aleister Crowley, when he was a member of something called the Order of the Golden Dawn."

Rita nodded. "The English magical group. Yeats was a member."

"Yeats the poet?"

She smiled. "No, Joshua, Yeats the chiropractor."

"Okay," I said. "Fine. Who holds the record for the most home runs hit during a single season?"

"Roger Maris."

"Okay," I said. "Fine. You wanna fuck?"

She laughed and I watched the muscles play beneath the smooth skin of her throat.

I said, "It's just I get so turned on when you point out my deficiencies."

She laughed again. "All right," she said. "We'll try it again. Yes, Joshua. Yeats, the poet."

"Thank you."

"And how did it come into the possession of this woman, this Eliza Remington?"

"I don't know. But I'll beat her up until I find out."

"You might try asking her first."

"Aha. That's just what she'd *expect* me to do."

She smiled—puzzled, maybe. "You're being unusually silly this morning."

"Unusually?"

"More so than normal."

I smiled. "Ah, well. Maybe the idea of talking to all these fruit loops is making me a little goony. And maybe it's just that I still get such a big kick out of seeing you here."

She smiled again. "I plan to be here for a long time, Joshua. It might be a good idea for you to get used to it."

I smiled. "Yes, dear. I'll certainly try."

"Can we get back to business now?"

"Absolutely."

"A card like that," she said, "assuming the provenance could be established, would be priceless."

"Eliza Remington apparently set a price. And Bouvier apparently paid it."

"Do we know how much?"

"No. But you just wait till I get my hands on Eliza."

"Stop it."

I grinned.

"How was it being carried?" she asked me.

"Bernardi says it was in a stiff leather binder, beneath a sheet of glassine paper. The binder was about a foot square. The card itself was about three inches by seven."

"Both the binder and the card are missing?"

"Yeah."

"And they were in Bouvier's bedroom before he was killed."

"They were supposed to be."

"So if Bernardi didn't kill Bouvier, then whoever *did* kill him presumably took the card."

"Unless Bernardi's lying about not taking the card. He could've found Bouvier dead, seen his chance, and ripped it off."

"If he had the presence of mind to do that," she said, "why didn't he have the presence of mind to remove his scarf?"

"Maybe he was squeamish."

"And taking the card would've made the case against him look even worse."

"Not if he hid it somewhere. Wrapped it in a garbage bag and buried it somewhere between the house and the interstate."

"He'd only hide it if he were working on the assumption that he was going to get picked up."

"Or that he *might* be picked up."

She frowned. "Is that what you think happened?"

"Not really. I'm just ratiocinating."

She smiled. "So we're back to the likelihood that whoever killed Bouvier was the person who took the card."

"Makes sense to me."

"Or. Person A kills Bouvier for an unrelated reason, and then, later, Person B wanders in and takes the card."

"Which would put at least three people in Bouvier's room that night, including Bernardi. Four, including Bouvier. It's beginning to sound like the ship cabin scene in *A Night at the Opera.*"

She smiled again. "Did the state police search everyone?"

"If they did, they probably didn't do a very good job. It looks to me like they decided from the beginning that Bernardi was the guy responsible."

"Not surprising," Rita said. "He was missing. The card was missing."

"Yeah."

She nodded. "The missing card. Which card was it? Which trump?"

"It was the Death card," I told her.

"How can I help you, Mr. Croft?" she asked me from across the white marble coffee table.

I had expected her to be short, probably because Sally had told me that her husband was short, but she was a tall woman, at least five foot ten. Her hair was silver—prematurely silver, and probably chemically enhanced, because I doubt that she was much older than thirty—and it was cut close to her skull, like a small boy's. It was the only thing about her that reminded me of a small boy. Above large brown eyes and long, thick lashes, her eyebrows were dark black arches that contrasted dramatically—as they were supposed to, I suspect—with the color of her hair. Her nose was small and even; her small round mouth was shiny with burnt-sienna lipstick, the lower lip slightly swollen, bee-stung, which gave her long oval face an expression that was at once petulant and sensual. Lithe and slender and high-breasted, she wore black pumps, black nylon hose, a black miniskirt, and a tight-fitting black jersey top that had a turtleneck but no sleeves. Her long tanned arms and her square shoulders were bare. New Age Mourning.

I said, "As I told you over the phone, Mrs. Bouvier, I'm working with Sally Durrell for the public defender's office. I need to learn as much about what happened last Saturday night as I can. And also about your husband. I know this is a bad time for you..."

The black arches of her eyebrows arched still more. She smiled slightly. "Why should it be a bad time?"

Because your husband just had his collar size reduced by fifty percent? I said, "Well..."

"I don't believe in death, Mr. Croft," she said, and took a drag from her cigarette. This was one of the ultrachic numbers, pastel paper and looking too thin for someone to suck smoke through it without sprouting a hernia. "Not in the sense you probably mean it," she said, exhaling.

"I mean it in the sense that you stop breathing."

"Exactly," she said, and slightly smiled again. "You're speaking, of course, of the corporeal body, which is merely one of the many vibratory forms taken by our ka."

I nodded. "Our ka," I said. As occasionally happens when someone starts explaining vibratory forms, I found my attention wandering around the room. This was the living room, an enormous space in an enormous and isolated and extremely expensive house in the hills to the east of Santa Fe. The wall of glass to my right, looking down over the town and the peasants who inhabited it, made the room seem even larger, and so did the broad mirrored wall behind the silver leather sofa that held Justine Bouvier. The rest of the furniture was silver, too, including the leather chair in which I sat. Probably it wasn't entirely a coincidence that the color matched the color of the woman's hair.

The basic motif here seemed to be Egyptian: a couple of pale blue scarabs the size of bullfrogs on the coffee table, a black bust of Nefertiti atop a white column, a large hieroglyphic tapestry on the wall to my left, a small marble statue of a stylized naked young man standing in one corner, his face blank, his arms held stiffly at his sides. The Siamese cat, sitting near the huge white marble fireplace, was clearly going along with the plan. He was trying to imitate a photograph of some cat god he'd admired while he was leafing through *National Geographic*.

There was enough marble in the room to slap together a life-sized replica of the Parthenon. Even the floor was marble, black, as shiny as obsidian. That floor might be pleasant in the summer, on the two or three days when the temperature in Santa Fe rose above eighty-five degrees. During the winter, it was probably a bitch to keep warm. But I suppose that if you could afford a marble floor, you didn't worry about heating the thing. You just marched your Nubian slaves in from time to time and had them breathe on it.

"You might think of the ka," she was saying, "as something like the soul, in Christian terminology. In addition to the corporeal body, it manifests itself both as an ethereal body and a spiritual body. Only my husband's corporeal body has left us. Quentin and I, his ka and my own, were karmically intertwined long before we met on this particular plane, and we'll continue to be intertwined, probably for many lifetimes to come."

Well, as Frank Sinatra once put it, whatever gets you through the night.

"I understand," I said, "that it was you who found him that morning."

"Yes." She inhaled, took the cigarette from her lips, opened her mouth, inhaled the little billow of smoke that was about to escape, and then, exhaling, she frowned. "It was..." She searched for a word. "Unpleasant."

A nice choice, I thought. "I'm sure it was. According to your statement, the door was shut when you arrived."

"That's right, yes."

"Who was it who actually discovered that the Tarot card was missing?"

"Me. As soon as I saw that dreadful red scarf around poor Quentin's neck, I knew that that nasty little Italian person had killed him. And I knew why, naturally. The card. I looked all over for it. Quentin brought it with him to the bedroom, the night before. It was gone. He took it."

"Bernardi."

"Yes, of course Bernardi."

"Who removed your husband's body from the beam, Mrs. Bouvier?"

"Someone from the state police. They told me, when I called them, not to touch anything."

"And did you search for the card before or after they arrived?"

"Before, naturally. It was the first thing I did. Even before I called them."

So she'd gone rummaging around the room, opening and closing drawers, or suitcases, or whatever, rifling through the shirts and the underwear, while the late Mr. Bouvier had silently dangled from his beam, watching her with empty bulbous eyes.

Maybe she guessed what I was thinking. Or maybe, being who she was, she read my mind. She took a drag from the cigarette, smiled, and said, "Are you shocked?"

"Shocked?" I smiled. "I haven't been shocked in a long time, Mrs. Bouvier."

She smiled again and those big brown eyes narrowed slightly as she nodded. "I sense that about you. I'm the type of person who can sense things intuitively. And usually, almost always, my intuition is right. You have a kind of internal armor, don't you? Emotional armor. Very strong, very powerful. It's something that serves a valuable purpose, by protecting you. But it's also something that limits you, too, reduces your possibilities for growth. It seems to me that it goes back for many lifetimes. Have you ever done a past-life regression?"

"Once. When I was audited by the I.R.S."

She smiled. "You have a sense of humor. I like that. You're a Virgo?"

"Intacta."

She frowned, puzzled.

"I'm an Aries," I told her.

Another smile. "Of course." Without missing a beat. "The ram. But you haven't, have you? You've never been hypnotized and helped to recall your former lives?"

"No."

Exhaling smoke, she leaned forward and stubbed out her cigarette. "How come?" she asked me.

"I've been too busy with this one."

"But you should try it. I think you'd find it intensely rewarding. Maybe even liberating." She drew her long legs beneath her, gently holding on to the slender calf of her right leg with her hand, and she sat back against the couch, her arm along its back, which provided me a three-quarter view of her upper torso.

"I could do it for you, you know," she said. "It's a skill, and I'm very good at it. I've helped people learn things about themselves that they couldn't *believe*." She smiled. "We could do it right now, if you want."

I've read somewhere that when men anticipate any sort of sexual activity, their whiskers begin to develop more rapidly. I believe it. Sitting opposite Justine Bouvier in her living room, across from those long shapely legs and those small perfect breasts unencumbered beneath taut black fabric, I could feel my beard growing.

"Some other time, maybe," I told her. Some other lifetime, maybe.

"Maybe," she said, smiling, "you'll discover that you were a king in ancient Mesopotamia."

More likely, I thought, an auto mechanic in ancient Newark. But I smiled pleasantly. Over the years I've gotten fairly good at smiling pleasantly. Even when I'd rather be in ancient Newark. "Getting back to last Sunday morning, Mrs. Bouvier. What made you so sure that Bernardi had taken the Tarot card?"

"You know about his jumping at Quentin the night before?"

"I understand that there'd been an argument."

"Worse than an argument. Much worse. He *attacked* Quentin. With his hands. He was trying to *strangle* him. And if it hadn't been for Peter and Brad, he would've. They pulled him away."

"That would be Peter Jones and Brad Freefall."

"That's right, yes."

"And why would Bernardi attack your husband?"

"He wanted the card, of course. He could never afford a thing like that himself, naturally. He was practically a pauper. But if he couldn't have it, he didn't want anyone else to have it. Especially not Quentin."

"Why especially not Quentin?"

"He envied him. Most people did. Quentin was a genius." I noticed that even though Quentin was still bobbing around in the etheric currents somewhere, she had no problem with the past tense.

"In what way?" I asked her.

THE MAGICIAN.

SHE SMILED AT ME. "Do you know anything about Magic, Mr. Croft?"

"Are we talking about pulling rabbits out of hats?"

She smiled again, and now there was a condescending sympathy in her smile. *The dear sweet soul simply doesn't understand.* "No," she said. "We're talking about High Magic. True Magic." I could hear the capital letters in her voice. "Putting ourselves in touch with the elemental forces and developing a power over them."

"Then, no," I said, "I don't."

"Quentin did," she said. "It was his life's work. He studied magic from the time he was a child. He learned Greek so he could read the works of Hermes Trismegistus—a collection of magical and mystical texts, very old. He learned Latin because a number of the ancient Grimoires— you know what they are?"

"Nope."

"Magical texts again, guides that explain the different rituals. Many of them are written in Latin, and so Quentin learned Latin. He learned Hebrew so he could study the

Kaballah. He spent an *enormous* amount of time and effort, Mr. Croft. He was an extremely dedicated man.''

I glanced around the huge living room, the expanse of black marble floor, the vista of a diminished Santa Fe down there beyond the pinon and the juniper, and then I glanced back at her. "Looks like it paid off for him."

She lifted her right hand from her calf and waved it lightly, dismissively. "Money is nothing."

I've noticed that the people who maintain this are generally the people with the most of it, and usually those among them who've never had to work for it.

"He inherited money from his family," she said. "And he made some good investments. But he spent most of what he had on the pursuit of knowledge. Naturally, there were people who resented his money, just as there were people who resented his knowledge. And there were people who didn't understand Quentin, who'd *never* be able to understand him."

I was beginning to wonder if there was anyone who'd actually liked poor Quentin. I asked her, "Would any of these people want him dead?"

She frowned. "Why ask that?"

"Because, as I told you, I'm working for the lawyer who's defending Giacomo Bernardi. She thinks he's innocent. And if he didn't kill your husband, then obviously someone else did. Almost certainly one of the other people who were there at the house in La Cienega on Saturday night."

"That's impossible. That horrible little man killed him. He used his own scarf to do it."

"That's the problem I have with this, Mrs. Bouvier. Even if Bernardi did use his scarf to kill your husband, how could he be stupid enough to leave the scarf at the scene of the murder?"

"He's an idiot. You should've seen him the night before, raving and ranting like a lunatic."

"Lunatics aren't always stupid."

"The police *arrested* him."

"The police aren't always right. I wonder if you could tell me something about Leonard Quarry."

She frowned again. "About Leonard? Tell you what?"

"Anything. I know he was there that night. I understand that he'd wanted to buy the Tarot card your husband purchased from Mrs. Remington. I've heard that he was a bit unhappy that your husband outbid him." All of this I'd gotten from Giacomo Bernardi.

"You don't think that *Leonard* killed Quentin?"

"I don't think anything, Mrs. Bouvier. I'm just trying to learn whatever I can."

She smiled. "Leonard is a disgusting man, absolutely revolting and I can't imagine how that brainless little wood nymph of a wife of his could *stand* to have him touch her"—she gave a delicate, feathery shudder, and her silver hair shivered—"but believe me, he's not the type of person to murder someone."

"It *is* true that he was unhappy about being outbid."

"He was unhappy, yes, that Quentin had bought the card. *I* was unhappy. I wish Quentin had never seen that horrible thing. I *knew* there was *something* about that card. I could *sense* it—I told you, I'm an extremely intuitive person. And the *money!* That Remington bitch is as tough as an Arab in a street bazaar."

This, I reminded myself, from the woman who'd just told me that money was nothing. "How much did your husband pay for the card, Mrs. Bouvier?"

She rolled her eyes in mock exasperation. "Oh, could we please *stop* with that *Mrs. Bouvier* nonsense." She put her hand, fingers splayed, to her chest—which had the effect, no doubt inadvertent, of drawing my attention to the same locale. "You're making me feel a million years old. My name is Justine. And yours is—Joshua, isn't it?"

"Joshua, right."

"Good." She leaned forward, picked up the pack of cigarettes and a slim gold Dunhill lighter. "Joshua. I like that." Smiling, she slipped a cigarette free, put it between her red shiny lips.

"About the card?" I said, smiling pleasantly.

She lit the cigarette, eyeing me over the flame. Cigarette jutting from between her small, even teeth, she exhaled through her nostrils and said, "Two hundred thousand dollars."

She said it flatly, to heighten the drama. I think I was supposed to say something like "Yipes!" or "Zowie!" I restrained myself.

"So you can understand," she said, exhaling, plucking away the cigarette, "why I might be a little bit concerned about it." She leaned forward and placed the pack and the lighter on the table. She sat back. "It was worth thousands more, of course. If that Remington witch had put it up for auction at Sotheby's, she might have gotten as much as half a million."

"Why didn't she?"

"A cash flow problem, Quentin said. She didn't want to wait. She couldn't. And neither could Quentin. He *had* to have the damned thing."

"Getting back to Leonard Quarry, Mrs. Bouvier."

"Now now now," she said, smiling, tilting her silver head to the side as she admonished me with the two fingers that held her cigarette. "What did we agree?"

I smiled pleasantly. It hurt some, but not enough to kill me. "Getting back to Leonard Quarry, Justine."

She laughed. It sounded light and musical and mostly artificial. "You *are* persistent." Her glance moved down my length, back up again. "Are you as persistent about everything as you are about asking questions?"

"Not usually."

She inhaled, then smiled as smoke streamed from her nostrils. "What a pity."

"Leonard Quarry?" I said.

She laughed her coy, musical laugh. "All right. What do you want to know about Leonard?"

"Why would he want the card?"

She shrugged. "To resell it, of course. And knowing Leonard, he probably already had a buyer lined up. Leonard's a dealer. Books and art. Most of it has to do with the occult, but not all. He pretends he's interested in the spiritual world, but at heart he's really only a petty little businessman."

"And why did your husband want the card?"

"It was part of a long magical tradition. I didn't want him to buy it, I sensed that it was karmically *wrong,* but I could understand his reasons for wanting it. You know that the Tarot itself, the symbols represented, go back to ancient Egypt?"

"No, I didn't."

"And this particular card has been handled by some of the most famous Magicians in the world. Cagliostro, Court de Gebelin, Aleister Crowley. Objects pick up vibrations, Joshua, from the people who handle them. They attract, they assimilate, some of the power possessed by the people who own them."

"And once he had it," I said, "what did he plan to do with it?"

"Use it. In his practice."

"His practice."

"In his rituals."

"And what sort of rituals were those?"

"I told you. Magical."

"I've heard it said, Justine, that your husband was involved in Satanism."

Her face pinched up with scorn. Scorn is seldom attractive, and it wasn't attractive now. "By who?" she asked. "By that grubby little Bernardi? You can't expect someone like him to understand Quentin and what he was doing. What does he mean by Satanism, anyway?"

"Beats me."

She leaned slightly forward "Satanism. It's a meaningless concept, Joshua. There is no *good* and *evil.* Those are relative terms—useful, yes, but only in this relative, dualistic world. On the cosmic level, everything is One. There are no opposites, no contradictions. The forces, the powers that exist out there, they're neither good nor evil, satanic nor godly. They simply *are.*"

I nodded. "Right." I had noticed something about her. Usually, and particularly when she talked about magic, the syntax and vocabulary of her language was refined, almost elegant. But occasionally, when she spoke about something for which she had no prepared script, her language slipped a notch or two. *How come* for *why*. *Who* for *whom*. I didn't know what this signified, or that it necessarily signified anything. I suppose I was merely exercising my incredible powers of observation. "Let's go back for a minute to last Saturday night," I said.

She sat back and sighed elaborately, then shook her head once again in mock exasperation. Or maybe this time it was real exasperation. "All right, Joshua. Yes. What?"

"I understand that you and your husband were sleeping in separate rooms."

She smiled, took a drag from her cigarette, and said, "Yes."

"You were with a man named Peter Jones."

She smiled again, nodded. "That's right."

"According to the police report, neither one of you heard anything that night."

"Yes."

"And you told them that neither of you left the room that night."

"That's what I said, yes."

I nodded. "Is that still your recollection?"

"Yes." She leaned forward, put out the cigarette, looked up at me, and smiled. "But are you sure that's all you want to ask? Aren't you a teensy bit interested in the sleeping arrangements?"

I smiled. "I hadn't thought that they were any of my business." And I hadn't thought that I'd have to ask. All I had to do was bring them up. She was an explainer, loved explaining the things important to her; and one of these, clearly, was herself.

"I told you," she said, putting her hand back on her calf, "that the link between Quentin and I was karmic. We had transcended, both of us, the physical link. When we did come together physically, we only did it as a part of Quentin's rituals, a way for him to draw upon my feminine strength, my feminine powers. You can understand that women have a specific type of power?"

I nodded. You bet.

"I was happy to help him. But I had a life of my own, just like he did, and sometimes"—she smiled—"you know the Cyndi Lauper song? Sometimes, you know, girls just want to have fun."

I nodded. "And so your link with Peter Jones was . . . ?"

"Physical." She smiled again, and again she tilted her head slightly to the side. "Still not shocked?"

"Not yet. How long have you been involved with him?"

She arched a jet-black eyebrow. "Involved?" A smile. "That's a very heavy word for something that was basically just an itch being scratched."

"How long have you two been scratching?"

Another smile. "Oh, a year or so. Quentin knew, naturally."

"Did anyone else know? Anyone who was at the house last Saturday night?"

She shrugged lightly. "They all knew, I imagine. I mean, we were *discreet* about it, naturally. Quentin and Peter and I. Quentin and I went to our rooms and talked for a while, and then, when the coast was clear, I tippy-toed off to Peter's room. It was just down the hall. But Santa Fe is a small town. There aren't many secrets here."

If she were right, and they did all know about her and Peter Jones, then any one of them would've known that Quentin could be raised to the roof beams without an audience watching.

I nodded. "Let's do this, Justine. Let me run these names by you, the names of the other people who were there that night, and you give me a brief description of each of them."

She rolled her eyes. "Oh God. How boring."

"Won't take long. And it would be helpful. Let's start with Peter Jones."

She smiled, raised her hand from her calf, and put her right arm, like her left, along the back of the sofa. Pressed tight against the black jersey, her breasts were looking less small than they had before, but just as perfect. "Poor Peter," she said. "He tries so hard to be a saint. But he's just so crazy about being a sinner."

I echoed Rita's questions to me: "What *is* a spiritual alchemist?"

"I don't have any idea. Something to do with meditation, according to Peter. But you'd have to ask him."

"He's never explained it to you?"

She smiled. "We're usually too busy with other things."

I nodded. "All right. You've told me something about
Leonard Quarry. What about his wife, Sierra?"

A bit more scorn. "*Sierra.* Can you imagine? I mean, if
you're going to invent a name for yourself, why not use a
little more imagination?"

"What kind of a woman is she?"

"One of those breathless, wispy little things who sob at
the death of the daffodils. She can't really be all *that* wispy,
if she's a psychic, and she's *supposed* to be. If she can see
inside Leonard's head, she must have an extremely strong
stomach."

I nodded. "What about Brad Freefall?"

"Brad? Brad's harmless, I suppose. Although God knows
I wouldn't want to trade places with Sylvia. Brad's into
drums, the harmonic vibrations. I mean, how would *you*
like to live with someone who was pounding on a tom-tom
all day?"

I smiled. I'd like it about as much as I'd like living with
Justine Bouvier. "And Sylvia Morningstar?"

"Sylvia's into crystals. She's all right. Scatterbrained. But
like Brad, she's harmless."

"Carl Buffalo?"

More scorn. "God. Carl Buffalo. The New Age Sioux
Indian. He takes sad little men up into the mountains and
teaches them how to get in touch with their warrior selves. I
can't imagine anything more dismal."

"You mentioned Eliza Remington. She's an astrologer?"

"She's a witch. A ruthless, conniving witch."

"What about Carol Masters?"

She tilted her head slightly to the side and shook it, smiling. "Poor Carol. Her career as an actress hasn't been

doing so well in the past few years, so she's discovered reincarnation. It's really too bad that Shirley MacLaine got there first. Carol's pathetic, really. Do you remember Carol Burnett doing her imitation of Norma Desmond? That's what Carol Masters always reminds me of."

"And Veronica Chang?"

For the first time, her face showed the shadow of something substantial. Like thought, perhaps. "Veronica," she said. She took her arms from the back of the sofa and folded them beneath her breasts. "She's a powerful woman."

"She's supposed to be a Saku master. What's that, exactly?"

"It's Brazilian. A healing technique. A type of laying on of hands."

"Chang doesn't sound like a Brazilian name."

"She's Korean." I could see her closing up on me, the small petulant mouth tightening.

"What's her relationship to Bernardi?"

She looked surprised. "Relationship? To that slob? No relationship at all. He didn't have a car, so Sylvia asked her to give him a ride."

Which is what Bernardi had told me. "Okay. What about Bennett Hadley?"

"Bennett?" she smiled. She leaned forward to pick up her cigarettes. I think that she was relieved to change the subject. "He's our resident expert. He knows everything. Just ask him. He'll tell you." She lit a cigarette, blew smoke out across the marble table. "He'd be attractive, really, if he weren't such a pompous jerk. Have you read his book?"

"No."

"*A Guide to the Invisible.* It's sort of an encyclopedia of the occult. He's done his homework, you can see that, but his understanding of the spiritual world is basically shallow. Second hand, out of books."

And that was all of them. All thirteen people who had been at the house in La Cienega that night. The number thirteen, at least in this instance, had proved unlucky. One of the thirteen had killed, one of them had been killed, and one was under arrest. All the rest, so far as I was concerned, were under suspicion.

"All right," I said. "Let's go back to last Saturday night again."

She blew out a small puff of smoke and exasperation. *"God,"* she said. "Haven't we been doing that?"

"I mean the party, specifically. What happened?"

"But I went all *through* that with the police." The petulance I had glimpsed in her face had moved to her voice and become more real.

"I know," I said. "And I appreciate your taking the time to do it again."

"Ugh," she said.

"We'll try to keep it as brief as possible."

She inhaled on the cigarette, exhaled. "It's a good thing I like you, Joshua."

I smiled. My debonair smile. "It's a wonderful thing, Justine."

She smiled. "Where am I supposed to start?"

"Whose idea was this party?"

"Brad and Sylvia's. Sylvia's, probably. Brad's not much in the idea department. You know about the arrest of Clayton Railsback last week?"

"Nope." I did, of course, from Bernardi. I wanted to hear what she had to say.

She frowned. "How could that be? It's one of the biggest things to hit this town in years."

"I was out of town last week."

"Oh. Well, Clayton's a healer, a psychic surgeon, studied for *years* in the Philippines with one of those little men they have there. Reaching right into the body and pulling out diseased organs? Nasty, *gruesome* stuff, and a lot of it is fakery, naturally, but Clayton is supposed to be *very* effective. I've never used him myself, but I'm hardly ever sick, not even a cold in the winter. I just seem to have this incredibly strong constitution. But a lot of people swear by Clayton. Anyway, he was arrested last week, for fraud. It's a put-up thing, naturally, the A.M.A. trying to get him, out of jealousy, mostly. So Brad's idea was for a group of us to get together and work out a kind of strategy.''

"A political strategy?"

"Well, that, too, naturally. Because, I mean, if it starts with Clayton, then where does it stop? The fascist mentality, Joshua. You remember the Jews in Germany?"

I did, and nothing she had said so far had angered me more than her comparing herself, and her friends, to the Jews in Germany.

"We were all threatened," she said. "All of us who've chosen alternative pathways, alternative ways of healing."

In New Mexico, anybody who wants to call himself a therapist can legally do so, and accept money for whatever therapy is provided. No training is required, nor is any sort of degree or certification. And in Santa Fe, it sometimes seemed that there were more therapists, and more varieties of therapy, than there could possibly be people in need of it. Possibly the therapists all provided it to each other.

"But mostly," she said, "to work out a spiritual strategy. What Brad wanted was for all of us to gather together in one place, so we could focus our energies and see what we came up with."

"And what did you come up with?"

"We never had time. The next day, poor Quentin was murdered, and then the card was gone, and then there were police all over the house. After we all talked to the police, everyone sort of dribbled away home."

"Okay. Tell me about Saturday evening."

And so she told me a story that I already knew, from the police records and from Bernardi's account. I would hear it again, and again, from all the others; and I would watch the teller and listen to the tale in the way I watched and listened now, waiting for some small detail altered or omitted or added, some small shift of voice or eye or emphasis. Observation, incredible powers of.

She told me that when she and her husband had arrived at the house in La Cienega, at about five in the afternoon, everyone but Bernardi and Veronica Chang was already there. There had been drinks out on the big enclosed porch, people milling about and gathering into clusters, most of them, she said, chattering about the recent arrest. Yes, Eliza Remington had brought the leather binder and had passed it to Quentin. Quentin had passed her a check for two hundred thousand dollars.

"Why conduct business there, at the house?" I asked her.

"The Remington witch's idea. She had to go to Houston the next day, she said. And Quentin hadn't been able to get all the money together until late on Friday."

Quentin had kept the card with him, showing it off to anyone who wandered up. Now and then, a small crowd of two or three or four had assembled around him and his prize. There were oohs. There were aahs. Leonard Quarry and his wife had stood on the other side of the room, looking stonily away.

"So everyone knew that Quentin had the card," I said.

"Yes, of course," she said.

"Did they know how valuable it was?"

"Quentin never mentioned what he paid for it."

"But he told them what it was. He told them its history."

"Yes. Naturally."

"And Quentin thought that was a safe thing to do?"

"But we knew everyone there. It wasn't like it was a room full of strangers."

Veronica Chang and Giacomo Bernardi had arrived only about fifteen minutes after the drinking had begun. "He's not the type," Justine Bouvier told me, "to miss out on free drinks." Veronica had joined her and Quentin while Bernardi had sat at the bar, drinking by himself.

A little after six, all of them had gone outside "to say goodbye to the setting sun," said Justine. All except Bernardi, who claimed to be suffering from asthma, which, he said, was aggravated by the cold. He remained at the bar. Justine, annoyed with Bernardi, maintained that he was simply unwilling to join in convocation with the others. I found that I was suddenly more fond of Bernardi.

Wine ("not too bad") was served with the vegetarian dinner ("dreadful sandy little bits of chick-peas or something floating in the sauce"). It was at dinner that someone asked Leonard Quarry how he felt about not having been able to obtain the Tarot card.

"Who asked him?" I said.

She shrugged. "I really can't remember now."

"According to the testimony of the other witnesses, it was Veronica Chang."

A bit snappish: "Well, if you already know, why ask me?"

I told her, "I need to know that everyone's in agreement, Justine. About what happened."

"Well," she said, reluctantly, her voice only slightly softer—she had been mollified, perhaps, but wasn't anxious to admit it. She wanted more. I suspected that she always wanted more, and that frequently she got it. She picked up the cigarettes, slid one out, lit it. "Maybe it was Veronica. I really can't remember. I mean, an awful lot happened that weekend. My husband was *strangled,* remember?"

It seemed to me that I wasn't the one who might be in danger of forgetting.

"I mean," she said, "even though I'm absolutely convinced that Quentin is still with us, the *essential* Quentin, it was still a terrible shock for me to wander into that room and see him hanging there."

"Of course it was," I assured her. "How would Veronica Chang know that Leonard Quarry had wanted the card?"

She shrugged. "I can't imagine."

"What did Leonard say?"

"Oh, the big fat fool tried to pretend that it didn't matter. Tried to pretend that he was being gracious about the whole thing. But you could tell, *anyone* could tell, that he was furious."

After dinner, she said, more drinks were served in the living room. Eliza Remington, who never drank anything stronger than tea or mineral water, went off to her room around nine o'clock. About fifteen minutes later, Justine Bouvier told me, the argument started.

THE HIEROPHANT

TO KEEP ITS wounded engine happy, I let the Subaru coast at fifty down the long winding run of the Ski Basin Road, past the adobe homes and the clutters of condominiums sprinkled amid the scrub pine. Most of these yuppie haciendas had been built fairly recently, after the California and Texas money flooded into the real estate market and sent prices floating skyward. Twenty years ago this had all been windswept arroyos and sunswept trees. The only occupants had been the coyotes and the rattlesnakes. The coyotes were gone now, and the rattlesnakes had become investment bankers.

At the bottom of the hill, at the Stop sign, the road met Washington Street, and I crossed this and drove along the asphalt entrance to the Fort Marcy sports complex. I parked the wagon in the lot, the engine coughing twice. It was two o'clock. The air was warm and the sky was blue. A few men and women in shorts and sweatshirts were running doggedly around the damp dirt track that circled the field.

Inside, I took a shower first, and sudsed myself up like Lady Macbeth on a bad morning, then spent a long time letting the scalding spray sluice off the soap. I didn't feel dirty, exactly, after my time with Justine Bouvier; but I didn't feel exactly clean, either.

The municipal pool was heated just enough to prevent sedentary types from leaping into cardiac arrest after they leapt into the water, and the air that had settled over it was warm and soupy and it held the tang of chlorine. At the moment, the pool was almost empty. A heavyset older woman in a floral one-piece and a floral swim cap wallowed in a tired but determined doggy paddle. A teenage girl, her eyes invisible behind her goggles, her body beneath the gleaming black nylon suit as sleek and graceful as a young seal's, went sliding by in a sturdy and deceptively slow-looking crawl. And in the center lane, a bemuscled lout executed loud and splashy power strokes, arms furiously flashing, feet furiously flailing, flat palms smacking against the water as though hating it, flogging it. Water spattered and splattered, great gouts of silver, into the lanes on either side.

I chose the lane at the far side of the pool and I dove in.

My own stroke is a fairly sedate, grandmotherly affair, a kind of aquatic jog. Swimming a mile—seventy-two lengths in a pool that size—is a tedious business if you see it merely as exercise. So what you do, you don't think about the exercise, or about anything at all. You concentrate on the sensations. The water supporting you and sliding like silk along your flanks. The smooth entry of each arm into its surface, the smooth downstroke against the density of liquid, the smooth exit. The stretch and pull of muscle. The steady suck and hiss of lung, the reassuring pump of heart. It's a kind of meditation, I suppose. I no longer count the laps. I know that once I've found my rhythm and reached my speed, a mile takes me exactly thirty-seven minutes, and now and then—when I remember—I glance at the big one-handed clock on the north wall. When the time is up, I'm done.

Today, though, my rhythm was off. I couldn't seem to empty my mind. Justine Bouvier and her story kept intruding.

"HOW DID THE argument start?" I had asked her.

"I told you," she said. "It was that Bernardi. We were all sitting around, having a very nice, very quiet conversation, when all of a sudden he gets up from his chair and he starts *bellowing* at Quentin. *'Why you want dees card? What you do with eet?'* " It was a cruel, mocking burlesque of Bernardi's accent; and, recognizing my own prejudice in hers, I felt more than a little guilty.

"He was drunk, naturally," she said. "So drunk that he could hardly stand upright. But that's no excuse. Quentin said something to him, I don't really remember what—"

According to the reports, what Quentin had said was, "Why don't you go away, you boring little man." Quentin had obviously been a better magician than he'd been a diplomat. Even if he'd been a terrible magician.

"—and Bernardi just *exploded!* He threw his drink away and he ran across the room and threw himself at Quentin. He hit me, too, with his arm, and I spilled my own drink. All over myself. It *ruined* my dress. It was silk, a Versace! And then he had his hands around Quentin's throat and he was *choking* him, and Quentin was sort of hitting at him, trying to get him away, and then finally Brad and Peter were there, pulling him off. They dragged him over to the corner, and his face was all red and loose and absolutely *crazed.* He was practically *slobbering,* like a dog. Brad was talking to him, probably giving him all that peace-and-love nonsense from the sixties. Brad's never really gotten over the sixties. And Sylvia was fluttering around the room, chirping away, trying to dry me off with some filthy rag she found someplace."

"Where was the card while all this was going on?"

"Quentin had it in his lap. In its leather folder. It fell when Bernardi attacked him, and I picked it up off the floor."

"Has Bernardi ever had any kind of dealings with your husband before?"

Indignant: "Of course not. Why would you even ask?"

"Just that it sounds like a fairly extreme reaction on his part." Even if Quentin had been, as I suspected, a gold-plated asshole.

"He's *Italian*. You know how excitable they are. And he's a lunatic."

Brad had given Bernardi a bottle of sambuca and Bernardi had gone bumbling off. Everyone had gathered around to commiserate with Quentin. ("Except for Leonard Quarry and his wood sprite wife. Leonard just sat there, gloating.") Shortly afterward, the party had begun to break up. Carl Buffalo had been the first to head for bed, Justine said, and he was soon followed by Leonard Quarry and his wife, Sierra. Then by Peter Jones, who was followed by Carol Masters, the actress. "Carol's been after poor Peter for ages. It's a shame she's not his type. He likes women who are still capable of breathing." This she said with a self-satisfied smile.

Veronica Chang had left last, and then Leonard and Justine had said their good nights to Brad and Sylvia, and they'd gone off themselves.

I said, "And you never saw Giacomo Bernardi again that night?"

"Not saw him, no. But I could hear that stupid soccer game he was watching. Peter's bedroom was right next to the library. It was still on when I fell asleep." She smiled. "You don't watch soccer games, do you, Joshua?"

"Every chance I get," I lied. "Quentin still had the card when you left his bedroom?"

"Yes. It was on the dresser."

"And about what time did you leave?"

"Oh, elevenish, I guess. Something like that."

I flipped my notebook shut. "Okay, Justine. Thanks very much."

"You're leaving?"

I stood up. "People to do. Things to see."

Still sitting, she smiled up at me. "Are you sure you don't want to try a regression? It wouldn't take long."

"Like I said, maybe some other time. Thanks anyway."

Slowly she unfolded herself up from the sofa and slowly, in profile, her eyes shut like a cat's, she stretched her long slim body. Arms stiff, hands balled in fists below and behind her hips, breasts thrusting outward. She sighed a long weary sigh, slowly rolled her shoulders, and then opened her eyes and saw me watching her. She smiled and turned to face me. "You're sure?"

"Yeah. Thanks."

She shrugged. "Your loss."

THE ELDERLY WOMAN in the floral swimsuit had pulled herself up the ladder and padded away, panting happily. The power stroker had burst from the water and swaggered off, dripping elaborately, looking for telephone books to rip up and pig iron to chew on. Or vice versa. The teenage girl still kept up her steady, sturdy crawl, and looked as though she could keep it up from here to China. A few new people had joined us, but I hadn't paid them much attention. I was too busy thinking about Justine Bouvier and why I had disliked her so much.

She was as predatory, in her way, as a coyote, although she probably lacked a coyote's depth. For all her talk of spirits and mysticism, she seemed to me about as deep, and as substantial, as a Burger King ashtray. She was selfish. She was a bigot.

But I had met selfish, shallow people before. I'd met bigots before—even, occasionally, in the mirror. And I didn't usually react so strongly against them.

I had reacted so strongly against her, I realized, because I'd reacted so strongly toward her. She was a woman who wanted men to be aware of her sexuality—needed them to be aware of it. And they would be. There was too much promise for them not to be: in the big brown eyes, the knowing smile, the lithe, limber, available body. And probably, if accepted, the promise would be kept. Probably she would be skilled and she would learn exactly what you liked and she would do it exactly as you liked it to be done. That would be important to her. She defined herself, I suspect, and she defined men, by their reactions to her. Their inner lives, and finally her own, didn't really matter.

And yet, despite her emptiness, perhaps even partly because of it, I'd found myself attracted to the package that held it. She might be, ultimately, dislikable. Probably she was. But that wasn't why I'd disliked her. I'd disliked myself for the attraction, and I'd projected the dislike onto her.

I've never thought that I would one day achieve a total lack of flaws. But occasionally I find myself thinking that it might be nice to stop discovering new ones.

BENNETT HADLEY LIVED to the west of town. From Fort Marcy, I took Washington to Paseo de Peralta, turned right up the Old Taos Highway, slipped between the traffic onto St. Francis, then quickly slipped off at Camino La Tierra. This area was newer even than the east side, and the homes were bigger and farther apart, riding the ridges of the rolling hills like castles and palaces. The sky was an upturned porcelain bowl, pale blue, its rim running all the way around the distant horizon. Patches of snow lay in purple shadows beneath the gnarled pinon and juniper. In the clearings, damp gray grasses lay flat against dark brown earth.

I drove on pavement for a couple of miles, then turned onto a road that in better times would be dirt, but that today with the thaw was mud. The engine coughed. I came to another mud road and turned right.

Bennett Hadley's was one of the newer houses. Although broad and handsome, it was a bit less grand than most of the others, and, because no landscaping had been done, a bit more stark—one tall story of khaki brown, buttressed adobe rising from what had obviously been, only recently, a construction site. Where the dank earth showed between lumps of snow, it was stripped and empty.

I parked the car, got out, hiked up the cement walkway, pushed the doorbell. After a few moments, it opened.

He was somewhere in his forties and he was an inch or so above six feet tall. His gray hair was parted on the left, above a ruddy, good-looking face that was, at the moment, smiling in welcome. He wore a plaid flannel shirt, gray

slacks, white cotton socks, expensive running shoes. In his
left hand he held an amber bottle of Pacifico beer by its
neck. He didn't look like an expert in the occult. He looked
like an actor, the kind of actor who plays the dependable
family doctor in a soap opera. A sensitive and caring man,
but still a manly man. And his voice, too, was an actor's
baritone as he said, "Croft?"

"Yes. Bennett Hadley?" I put out my hand.

"The one and only." We shook hands. His grip was un-
necessarily firm; but manly men, in the midst of ritual, can
sometimes forget themselves. "Come on in. You drink
beer?"

"I've been known to."

"This way."

I followed him down a tile-floored passageway into the
kitchen. A high ceiling with square wooden beams and
clerestory windows. More tile on the floor. A big butcher
block table in the center. Oak cabinets all around. Hadley
set his beer bottle on the table, opened the door to a large
refrigerator, took out another bottle, used a church key to
snap off the cap, handed the bottle to me. I thanked him,
and he lifted his own bottle by the neck and said, "Let's go
outside. Nice out there today. No wind."

Once again I followed him. Down another tiled passageway and then through a glass door, out onto the semicircu-
lar flagstone patio. Hadley shut the door behind us and
waved his bottle toward a wooden picnic table and two
wooden benches. "Grab a pew."

The patio was warm and dry because it took the southern light and because it was mostly enclosed, a viga ceiling
overhead and two low adobe walls that would cut off any
wind from west or east. It was bisected, south to north, by
a line of three upright, stripped pine logs that served as pil-
lars. Hadley positioned himself against one of these, the
outermost, three or four feet from where I sat. He leaned
back against it, in profile to me, his arm folded across his
chest, the beer bottle dangling loose. He narrowed his eyes
and looked out across the unfolding hills. "Beautiful here,
isn't it?" In his voice was the same comfortable pride of

possession you sometimes heard in Ben Cartwright's voice when he gazed out at the Ponderosa.

"It's a mighty fine spread," I said.

He nodded. He hadn't heard the irony. "You know," he said thoughtfully, "an old Sufi master once told me that there was nothing so wonderful, and nothing so mysterious, as the world. Turns out he was right." He nodded again, pleased with the notion, or pleased with himself for appreciating it.

Although it meant shattering what was clearly a deep mystical communion between man and real estate, I said, "I wonder if I could ask you a few questions, Mr. Hadley."

He roused himself from his contemplative state, looked over at me, and smiled. "Ask," he said, "and you shall receive." He leaned away from the pillar and came and sat down opposite me, sideways, then swung his legs over the bench to face me, beer bottle on the table and held between both hands, fingers interlocked around the neck.

I said, "Do you think Giacomo Bernardi killed Quentin Bouvier?"

"Sure."

"Why?"

He shrugged. "Bernardi's killing him was appropriate. Killing him that way, hanging him. In Bernardi's eyes, anyway."

"Appropriate?"

He took a sip from his bottle of beer and eyed me speculatively. "Do you know anything about the Tarot?"

"Not much."

"All right." He leaned forward, into the story he was about to tell. Like Justine Bouvier, he enjoyed explaining things. "There's a Major Trump called The Hanged Man. It shows a man hanging upside down from a gibbet, with the rope tied around his left ankle. In the Italian Tarot tradition, which is historically the earliest, this card is called El Gobbo. But it's also called Il Trattore. The Traitor. Italy's got a long history of hanging traitors by their heels. Goes back to the Renaissance, and probably beyond. And look

at World War Two. That's exactly what the partisans did to
Mussolini after they caught him.''

"Quentin Bouvier wasn't hung by his heels."

Hadley shook his head, abrupt, impatient. "That's not
the point. The point is that from Bernardi's point of view,
Bouvier *was* a traitor. The distinction between black and
white magic is a great deal more arbitrary than most people
think, certainly more so than Bernardi tends to think. But
the fact is that Bernardi saw himself as a white magician,
and he saw Bouvier as a black magician, a man who dealt
with spirits and devils. Bernardi's not sophisticated enough
to realize that these devils, more often than not, are merely
metaphors, symbols for certain mental processes and certain hidden aspects of the self. For him, they're real. And
for him, anyone who deals with them is by definition evil.
By definition a traitor to the ideals he cherishes. He didn't
want Bouvier to have that card."

"And so he killed him."

"Exactly." He sipped at his beer. "Death by hanging. The
perfect death for a traitor. From Bernardi's point of view,
that is. He saves one card, and he turns the black magician
into another card." He nodded, more to himself than to me,
as though satisfied by his exposition. "Appropriate."

"If you're right," I said, "why *didn't* Bernardi hang
Bouvier by his heels?"

Hadley shrugged. "Who knows? Too drunk, probably.
He was drinking like a fish from the time he arrived at the
house."

"If he was so drunk, how did he manage to sneak into
Bouvier's room, knock him out with a lump of quartz, hoist
him to the rafters, steal the card, and then leave the house
and hide the card?"

As I spoke, Hadley had begun to frown slightly. He let go
of the beer bottle and began to rub his right temple lightly
with the fingertips of his right hand. When I finished, he
said, almost curtly, "Look. I can't speculate about that. You
asked me what I thought. I told you."

Testy. A man who was happy, who was delighted, to provide answers, but only so long as he was personally pleased by the questions.

I nodded. I asked him, "What would Bouvier have done with the card?"

Hadley suddenly grinned. This was a question he liked. "Nothing. That's the terrific part. Oh, no question, he would've used it in one of those idiotic ceremonies of his. He would've chanted his Latin chants and invoked the demons—Astaroth and Baphomet and the rest. And the same thing would've happened that happened *whenever* he conducted a ceremony. Nothing. A big flat zilch."

"You don't believe in magic," I said.

"I don't—I didn't—believe in Quentin Bouvier. As I say in my book, I believe that magic, like any other belief system, properly understood, provides a channel through which an individual can focus his energies. But in order to focus them, you've got to develop them. In order to become a mage, a master, a sadhu, a yogi, whatever, you've got to bring to bear enormous amounts of self-discipline. Quentin didn't have that. Never had it. He was a dilettante."

"What about his wife?"

"Hah!" He grinned. "The Dilettante's Apprentice. You talked to her? She lay her Egyptian number on you?"

"She mentioned something about the cards being originally Egyptian."

"Typical Bouvier bullshit. Bullshit that's been handed down by pseudo-scholars for centuries. People like de Gebelin and Eteilla believed that the cards were introduced into Europe by the Gypsies, and that the Gypsies were originally Egyptian. Wrong on both counts. The Gypsies are from India and the cards are originally Italian. But Quentin had an Egyptian bee in his bonnet, thought he was the reincarnation of Akhenaton. And Justine, who's never had an original thought in her entire life, bought his story. She liked the idea of being Mrs. Pharaoh."

I said, "She believes, or says she believes, that this card possesses a power it picked up from the magicians who handled it."

For a moment his face was as scornful as Justine Bouvier's had been, earlier today. "Justine believes anything that her idiot husband believed. Well, let's face it, the woman is not a giant of the intellect—she was his bloody *secretary* before she was his wife. But all right, sure, the card probably did pick up vibrations from whoever handled it. A sensitive psychometrist might even be able to identify some of them. But personal vibrations become attenuated over time. And they get overlaid by the vibrations of the people who handle an object more recently. The strongest vibrations on that card would've been the vibrations of Eliza Remington." He grinned. "So Bouvier paid two hundred thousand bucks for the vibrations of an anemic little old lady who pretends to be an astrologer."

"How did you know how much Bouvier paid for the card?"

"What?" His eyes narrowed, in pain or in thought, and his fingertips touched delicately at his temple again, and began kneading. "I don't know. Someone mentioned it that night."

"Do you remember who?"

"No," he said. Lightly, his fingertips made small circles in the gray hair.

"Who else might've known how much the card was worth?"

Gruffly: "How would I know?"

I said nothing. I let his anger lie between us, across the wooden table, and I waited to see what he did with it.

He stopped kneading, held up his hand, showed me his palm. "Sorry," he said. "I had a rough night last night. My head's killing me. I just don't know, all right?" It wasn't particularly gracious, but it was an apology.

"No problem," I said. "What do you think of Leonard Quarry?"

He frowned. "Why?" He lifted his bottle, took a hit of his beer.

I said, "I need to learn everything that I can about these people. You know them. I'd appreciate any insights you might be able to offer."

He shook his head. "You're trying to help Bernardi. I understand that. But you're wasting your time, my friend. There are two kinds of people in this world. There are winners and there are losers. And Bernardi is definitely a loser."

Whenever I hear someone express a sentiment like this, I'm reminded of Robert Benchley's observation about the two kinds of people in this world: there are those who divide the world into two kinds of people, and those who don't.

"Maybe," I said. "But I'm being paid to learn what I can."

"And you think one of the others killed him."

"I'm not being paid to think."

He grinned. "That's good. Because if you think Bernardi's innocent, you're wrong."

"Maybe. It happens fairly often. Leonard Quarry?"

He shrugged. "But this is all off the record, right? The last thing I need right now is one of these clowns coming back at me with a lawsuit."

"I'm not a reporter," I said. "Nothing you tell me is going to end up in the *New York Times*. And I won't be giving out names."

He nodded. "All right. Leonard Quarry. Another dilettante. Worse than Bouvier, in fact, because at least Bouvier believed the bullshit he was spouting. I don't think that Quarry believes in anything except Mammon." He sipped at his beer. "That's money."

"Right," I said. "Thanks."

Once again, he hadn't heard the irony. Maybe he never did. "He lives out in Agua Caliente," he said, "near the hot springs, with his wife, a frail little number who calls herself Sierra. She's a psychic, allegedly. Quarry's a dealer—in esoterica, primarily, but when push comes to shove, he'll move anything that'll turn him a buck. He likes to pass himself off as an expert on the occult. He's anything but. He talks the talk, but he can't walk the walk."

I said, "You knew that he wanted to get that Tarot card from Eliza Remington?"

"Sure. And I know he was pissed off that he didn't get it. But look, Quarry didn't kill Bouvier. Quarry weighs in at about four hundred pounds, and on top of that he's got emphysema. He has a hard time lifting his gin and tonic. He'd *never* be able to lift Quentin Bouvier."

"How did you know that Quarry wanted the card?"

"What?" Wincing slightly. We were back to the routine with the fingers at the temple.

"How did you know that Quarry wanted the card?"

"I don't know. Someone mentioned it at dinner that night."

"Okay," I said. And then, one by one, as I had with Justine Bouvier, I went through the names of the other people who'd been at the house in La Cienega last Saturday night. Hadley's responses, although he didn't know it, were nearly identical to Bouvier's, and as glibly dismissive.

Peter Jones: "He's into a kind of alchemical meditation. Transmuting base elements into spiritual. And he's got plenty of base elements to work with. You know he's been having an affair with Justine Bouvier for over a year?"

Brad Freefall and Sylvia Morningstar: "Sylvia's a crystal maven, Brad's into drums. They're both relics. Debris left over from the sixties."

Carol Masters: "The poor man's Shirley MacLaine. She's into reincarnation and she's a channeler, channels a celestial being named Araxys. Funny, but a lot of what he has to say is lifted straight form the dialogue of Carol's old movies."

Carl Buffalo: "Chief Thunderthud, I call him. One of the local gurus of the men's movement. A muscle-bound clod."

Eliza Remington: "A fraud. But a sharpy, no question. You make an appointment, Little Liza takes your name and your birthdate and your place of birth. She uses those to get your social security number—she's got a computer, and she's hooked up to a database—and then she can find your medical history, your employment record, credit standing, retty much anything she wants." He grinned. "Well, shit, ou're a private eye, right? You know how that works."

"Yeah." But only because Rita had told me.

"And then, when you show up, she dazzles you with how ccurate she is. She's a sharpy, all right." He grinned and hook his head, almost in admiration.

I asked him, "How did she get the Tarot card?"

"Been in her family for years, apparently. She only sold . now because she needed the cash. That's the story, any-vay."

"And what about Veronica Chang?"

As it had earlier today, when I was speaking with Justine 3ouvier, Veronica Chang's name abruptly changed the tex-ure of the conversation. Hadley frowned, and started once gain to do his trick with his temple. "Veronica," he said. "Interesting woman."

"How so?"

"Very bright, very attractive. I never understood how she ot involved with Bouvier."

"She was involved with Quentin Bouvier?"

He frowned, puzzled. "Quentin?" Then he grinned. "No, not with Quentin. With Justine."

THE LOVERS.

"I NEED A NEW CAR," I said.

Rita said, "I told you, Joshua. I think you should lease one."

"Obviously, Rita, you don't understand the intimate relationship that exists between a man and his motor vehicle."

"Obviously not. But I do understand the intimate relationship that exists between a man and the Internal Revenue Service. If you lease the car and put it in the agency's name, you can deduct your payments."

"There are some things whose importance transcends financial considerations. A car, Rita, is more than just a means of transportation. It's an expression of a man's inner being, his true essence."

"Joshua?"

"Yeah?"

"I don't want you to be offended."

"You don't buy that, huh?"

"Well, yes, as a matter of fact, I do. It's pathetic, of course, but I buy it. But I'm not talking about that."

"What are you talking about?"

"Your feet. They're cold."

"Oh," I said, and I laughed. "Sorry."

We were in Rita's bedroom, lying in Rita's big canopied bed, the down comforter pulled up to our waists. Propped up against a pair of pillows, her hair jet black against the white Egyptian cotton, Rita was wearing a black silk nightgown that I found, as always, profoundly interesting. Lying on my side, my elbow against the mattress, my cheek notched against my fist, I was wearing what I usually wore in these circumstances. A silly grin. In the soft light from the nightstand lamp, she looked about twenty years old, and more beautiful than anything I'd ever seen.

"Speaking of inner beings," she said.

"Yeah?"

"Were you able to locate Carl Buffalo?"

"Locate, yes. Talk to, no. He's up in the mountains with a flock of happy campers. He'll be back in a couple of days. I spoke with some woman at his house—wife, girlfriend, I don't know."

"Not a wife. The land tax records have him as single."

"You got that from the computer?"

"Yes. What about Carol Masters?"

"She's out of town, too. Probably visiting Alpha Centauri. That's where this guy she channels, Araxys, is supposed to live. What do you figure Alpha Centauri is like this time of year?"

"Warm. Who will you be seeing tomorrow?"

"Brad Freefall and Sylvia Morningstar. I've got an appointment out in La Cienega at ten."

"When you're in the house, make certain you take a careful look at the fireplaces."

I took a careful look at Rita. "And why would I do that?"

"That Tarot card would be easier to conceal if it weren't inside its leather binder."

"Ah. Right. And leather can burn."

"And leather can burn."

"Hey," I said. "I knew that."

She smiled. "But possibly, if the binder *has* been burned, some of it remained."

"I'll take a careful look at the fireplaces," I said.

"What about Leonard Quarry?" she asked me.

"He hasn't returned my call. But Peter Jones did, the guy who's been playing around with Justine Bouvier, and I'm seeing him at four tomorrow. He lives in Mesa Roja. What I thought I'd do, after I talk to Brad and Sylvia, was shoot up to Agua Caliente and see if I can find Quarry. Afterward I can drive over to Mesa Roja. It's not far."

"And Veronica Chang?"

"Tomorrow night."

"Eliza Remington?"

"I see her on Thursday. I told you about her using the computer to fake the astrology stuff?"

"Several times." She smiled. "You know, Joshua, this affection you have for petty fraud is a little bit worrisome."

"I get a kick out of a sixty-one-year-old woman who uses a computer base to scam people."

"You've only got Bennett Hadley's word for it that she does, you know."

"I know," I said. "But even if she doesn't, it's a good story."

"What do you think of his story about Bernardi killing Bouvier?"

"I don't like that one as much. If the whole point is that Bernardi killed Bouvier because Bernardi saw him as a traitor, then why didn't he hang him up by his ankles? Which, on Hadley's argument, is what Bernardi would've done. *Should've* done."

"The argument is specious, obviously."

"I love it when you talk dirty."

She said, "Hadley feels that no one else makes a likely suspect?"

"So he says. He admits that no one liked Bouvier, but he's convinced, or says he is, that no one disliked him enough to kill him. Except Bernardi."

She said, "What about the connection between Bouvier's wife and Veronica Chang?"

"Hadley says they were an item for a while last year. Before Justine Bouvier became involved with Peter Jones."

"These people lead complicated lives."

"They surely do."

"Ma'am."

"What?" I said.

She smiled. "When you say something like *They surely do,* aren't you cowboys supposed to add *ma'am?*"

"Yes, ma'am," I said. "I plumb forgot."

She laughed. She reached out and, lightly, she put her hand on the back of my head. "Give me a kiss, you big galoot."

"Yes, ma'am," I said, swooping slowly down off my elbow. "I surely will."

LA CIENEGA IS A small community south of Santa Fe, hidden behind the hills to the west of the interstate. The older homes, built and still owned by Hispanic families, sit close together among the tall cottonwoods that crowd the banks of the narrow creek. Today the neat vegetable gardens, the carefully constructed chicken coops, were beginning to poke themselves out from beneath the flimsy pelt of melting snow. The trees, winter-stripped and streaked with meltwater, groped with gray spidery branches toward the faraway blue sky.

The newer homes, most of them built by latecomer Anglos, sit farther out on the plateau, away from the water and the trees, isolated from each other by the open spaces of high desert. The house of Brad Freefall and Sylvia Morningstar was probably the largest of these. A huge compound encircled by a pale brown adobe wall, it sprawled like a fortress along the top of a long bare hill where snow lay in veins along the gullies. The rutted mud of the driveway swung through a broad wooden gate in the south wall. A sign over the gate announced to the weary, and possibly puzzled, traveler that he was entering Rancho Nirvana.

In the courtyard, I parked the Subaru between an old Dodge pickup truck and a boxy Mercedes-Benz four-wheel-drive wagon, a vehicle that had cost more money than I earned in a successful year. Financially, these New Agers seemed to be doing okay for themselves. Justine Bouvier lived in an Egyptian eagle's nest paneled in marble, Bennett Hadley in a dandy La Tierra minimansion, and the Freefall-Morningstars in an adobe version of Xanadu. It occurred to me, and not for the first time, that perhaps I was in the wrong line of work. Maybe it wasn't too late for me to begin a new career—fortelling the future, maybe, by squinting thoughtfully into a handful of chicken gizzards. If worse came to worst, and I bombed, I could always make gravy.

I clambered out of the Subaru, clomped up the damp flagstone walkway that ran through the spindly Russian olive trees to the long territorial-style wooden portico. I pressed the glowing button to the right of the heavy oaken door.

The woman who opened the door wore a white peasant skirt and a ruffled white peasant blouse that exposed a bit more bony brown shoulder and a bit more bony brown sternum than perhaps it should have. Medium tall, she was very thin, and her quick, nervous movements made the thinness seem almost febrile. But despite the gauntness, her face was an attractive one, deeply tanned, animated, her brown eyes round and lively, her nose elegant, her lips full and quick to smile. Her teeth were large and white, and her hair was a thick brown frizzy cascade, threaded with silver. She was perhaps forty-five years old.

"Mr. Croft?"

"Yes. Sylvia Morningstar?"

"Yes, please come on in, it's *such* a pleasure to meet you." She was shaking my hand rapidly, pumping away, her thin fingers strong against mine. She emphasized quite a few of her words when she talked, like Justine Bouvier, or like someone who's read a lot of *Cosmopolitan*. And she strung her sentences together, plaiting them into a single bright encircling lariat of chatter: "This way, Brad's in the living room, I'm *so* glad you've come." As I followed her down a tiled hallway, she said over her shoulder, "I'm just so *pleased,* I can't tell you, that someone's trying to help out poor Giacomo, it's terrible what happened to Quentin of course, but Giacomo *couldn't* have done that, we've known him for *years,* he's been a *wonderful* friend, and I just *know* in my heart that this is all some kind of terrible mistake. Brad? Look who's here, darling, it's the private detective I told you about, Mr. Croft, from the public defender's office.''

The living room had been built on three levels, each two feet lower than the last, connected one to the other by wooden steps and creating a kind of broad amphitheater that circled a huge kiva fireplace where a sprightly yellow fire fluttered. Floating across the air was a faint smell of sandalwood and some soft melodic guitar music I didn't recognize. The curved white stucco walls towered up to a ceiling of dark brown shiny vigas and latillas. Except for a large cream-colored carpet on the lowest level, before the fireplace, the bleached and polished hardwood floor was bare. Sylvia Morningstar and I stood on the upper level, and Brad Freefall was lying on a long blue sofa against the wall on the middle level, his head against its arm, his knees raised, his bare feet flat against its cushion. Behind him, a curved picture window displayed a panoramic view of the courtyard and its Russian olives. He had been fiddling with a small drum, the size of a bongo, made of leather and wood. Now he grinned and set the drum on the floor, swung his feet down and stood, holding out his hand as I approached. "Hey, man, glad you could make it."

About the same age as his wife, just as tanned, he was tall, my height, and comfortably overweight, his rounded belly drum-taut against a Grateful Dead T-shirt. His eyes were blue and very clear, his face boyish and pleasantly fleshy. With his long blond hair held in place by a beaded headband, he looked like a surfer going amiably to seed. "Sit, man, sit," he said, and waved a big flat hand toward an upholstered armchair. I sat.

Sylvia Morningstar asked me, "Can I get you some tea? We've got some regular, English Breakfast, I think, and we've got some really nice herbal tea. Red Zapper? Heavenly Herbal? Citrus Surprise?"

Hands in his back pockets, Brad Freefall offered, "Beer, maybe? Whatever."

"Thanks," I said. I told Sylvia Morningstar, "The English tea will be fine."

"Good, that sounds lovely, we'll all have some. Brad, darling, I'm sure Mr. Croft's a busy man, why don't you start without me, dear, and tell him everything that happened last Saturday—that's what you wanted to talk about, isn't it, Mr. Croft?"

"Among other things, yes," I said.

"Sugar?" she asked me. "We've got Equal, too, if you want it. Or date sugar? And I think we've got turbinado, too."

"Plain sugar's just fine."

"Lemon? Milk?"

"Lemon. Thanks."

She bobbed her head at me. "I'll be right back."

Brad Freefall sat back down in the corner of the sofa, left arm along the sofa's back. He extended his long legs out along the floor and crossed them at the ankles and he grinned at me. "A private eye," he said. "Far out. Is it ever like they make it look on TV?"

"Not very often."

He nodded. "Running around and shooting people, car chases, all that good shit. Never really happens, right?"

"Almost never."

"Way I figured. Hype, man. Media moonshine. Anyway, no shit, I'm glad you're here. We both are. We've been talking about it a lot. Only natural, right? Considering it all went down right here at the house. Quentin getting offed and all. But I don't care what the cops say, man. Giacomo never did it. Never happened. The guy may be kind of a slob—who's perfect, right?—but he's got real purity of heart, man. He's got soul. He wouldn't be *able* to do something like that."

"How long have you known Bernardi?"

He shrugged his heavy shoulders. "Years, man, Giacomo's been around forever, seems like."

"When did you first meet him?"

"I dunno. Ten years ago? You should ask Sylvie, she's good with dates and like that. We met him at a party or something. No, wait, I take that back—it was at a psychic fair at Le Fonda. I was there with my drums and Sylvie was there with her crystals. We had a booth together. Giacomo was doing readings in the next booth and it was kinda slow. Dead, in fact. Back then, the psychic fairs were just starting up, and we didn't get the kind of traffic we get now. So, anyway, Sylvie asked him to do a reading for her. As a goof, mostly, you know? And so he did Sylvia's cards for her, and then he did mine. He was good, man. I mean really good. Intuitive. Way I see it, the cards are like a vehicle, you know? A channel, man, for you to focus your own energies."

Hadn't Bennett Hadley said exactly the same thing, in almost exactly the same words?

"And Giacomo's intuition," Brad said, "was right on. We were both kinda down about then, Sylvie and me. Things weren't working out, moneywise. We were even thinking of splitting, leaving town and heading back to California. But Giacomo said to fade that. He said that everything was gonna turn around for us, in a major way. And he was right on, man. Totally right on. Hey, Sylvia, I was just saying how Giacomo told us to chill out on the idea of splitting Santa Fe, back when we first met him. Remember, babe? The psychic fair?"

"Giacomo is *extremely* sensitive," Sylvia Morningstar told me, lifting a mug filled with steaming tea from a round red metal tray and handing it to me, "and *extremely* talented, and probably, if we hadn't asked him to read our cards, we would've made a *terrible* mistake and gone back to California." Holding the tray carefully, she sat down beside Brad and handed him a mug. "Here you are, darling." She took the last mug for herself, and laid the tray to her left, on the sofa cushion. "And then *none* of these wonderful things would've happened." She waved her arm lightly, to take in the wonderful lavish house, the wonderful high desert, the wonderful world.

I asked, "How did the wonderful things happen?"

"Well, it was incredible," she said, "because the very next week, the week after the fair, I accepted a new client, a referral from a friend. She was a Swiss woman, the client, from St. Moritz, and she'd come here for the skiing and she was having these *terrible* pains all up and down her left hip, really *agonizing* pains. She was a wonderful woman, but *no one* had been able to help her, not the medical doctors, not the chiropractors, not even my friend, who did body work and who was just *wonderful* with it. So I worked with her, we were living in town then, off Agua Fria, and I had this little tiny office space with a rickety little massage table, the whole thing wasn't much bigger than a closet, and I set up the crystals along her body—you know how crystals work?"

"They vibrate?"

"Exactly!" she said, delighted. Beaming, she turned to Brad and put her hand atop his thigh. "You see, darling, I *told* you he'd understand." She turned back to me. "I'm so *glad*. But of course, I'm sure you realize that it's just a teeny weeny bit more complicated than that, you've got to *sense* exactly where the blockage is, in your client, where the problem lies along the meridians, and you've got to *know* exactly which vibrational frequency is the proper one, and you've got to know *exactly* how much exposure to that vibration will produce the results you want."

Before she could explain any further, I said, "But it worked. You healed her."

"Oh no," she said, "not *me*. The crystals, the crystals and her own recuperative powers, her own vital energy. No, I was merely an assistant, an agent."

Brad Freefall grinned and ran his flat hand gently along her frizzy hair. "Yeah, babe, but you were the one who knew how to use the crystals."

She looked at him, smiling happily, and she actually blushed with pleasure. He leaned forward and kissed her lightly on the temple. She squeezed his thigh.

Feeling somewhat like a voyeur, I said, "And how did that make the wonderful things happen?"

She turned back to me, blinking. "Oh." She said it as though she'd forgotten I was there. She blushed again. "Oh dear, I'm so sorry. Margarite, that's my client, she was so pleased with what'd happened that she moved here, to Santa Fe, and she built this house and put it into trust for Brad and me. And then while she was alive, we all lived here together and we set up a foundation, the three of us, the Crystal Center, to investigate and promote alternative healing. We've done some *wonderful* work here, Brad and I. And we couldn't have done any of it without Margarite's help.''

''While she was alive?'' I said.

She took in a deep breath and she sighed it slowly out. ''Yes.'' She nodded. ''It was a *terrible* tragedy. Poor Margarite died five years ago, cancer, ovarian, there was nothing anyone could do.''

I took a sip of tea and then I asked what might have been a rude question. ''She didn't have the cancer when you first used the crystals on her?''

She looked shocked. ''Oh no! She'd been examined by *hundreds* of medical doctors and none of them had ever found a thing, no, the cancer was something that happened later—it just suddenly appeared like some horrible monster and it took poor Margarite away from us.''

I nodded, but I was wondering whether poor Margarite might have survived her cancer if she'd sought out another medical doctor soon enough. And hadn't I read somewhere that ovarian cancer was sometimes difficult to detect? Despite what Sylvie believed, or said, had the dark unruly cells of Margarite's body already begun their deadly blossoming, unnoticed, undiscovered, when she first showed up at Sylvia Morningstar's door?

I hoped not. Against all expectation, and my better judgment, I found myself liking both these people. I didn't believe, myself, in the miracle of crystals; but it seemed clear to me that they did, sincerely. Whether that made them naive, or foolish, or absolutely right, or—as I suspected but preferred not to admit at the moment—fairly dangerous, those were questions for which I didn't at the moment have the answers. And questions to which, at the moment, the answers were irrelevant.

"Okay," I said, "let's talk about last Saturday night. How long have you known Quentin Bouvier?"

Brad shrugged. "Four, five years?" He looked at Sylvia.

"Six, darling," she told him. "Don't you remember? He and Justine came to the convocation out in Galisteo. Veronica's thing." She turned to me. "Did you ever meet Quentin?"

"No."

"Well, if you didn't know him well, he could seen a bit, oh, difficult, I suppose. He was extremely bright, and he'd spent all his life learning about High Magic, he'd really made a *tremendous* study of it, and I suppose he didn't have much patience with people who didn't share his interests, or know as much as he did. But, really, basically, he was a good person, I think. It's just awful, a terrible thing, that someone could kill him like that."

I asked her, "Who do you think could've done it?"

"Well, of course, it couldn't have been anyone who was here that night. We know all of them, they're all good friends of ours and wonderful people, *spiritual* people. Brad and I've been going over it, trying to work out how it might've happened, and we've come up with a theory."

"Yes?"

"Well, we never lock our front door, we've been living out here now for seven years and we've *never* had any trouble, none at all, but there's always a first time, isn't there? And it wasn't locked last Saturday night. What must've happened is that someone, a burglar, came in that night, looking for something—valuables, jewels, I don't know, maybe the stereo or the TV—and he went into Quentin's room and Quentin woke up and saw him, and the burglar got frightened and hit him with my quartz crystal, which would've been the first thing he found, it was right there on the nightstand, practically *begging* to be picked up."

"Why," I said, "after he hit him, would the burglar hang him?"

"Because Quentin had seen him. Quentin could identify him."

"Ms. Morningstar—"

"Sylvie, please."

"Sylvie. Burglars don't usually enter a house at night. They generally go in during the day, when no one's home. And how many cars were parked outside your house that night?"

"How many? I don't know." She looked at her husband.

He shrugged. "Six or seven?" he asked her.

"Nine," I told them. "According to the state police reports. A burglar isn't very likely to hit a house that has that many cars outside."

"But it *had* to be a burglar," she said. "Nothing else makes any sense. It *couldn't* have been one of our friends."

"Did any of them have any reason to dislike Quentin Bouvier?"

"None of them!" she said. "Really, Joshua—do you mind if I call you Joshua?"

"Not at all."

"Really, Joshua, you have to understand that these people all treasure life. Most of them are healers, and caring for others, caring *about* others is the most important thing in their lives."

I said, "What do you think about Justine Bouvier?"

She smiled happily. "You've met her? Isn't she *wonderful?* So beautiful and so chic! All those lovely clothes she wears, and she wears them so well, she has such *style,* I'd give *anything* to be able to wear clothes the way she does."

I had been watching Brad Freefall out of the corner of my eye as I asked the question, and I noticed that he very quickly pressed his lips—it might have been a frown, but it was too fleeting to identify. When I glanced over to him, his own glance skittered away.

Something there, something about Justine Bouvier.

But to learn what it was, I'd have to chisel Brad loose from Sylvie. Which would probably be as easily accomplished as separating Siamese twins.

I tried something, and it worked. "I wonder," I said, "if I could take a look at the room where Quentin Bouvier was sleeping that night."

Sylvia scrunched up her thin shoulders, put a hand to her thin neck, and gave a feathery little shiver. "I'm sorry, Joshua, but I can't go in there again. After the state police took away all the bedding, I had to go in there to clean up, and it was a *terrible* mess, and I got physically *ill*. I've been keeping it locked ever since, and I just *can't* go in there again." She turned to Brad. "Darling, do you mind?"

He nodded bravely, squeezed her shoulder. "Sure, babe. We'll be right back." He stood up. "This way, man."

I set my tea on the floor and followed him from the living room. We went back the way I'd come, through a high-tech kitchen with an oven big enough to roast a Cadillac, and into the west wing of the building. A corridor ran down its length, floored with red Mexican tiles and walled to the right with stuccoed adobe and vertical panels of double-glazed glass. Through one of the panels, I looked out across the courtyard and saw that the house's east wing seemed to be a mirror image of this one.

Brad showed me the first room, the library, where, last Saturday night, Giacomo Bernardi had sat swilling sambuca while he watched a soccer match. The television, flanked by two tall speakers, was only a shade smaller than a drive-in movie screen. A burglar would've needed a U-Haul truck, and a derrick, to cart it away.

Brad told me that the next room had been occupied by Peter Jones. He didn't mention that Jones had shared his accommodations with Justine Bouvier.

The next room had been Veronica Chang's, and the room after that, Brad said, had been the Bouviers'. I noticed that small spotlights ran on tracks near the hallway ceiling.

As he unlocked Bouvier's door, I asked him who had been sleeping in the last room, the room beyond the Bouviers'.

"That was Carl's, I think," he said. "Carl Buffalo." He shrugged. "But you should ask Sylvie. She arranged all that." He opened the door and stood back to let me enter.

A fair-size room. White walls decorated with a couple of abstracts that had been painted by an interior designer, brightly colored and immediately forgettable. A thick white shag carpet. A small kiva fireplace in one corner. A twin bed, stripped down to a bare mattress and flanked by two pinewood nightstands. A low pinewood dresser running along one wall. Two doors on the far wall. Overhead, sunshine filtered in through an opaque rectangular skylight and splashed in from a clerestory window as long as the room, facing toward the courtyard.

And overhead, too, supporting the stained and polished vigas, was the beam from which Quentin Bouvier had been draped.

It was a good solid beam. It would be able to hold quite a bit more weight than the one hundred and thirty pounds that Bouvier had weighed.

I turned to Brad, who stood just inside the doorway, heavy shoulders slouched, his hands once again in his back pockets.

"The rest of them were sleeping in the other wing?" I asked him.

He shrugged again. "Most of them. The Quarrys were in the guest house, up ahead." He jerked his head to the right.

"So a total of how many bedrooms?"

"Nine, counting the guest house."

"Guest house is connected to this wing?"

He nodded. "Right. There's a door up the hallway, by the last bedroom."

"The lights out in the hallway. The spots. Were they on last Saturday night?"

"Yeah. But dim, man. They work off a rheostat. I turned them on before dinner."

I nodded. I crossed the room, opened one of the two doors. A closet, empty. Opened the other. A small, tidy bathroom: sink, toilet, shower stall.

I walked over to the beehive-shaped fireplace. It had been swept clean.

I said, "The fireplace hasn't been used recently?"

"Yeah, it was, man. Quentin used it. We had wood in all the fireplaces last Saturday. The state cops cleaned it out."

"Were all the fireplaces used?"

"Most of 'em. There's no other heat in this part of the house."

"The cops swept them all?"

"Yeah. Looking for evidence, they said."

And if there had been any, they had found it.

"What about the drains?" I asked him. "In the showers."

He nodded. "Yeah. They checked those, too."

"They find anything?"

"They didn't tell me, man."

"The chunk of quartz," I said. "The one that was used to clobber Bouvier. The cops have that?"

"Yeah," he said. "It was one of Sylvie's favorite pieces."

"That's a shame."

He nodded. "Bummer, man."

I nodded. I looked around the room. "This is a terrific house, Brad."

He grinned. "Thanks, man. We like it."

"It's huge, isn't it?"

"Yeah. Great for meetings. And now and then we rent it out. Groups, you know? The Sierra Club. Greenpeace. Like that. Gives us a nice little income."

I nodded. "So what's this I hear about you and Justine Bouvier?"

Beneath the tan, his face went pale.

THE EMPEROR.

I TOOK THE INTERSTATE north, past the racetrack, past the Cerrillos exit, then swung off onto St. Francis. That street, one of the main commercial routes into town, was today choked with lumbering trucks and splenetic, honking tourists as it wound through the western part of Santa Fe, sloped down to the Alameda and the Santa Fe River, and then rose up after it crossed Paseo de Peralta. Traffic didn't thin out until the road sloped down again at the ridge beyond La Tierra, sliding through the pine trees toward the stony brown bluffs and twisting arroyos north of town, wild ragged badlands flung out east and west as far as the eye could see.

Every year there was more traffic, there were more tourists, more trucks hauling ground beef and chiles and salsa to feed the tourists. The locals fret about it, call it the Aspenization of Santa Fe, howl at the city council. The Plaza, they say, has become an upscale shopping mall of pricey, precious boutiques where dullards from Duluth dress up like nouveau riche cowboys and affluent Apache Indians. Which is an interesting grievance, since this is how many of the locals themselves prefer to dress.

But the locals are right: there's a point where chic slips over into crass, and Santa Fe seems destined to reach it. So long as people, including the dullards from Duluth, hunger for something with even a semblance of grace and tradition and spare uncluttered beauty, and so long as they're prepared to pay for it, there will be affable sharks who will be more than happy to provide the semblance and take the cash. And Santa Fe, like many an American city, will continue its slow, relentless transformation into a theme park—dull, drab, and dead.

But outside town, the countryside is still spare and uncluttered, the sunlight still reels down from a clear blue silky sky, the mountains and the buttes still soar wild and reckless from a landscape so nonchalant about its lean rugged beauty, so indifferent to the passage of time, and the passage of man, that it takes the breath away. Driving through this country can be, should be, an exercise in humility; and that may be one of the very best exercises possible.

And so I drove north toward Agua Caliente and I admired the scenery and I felt properly humble and I thought about what I'd learned from Brad Freefall and Sylvia Morningstar.

Once again, when Brad and I returned to the living room, it had been Sylvia who had done most of the talking. Her account of the get-together last Saturday night didn't differ, in any significant way, from the accounts given by Justine Bouvier and Bennett Hadley, or from what I'd read in the police reports. Except that Sylvia minimized the violence of Bernardi's attack on Bouvier, tried to make the confrontation sound less like an actual physical assault than a spunky debate that had gotten a bit out of hand. Brad had sat there, quietly deferring to her. I got the impression that he usually deferred to her: that she provided the strength in the relationship.

When I asked her about her guests that night, I learned that Sylvia, unlike Bouvier and Hadley, didn't have an unkind word to say about anyone, anyhow, in this life or any other. According to her, all the people who had been there when Bouvier was killed were paragons of probity and kindness, selfless souls dedicated to the betterment of mankind. After the earlier interviews, it was refreshing to listen to someone from whom derision wasn't a hobby. But it was also less than illuminating.

Brad, when I talked to him alone in Bouvier's bedroom, had been a bit more helpful.

I had set him up, of course, put him at ease and then sandbagged him with the question about Justine Bouvier. And, as I'd thought, Brad didn't possess the emotional equipment—duplicity, we call it in the trade—to carry off a convincing denial.

As he went pale, he had said, "What?" He tried for a smile, and it came off sickly.

I grinned at him, man to man. This didn't come off too well, either—it was almost a leer, and it made me feel slightly tainted. "Come on, Brad," I said. "It was probably no big deal. A quick roll in the hay, right?"

He surprised me then by blushing. A lot of people in Santa Fe did things that deserved a blush or two, but Brad and Sylvia were the first people I'd seen in a long while who actually came through with one. For a moment, he said nothing. He blinked. He took a deep breath. He sighed, and then he said, with more sadness than anger, "The bitch."

My turn to say nothing.

He said, "She's the only one could've told you." But there was a thin note of doubt running through his voice, and a questioning, almost anxious look on his healthy, open face.

Still I said nothing. Brad had the ball and I let him run with it.

"I begged her not to tell anyone," he said. "I warned her. I told her that if Sylvie ever found out, I'd…" He frowned, looked away.

Kill her? Make her listen to rap music?

He sighed again, looked down, shook his head. "Ah shit, man." He took his hands from his back pockets and sat down on the bare mattress, arms on his thighs, shoulders bowed, head down.

I sat down myself, atop the dresser. "She didn't tell me, Brad."

He looked up, puzzled, perhaps a bit alarmed, afraid it might have been someone else.

"No one did," I said. "It was a guess. A shot in the dark. I saw how you reacted when I mentioned her name. And I've met the woman."

Not quite believing me, but clearly wanting to, he said, "She didn't say anything about me?"

"Nothing about any kind of relationship."

His face went suddenly sour. "Shit, man, it wasn't *any* kinda relationship. It was a one-shot deal. She showed up here one night when Sylvie was out of town. Came to the door wearing a fur coat and nothing else. Even then, man, nothing would've happened, probably, except that I was feeling down, you know? Missing Sylvie and all. I had some weed in the house, not much, an old joint somebody left, like years ago. But I did it, and that just made me feel more down, and then *she* showed up. Invited herself in, told me she knew I'd be lonely with Sylvia off in Mill Valley. And it just happened, man. She got what she wanted."

He flushed again, remembering. "Well, shit, man, I wanted it too, I guess. Hard not to. She's—well, like you say, you met her. You know what she's like, I guess. But it was just that one time. Never again. And I told her, man, I told her I never wanted Sylvie to find out. She just laughed at me. And so I had a beer can, empty, you know? And I tore it in half, right across the middle, and I told her that's what'd happen to her if it ever got to Sylvie what'd happened. She believed me. I must've sounded pretty spooky."

I nodded.

He frowned at me. "What *is* it with her, man? Why does she do that shit? Is she, what, like a nymphomaniac?"

I shrugged. "I think that Justine uses sex," I said, "uses her body, to control her world, to give herself a sense of power. Or she tries to."

He shook his head. "She's a flake, man."

I nodded. "Probably as good an explanation as any."

He looked at me. "You're not gonna . . ."

"Tell Sylvie? No."

"Jeez," he said, and shook his head sadly. "It was just that one time, man. And it never happened before, not with anyone."

I nodded. "Who else has she been involved with, Brad?"

He frowned again.

"Brad, you don't believe that Giacomo killed Bouvier. I don't either. It had to be one of the others."

He nodded, looked away. "Yeah. I could see you didn't go for the burglar bit." He looked back at me. "I guess I don't either. I wanted to, because Sylvie does. But, Jesus, man, that's *heavy*. That means that someone we know is like a *murderer*."

"That's right. And you do know these people, Brad. I don't. I don't have any kind of handle on them. Who else has Justine been involved with?"

"But it doesn't make any difference, man. Quentin didn't give a shit. He knew she played around. He did, too. I think they got turned on, the two of them, telling each other about it. I think that was their number."

"Maybe. But I still have to learn as much as I can."

He took a deep breath. "Shit, man." He shook his head again. "I don't feel right, talking about other people."

I respected his sense of honor, but I had a job to do. "I already know about Peter Jones," I said. Taking the first olive out of the jar, trying to make it easier for him to give me the rest. "Who else? Carl Buffalo?"

He looked surprised. "Jesus, man, how'd you know about Carl?"

I hadn't known; I'd picked a name at random. Maybe that was also the way Justine operated. "I heard something," I said. I didn't mention that I'd heard it right here, and right now.

"Yeah," he said. "Carl told me she came over to his place and did the same deal with him that she did with me. But Carl got off on it—this is before he had an old lady of his own. A couple of years ago. Carl fell for her, man. He was gonzo for her, and when she cut him off, he kinda flipped out for a while. He kept calling her, you know? Asking her

to see him. She'd just laugh. Like you say, man, she's a
power tripper. She gets off on it. Carl couldn't see that. Finally Quentin had to go over to Carl's and ask him to cool
it."

"Quentin went to Carl's place?"

"Yeah, like I say, Quentin knew what she was doing. That
was their game, man. Being, like, secret swingers."

"When did she cut it off?"

"I told you. Couple years ago."

"Who else was she involved with?"

"Shit man, she's not the one who's dead. Quentin is."

"And I won't know why unless I understand the connections between all these people. What about Bennett Hadley? Was she ever involved with him?"

He looked at me, frowned, shook his head. "Don't think
so, man. Bennett's not her style. Too spooky, maybe."

"Spooky?"

"He gets these headaches, like. Migraines, I guess. And
he weirds out. It's like, you know, people who drink too
much and get blackouts? But Bennett, man, he doesn't need
to drink. He gets one of those headaches, like when he gets
upset, and he starts talking weird, and then later on he can't,
like, remember any of it."

I remembered Hadley massaging his temples. "Weird
how?" I asked.

"*Weird,* man. I was out with him once, me and Peter
Jones and him, we were at Vanessie's having a drink. Just
beer, right? That's all I ever drink. And so Peter asks him
something about his family, right? About his father. What'd
his father do, you know? What kind of job did he have?
And Bennett starts rubbing his head and wincing, sorta, and
then the next thing you know he's shouting at us, me and
Peter. Stuff about ingratitude and envy, crazy stuff. Came
out of nowhere, man. And *loud.* The bartender had to ask
us to leave. Bennett's still babbling away, right? And then,
when we get outside, Bennett sorta stops and looks like his
knees are weak. And he rubs his head some more and then
he looks around like he can't figure out where he is, you
know? And then he asks what happened and Peter tells him.

Peter's good with that stuff, real gentle. And Bennett, he says he musta had a flashback. From the war, you know? Vietnam. He was there.'' Brad shook his head. ''Spooky, man.''

''How often does he get these headaches?''

''I dunno. Peter told me he's seen him do it before. But that was the only time *I* ever saw it happen. Only time I *want* to see it happen, man.''

''You've read his book?''

''Sure. Good book. He's okay, he's cool, he knows what he's talkin' about. It's just those headaches, man. They're spooky.''

''What about Leonard Quarry?''

''What about him?''

''Was Justine ever involved with him?''

''With Leonard? Are you kidding? He weighs like a million pounds. He looks like Jabba the Hut, man. Justine can't stand him.''

''What do you think about him?''

He shrugged. ''I dunno. He's always been okay to me.''

''Does that mean he hasn't been okay to other people?''

He shrugged. ''I don't know about other people, man. All I know is how the guy treated me.''

''No way he might be responsible for Bouvier's death.''

''No way, man. All Leonard wants to do is buy and sell things and lie around in the hot springs. The heat is good for his emphysema. That's why he moved to Agua Caliente.''

I nodded. I said, ''I've heard that Justine had a relationship with Veronica Chang.''

His eyebrows went up. ''No shit. I didn't know that.'' He grinned. ''Far out.'' A thread of admiration, perhaps even envy, ran through his voice.

''What do you think of Veronica Chang?''

''Amazing lady, man.'' He nodded. ''Amazing.''

''How so?''

''First of all, she's like drop-dead gorgeous. I mean, you remember the Dragon Lady, from the old 'Terry and the Pirates' thing on TV?''

"Sure." Brad was, on that evidence, a few years older than he looked.

"Really? You remember that? A million years ago, it seems like now. But I still remember the Dragon Lady. And Jesus, man, was I in love with that chick. Those eyes and that slinky body, you know? Well, that's Veronica. And I know it's like a stereotype and all, but Veronica, well, she really is, like, *inscrutable,* you know? She sits there, man, with this little Dragon Lady smile, like she knows exactly what you're thinking. She doesn't say much, most of the time. Hardly says a word. But when those eyes of hers lock on, man watch out. This is a lady with some serious charisma."

"Has she been involved with anyone besides Justine?"

"Shit, man, I didn't know she *was* involved with Justine. Far as I knew, the only person she ever hung out with was her brother."

"Her brother?"

"Paul. He lives with her. Better watch out for him, too, man. He's a Bruce Lee clone. Except that Bruce Lee was like, what, only about three feet tall? Paul is like six feet if he's an inch, and he's built like a brick shithouse. And he does some kind of martial arts thing. I dunno, karate, kung fu, some kinda Oriental thing like that. Chop chop." He chopped his hand at the air.

"Paul wasn't at the party."

"No. He doesn't go out much. Probably hangs around the house all day and punches sandbags. Or whatever is it they do, those karate guys."

I asked him about the others who'd been there last Saturday night. He liked them all, not perhaps with the blanket exuberance that Sylvia would later show, but genuinely, it seemed to me.

So, as I drove northwest through the rolling hills, I ticked off what I'd learned that was possibly important. The state police had checked the drains and the fireplaces in the La Cienega house. Bennett Hadley had headaches from time to time. Justine Bouvier, from time to time, had had Carl Buffalo. And had once had Brad Freefall. Veronica Chang had a brother. I didn't know yet whether any of this was actually important, and maybe I would never know.

AGUA CALIENTE LIES in a narrow valley bordered by low-lying brown hills, the hills striped today with irregular bands of melting snow. I passed the entrance to the commercial hot springs and drove another quarter of a mile, following the directions I'd received from Brad Freefall. Found a large aluminum mailbox, battered and unmarked, listing atop its wooden post as it guarded the entrance to a small dirt track that wound off to the left, through a snow-splotched field and down into the pale spidery cottonwoods. I turned off the main road and followed the path along the slope. The station wagon coughed discreetly once or twice, a professor clearing his throat before his lecture on semiotics.

Surrounded by tall trees that filtered out some of the sunlight, Leonard Quarry's house squatted at the end of the road, a two-story, chocolate brown adobe rectangle with a steeply pitched zinc roof. There were no cars parked in front. Black brittle weeds leaned out of the thinning snow. Shadowed, solitary, the old house seemed gloomy and abandoned. Water streaked the plaster, staining it the color of old blood. Beneath the roof's overhang, to the left of the cement steps, sat an unruly stack of pinon firewood. A few logs had escaped the pile, but hadn't made it back to the safety of the forest. They lay black and twisted atop the snow. Over the wooden door brooded a large bleached steer's skull.

I eased out of the Subaru, walked up the steps, knocked on the door. Meltwater dripped from the skull's shattered sinus cavity, as though the thing were suffering from influenza. I stood away from the drip.

After a moment, the door opened. Halfway. Cautiously.

Peeking around the door, bent slightly forward, she was medium tall, in her late twenties, and as thin as Sylvia Morningstar but very pale. The paleness was highlighted by the jet black makeup outlining her large, expectant brown eyes. Her hair was also black and it hung in soft, Pre-Raphaelite curls to her delicate shoulders. She wore a long-sleeved dress of white lace that fell loosely to the gathered waist, then continued its fall to her ankles. Her feet were bare, the skin so translucent that I could see the blue of veins. She was very beautiful—an earlier and more ethereal version of Cher.

"Oh dear," she said, as though mildly surprised, and she put the slender fingers of her right hand lightly to her throat. Her wrist was fine-boned, not much thicker than my thumb.

"Sierra Quarry?" I said.

"Yes?" Sounding faintly uncertain, as though she were unsure of my intentions, or her own identity.

"My name is Joshua Croft. I'm an investigator working for the Santa Fe public defender's office."

"Yes," she said, her soft voice low and solemn. She nodded. "I know who you are."

This caught me off guard. Maybe it was supposed to. "Really?" I smiled. "How?"

"Sylvia called. Sylvia Morningstar. She said you might be coming by."

Ah.

"Oh dear," she said again. She blinked and glanced around me, left and right, as though checking to see if there were any more of me lurking about.

"Yes?" I said.

She removed her hand from her throat, put it along the edge of the door, elbow out, as though barring me. Her fingernails were bright red, the only touch of color she apparently allowed herself. Like Giacomo Bernardi's, they'd been bitten to the quick. She stood up straight. "Leonard's not here," she told me. She said it bravely, the mistress of the castle denying entrance to the Saracens. "I don't know when he'll be back."

"Do you know where I could reach him?"

"No," she said with that low, fluting solemnity of hers. "No, I don't."

"May I come in for a few minutes and ask you a few questions?"

"Oh no," she said, and her bravery vaporized. Her eyes widened slightly and her fingers went again to her throat. "No, I couldn't do that. Not without Leonard here."

"It won't take long, Mrs. Quarry."

She shook her head. "No. No, I'm sorry. It wouldn't be right. Not without Leonard here."

"Mrs. Quarry, you're welcome to call the public defender's office if you like, to verify my credentials."

"No, no, no. It's not that. It's just that it wouldn't be right without Leonard."

"I see." I didn't see much of anything, except her, and her I didn't understand. I reached into my coat pocket, slipped out a business card, held it out to her. "Could you give this to Mr. Quarry, please, and ask him to call me?"

She took the card. "I will. Of course. *Thank you.*" The gratitude seemed genuine, but I couldn't tell whether she was thanking me for leaving the card, or simply for leaving.

I told her, "But I'll try stopping by again, later today." After I talked to Peter Jones.

Her eyes widened again. "Oh no, you really shouldn't. I don't have any idea when Leonard will be coming home."

I didn't point out that she was supposed to be psychic. I thought that this was very sporting of me.

"It might be very late," she said. "You'd probably just be wasting your time."

I was probably wasting it now. "Right," I said. "Thanks."

I climbed down the steps and into the Subaru. She stood there, peering solemnly around the door, and watched me until I drove out of sight. Before I did, I waved at her. She didn't wave back.

I was irritated. First the guy doesn't return the calls I leave on his machine. Then, when I very cleverly show up on his doorstep, he's not there.

I was irritated enough to play a hunch. Playing it would cost me only a couple of minutes, anyway. So, instead of driving past the gate to the hot springs, I turned into it. Drove down the gravel road, across the narrow bridge, parked the wagon at the main building, thumped up the wooden steps, entered the office. The woman behind the counter—attractive, blue-rinsed, in her fifties—smiled brightly and brightly said hello.

"Hi there," I said, even more brightly. "I've got an appointment with Leonard Quarry."

She blinked against this gust of cheeriness, but her smile endured. "He's in the pool." She riffled through some papers on the counter, looked up. "I'm sorry," she said, and seemed to be. "It looks like Mr. Quarry didn't leave you a pool ticket."

"That scamp." I smiled. "No problem. I'll spring for the ticket."

I paid her, took my ticket, and stepped back outside.

The place had changed in the three or four years since I'd last been here. Back then it had been simple and rustic, pretty much the same way it'd been for thirty years. A large weather-beaten wooden structure, set back into a notch in the rocky hillside, containing the men's and the women's hot pools. In front of this, a rusty hand pump which guests could use to suck the potable mineral water up from its secret channels beneath the gravelly soil. To the left, a line of weather-beaten wooden cabins that held the people who were staying longer than an afternoon. Few people did, back then.

It was a shade more upscale now, as though it were trying to attract the Perrier crowd. The cabins and the pool building had been painted an unfortunate mustard yellow. an outdoor swimming pool had been built of concrete, fifty feet long, twenty feet wide. Pale fingers of steam fluttered slowly along the surface of the still, blue water. The pool was empty. So, apparently, were the cabins. Maybe the Perrier crowd hadn't heard yet.

The pump was still there, and still rusty. Either the renovation money had run out too soon or the owners had decided to leave it as it was. A touch of rural authenticity.

I entered the hot-pool building, gave my ticket to a slight, slim Hispanic man, then went into the small locker room, stripped, stuffed my clothes into a locker, locked it, and stepped out into the shower room.

The shower room hadn't changed: a warm fog of air, a smell of mildew, gray cement floors, gray cement walls, white metal stalls blistered along their edges with rust. In the stall next to the one I chose, a fat man too young to be Leonard Quarry washed himself with a small amount of soap and a large amount of zeal. The black tufts of hair at his shoulders looked like epaulets. On the floor outside his stall stood a plastic gallon jug, half filled with mineral water—like many of the guests, he apparently liked to replenish the fluids he sweated away in the pool.

I washed, then padded past the fat man, who was still lathering exuberantly, and into the resting room, where there was a row of white padded tables. Two of them were occupied, each supporting an unidentifiable form swathed in sheets from head to toe. Neither was fat enough to be Leonard Quarry.

The pool attendant, the same man who'd taken my ticket, sat on a stool in the corner, reading *TV Guide*. He looked up, nodded to me.

In front of the pool, which was hidden behind a wall of glass milky with condensation, the cement floor gave way to rough steps chiseled out of the living rock, slick beneath my feet. I opened the glass door and looked around.

Two hundred years ago, when the local Indians used it, the pool had been open to the wide New Mexico sky and the dazzling New Mexico sun. Now it was roofed with corrugated metal and illuminated with electric lights. Progress. A natural formation in the rocks, it was roughly elliptical, fifteen feet wide by about twenty feet long. Steam unfolded from its greenish surface. The air was soupy and smelled still more strongly of mildew.

There were only four people inside here. Two young men stood off to the left, standing chest deep, their hair slicked back, sweat streaming off their shoulders as they discussed Santa Fe property values. An elderly Hispanic man, wrinkled brown skin sagging at his chest and hips, sat in thoughtful silence on a small ridge of rock, only his lower

legs in the water. And in the corner off to my left, rising out
of it like an iceberg, was a mountain of loose white blub-
bery flesh that had to be Leonard Quarry.

He was bald except for some gray hair fringing the back
of his skull. His face was an assortment of circles and
spheres: domed forehead, globular cheeks, round snout of
a nose, plump drooping lower lip, three or four pale white
chins. Thick pendulous breasts and pudgy shoulders above
water level, bulky arms beached along the rock ridge that
ran around the pool, he sat with his big round head leaning
back against the rock, like an emperor patiently waiting to
learn whether Rome had burned down.

I stepped into the pool, felt its heat ride up my thighs, my
stomach, my chest, then I set off toward him, the granular
sand nuzzling against the soles of my feet.

THE EMPRESS.

HERNANDEZ SAID, "And you just happened to be there."
He put enough sarcasm into the word *happened* to curl it
along the edges.

"No," I said. "I told you. I came up here to ask Quarry
about last Saturday night."

Dressed again, I was sitting in a chair in the office of the
manager of the Agua Caliente hot springs. Hernandez was
also dressed, in a navy blue suit, a white shirt, and a blue tie
striped with red. He sat atop the manager's metal desk, his
right foot off the floor, and he was swinging his black
tooled-leather cowboy boot impatiently back and forth. His
partner, Green, wore a gray suit and sat on the far side of the
room, which in fact wasn't very far, in a padded leather
chair identical to mine. Although he seemed less impatient
than Hernandez, he didn't appear any happier with me.

The office was pleasant enough, knotty pine walls and
hardwood floors, but it was small and it was getting smaller
all the time. I had been there, with Hernandez and Green,
for over an hour. Green's Sony Walkman, lying on the desk,
had been recording it all. Through the window behind Her-

nandez I could see three state police cars, two cruisers, and the unmarked Chrysler in which Hernandez and Green had arrived, all parked helter-skeleter in front of the pool building.

"Why'd you do it?" Hernandez said.

I shrugged. "I don't know. I got tired of the usual stuff. Video games. Bungee jumping."

"Cute. You're very cute."

"So are you," I said. "Did you know that you've got little flecks of gold in your eyes?"

Hernandez nodded. "You'll have plenty of time for that shit later. Lots of pretty eyes up in the state pen. And that's where you'll be getting your mail for a long time. We've got means, we've got opportunity." He grinned. "And we've got you, pussycat."

I nodded. "And where's my motive?"

"That's what we're trying to establish." He spoke in tones of great reasonableness. "That's why we're having this little conversation. This pleasant little chat."

"Oh," I said. "Right. I wondered."

"So why'd you do it?"

"Come on, Hernandez. Get real."

Hernandez sat back, looked over at Green. "What do you think?"

Green, expressionless, glanced at me, looked back to Hernandez, and said, "I think maybe he should resist arrest a little bit."

I laughed. I said to Hernandez, "You guys get this stuff out of a book?"

Hernandez leaned forward. He smiled. "You think this is funny, sweetheart?" He had eaten garlic recently. Several pounds of it. Garlic is never at its best when it arrives secondhand.

"No," I said. "I think it's a waste of time. For all of us."

Hernandez sat back, looked at Green. "He thinks it's a waste of time."

Green nodded. "Gee."

"Look," I said, "I told you—"

"Tell us again," Hernandez said. "Start from the beginning. You went up to Quarry in the pool."

I WENT UP to Quarry in the pool. His breathing was rheumy; I could hear the air rattling in his lungs. "Mr. Quarry?" I said.

The big round head slowly lifted itself away from the wall. The eyelids slowly rose. Two small gray eyes, squeezed even smaller by horizontal folds of flesh, looked out at me without much interest. "Yes?"

"My name is Joshua Croft. I'm an investigator working for the Santa Fe public defender's office. I'm sorry to bother you—"

"Then don't." The eyelids dropped and the head fell gently back to the wall. Somewhere deep inside that mass of chest, phlegm rasped and gurgled.

"Mr. Quarry, I have to ask you some questions about last Saturday night."

"I've already discussed that with the police, and at great length. I have nothing more to say." His eyes were still shut.

"Mr. Quarry, do you believe that Giacomo Bernardi killed Quentin Bouvier?"

The eyelids rose, and then the eyebrows did. "Are you still here?"

"I like it here. I'm thinking of moving in."

He closed his eyes. "There goes the neighborhood."

The door opened, off to my left. I glanced over. It was the fat man from the shower, carrying his plastic jug. He dipped his toe tentatively into the water, testing it.

I turned back to Quarry. "Mr. Quarry, if I had that Tarot card in my possession, the Death card, how much would I be able to sell it for?"

The eyelids didn't move. "But you don't have the card in your possession."

"Someone does."

He opened his eyes. "What grave psychological flaw compelled you to believe that you have the right to disturb me?"

"I don't see it as a right. I see it as a privilege."

He raised an eyebrow. He looked me up and down. This wasn't as effective a display of contempt as it might have been, since there was only about two feet of me above water. He said, "Are you always this unpleasant?"

I shook my head. "I haven't even started yet."

He lowered his head. His chins lapped out across his chest. "Is that a threat?"

"Yeah."

"I *could* call the police, you know."

I shrugged. "I paid for my ticket."

"Perhaps. But you're a nuisance. Even worse, you're a bore."

"Right. You call the police. Maybe they'll ask me to leave, maybe they won't. Say they do. I park outside your driveway and I wait there until you talk. You go into town, I follow. You eat at McDonald's, I'll be in the next seat with my Big Mac."

Once again, he looked me up and down. "Yes," he said. "I should imagine that McDonald's is exactly the sort of place you'd frequent."

"You could probably get a restraining order. But it would take time. It would mean going to court."

"The idea is beginning to tempt me."

"Or," I said, "instead, you give me ten minutes. I ask you my questions and then I leave."

He took a deep breath. Air rattled inside him, and he coughed and put his hand to his mouth. His breasts wobbled and water rippled away from him in frantic little waves. It was a long, raspy, liquid cough, and when it ended, his face was red and his eyes were watering. He looked over to me, irritated, as though I'd somehow been responsible for the attack. "I don't like you, you know."

I nodded. "I can probably live with that."

He leaned his head back against the wall, shut his eyes. He pressed his meaty lips together. "Very well," he said. "Ten minutes."

"If I had the card, how much could I get for it?"

"Nothing," he said without opening his eyes. "Unless you happened to know a buyer who was willing to purchase it illegitimately."

"Do you know any buyers like that?"

He smiled faintly but kept his eyes shut. "Of course not."

"Hypothetically," I said, "what could the card bring in an illegitimate sale?"

He shrugged. Pale flesh quivered on his upper arm. "No way of telling. The buyer would know, of course, that the card was stolen, and that a murder was connected to its theft. That would give him a certain amount of leverage, I should think. Bring the price down rather a lot. Who can say? A hundred thousand dollars?"

"I understand that you wanted to buy the card from Eliza Remington."

"Did I?"

"The ten-minute deal only works if you actually answer the questions."

"You really are a dreadful bore."

"Yeah. It's something I'm working on."

"You've gotten quite good at it."

"You wanted the card," I said.

"Not for myself."

"For whom?"

"A buyer who shall remain nameless."

"Would he still be interested?"

"The card is stolen property."

"That doesn't answer the question."

"No," he said. "He would not be interested."

"Do you think that Giacomo Bernardi stole it?"

"The police do, obviously."

"But do you?"

"I think that the theft of the card and the clumsy murder of Quentin Bouvier are entirely in keeping with Bernardi's general level of incompetence."

"He was clumsy enough to get caught, therefore he's guilty?"

He smiled. "Exactly."

"In your opinion, was there anyone else who might've been happy to see Bouvier dead?"

"I can't imagine that there was anyone who wasn't perfectly delighted. The man was an insect."

"What about his wife?"

He smiled again. "She inherits, does she not? A tidy little sum, I'll wager."

"Do you know of anyone in particular who disliked Bouvier?"

"Everyone disliked him."

"Sylvia Morningstar says she liked him."

"Sylvia Morningstar says she likes everyone. She's the Mother Teresa of Santa Fe, to hear her tell it. Mother Teresa dresses better, of course."

"So there's no one—"

"No one in particular, no. The man was universally despised. Quentin Bouvier is the man that Will Rogers never met. He was a charlatan. He was a self-serving, self-aggrandizing lout. Dying was the one decent thing he did in his life."

"You weren't very fond of him."

"How acutely perceptive of you."

"What do you know about Veronica Chang?"

"Nothing. Your ten minutes are up, surely?"

"One more question."

He sighed a low, rattling sigh. "One." He cleared his throat.

"Who wanted to buy the card?"

"I'm not at liberty to reveal that." He opened his eyes and lifted his head from the wall. "I wish I could say that it's been a pleasure, but of course it hasn't."

With a great wobbling of flesh and splashing of water he lowered himself into the pool. The trembling surface reached just to his second chin. He didn't say goodbye before he turned and began to wallow toward the entrance. I watched him clamber slowly up the steps, his hand clutching at the metal rail, and I realized that probably, for the rest of my life, whenever I debated having a second beer, the view of his naked backside would return to haunt me.

He was still in the resting room ten minutes later, when I emerged from the pool area: a mountain of blubber lying beneath a white cotton sheet that rose and fell with his wheezing breath. The table next to his was empty and I lay down on it. As the attendant swaddled me in cotton, I looked over to the mound that was Quarry and I said, "Sooner or later I'll find out who the prospective buyer was. Why don't you save me some time?"

From beneath the sheet he said, "I have no interest whatever in saving you anything. Paco, please tell this man that I don't wish to be disturbed."

Paco smiled at me and shrugged. "Is better be quiet now," he told me. "Is better, the resting after the water." He drew the sheet up over my head and tucked it in.

I lay there, wrapped up and steaming like an enchilada. My body throbbed. Sweat poured down my skin. I drifted off for a while, hearing from a distance the slow asthmatic wheeze of Quarry's breathing. I was lying on a beach in Cancun, Rita beside me, the air candied with the scent of coconut oil. Quarry coughed again, another liquid, rattling eruption. The weight of the sunlight pressed me flat against the sand. The fronds of palm trees flickered in the breeze, a faraway seagull fluttered off into the blue...

I suddenly realized that something was missing. Not from the fantasy, from the current reality. The room was silent.

Quarry's wheezing had stopped.

I hadn't heard him leave. I tugged my hand away from my side, where the sheet held it, and pulled the damp cotton material away from my face. I pushed myself up from the table and turned to him.

He lay there. He was absolutely still. In the center of his chest, surrounded by an irregular stain of bright scarlet, a transparent rectangular chunk of plastic jutted up at an angle from the sheet, like an electric switch set to Off.

"SO HOW'D YOU GET the ice pick into the resting room?" Hernandez asked me. "Everyone's naked in there, right? How'd you do it without someone seeing it?"

"I didn't," I said.

"You concealed it in some bodily orifice?"

I winced. "Did you ever try concealing an ice pick in a bodily orifice?"

"Uh-uh. Tell me about it."

"Hernandez, why aren't you looking for the other guy. The guy the attendant saw?"

He shrugged. "Why should I bother with him when I've got you?"

"Because he's the one who probably killed Quarry."

"Yeah? You're so smart, why didn't you nab him?"

"I told you. I was a little busy at the time."

"Tell us again."

The attendant, Paco, had come around the corner, seen Quarry, and had immediately wanted to do three or four things at once, including run around in circles. He had wanted to give Quarry CPR, which would have been futile in this case, and, in the case of puncture wounds to the chest, is seldom a very good idea. He had wanted to pull out the ice pick, which would have destroyed any prints on the handle. He had settled for giving Quarry mouth to mouth. A braver man that I. By the time I called the police and an ambulance, and learned from Paco about the man, the man was gone. "A skinny guy," I said. "Anglo. Dark brown hair. Very tanned. No scars. And he wasn't circumcised, Paco says."

Hernandez nodded. He turned to Green. "He wasn't circumcised."

Green nodded. "Then I guess we don't have to worry about Israeli spies."

Their routine, I thought, was beginning to wear a bit thin. I said, "Hernandez—"

Someone knocked at the door. Hernandez called out, "Come in."

The door opened and a trooper stood there, holding a Smokey the Bear hat in his hand. "Talk to you, Sergeant?"

Hernandez nodded, pushed himself off the desk, walked across the room, followed the trooper out, pulled the door shut.

Agent Green was studying me. I studied him. Early thirties, tall, heavyset, balding. Eyes that missed nothing in a blank face that expected nothing and would be surprised by nothing. After a moment he said, "What was the name of that woman up in Hartley?"

I was certain that he knew the name as well as I did. "Polk," I said, "Deirdre Polk."

"Polk, yeah. She died, too, didn't she."

"Yeah."

He nodded. "Seems like a lot of people end up dead after they talk to you."

I ignored that. Or tried to. When I thought about it, I still felt rotten about the death of Deirdre Polk. If I had been a little more careful, she might still be alive.

I didn't feel very good about the death of Leonard Quarry. I hadn't especially liked him. He had struck me as one of those clever, waspish, self-created figures who like to believe that they're superior to the concerns of lesser mortals—things like kindness, compassion, simple courtesy. But I hadn't wanted him dead.

Who had? The man described by Paco looked, so far as I knew, nothing like any of the people who'd been in La Cienega last Saturday night. And he was an Anglo, which eliminated Veronica Chang's brother, Paul.

Could he have been Peter Jones, the man who'd told the police that he spent Saturday night with Justine Bouvier? It didn't seem likely. Why would Jones put himself in a position where he could be identified by Paco? So who was he? The mysterious buyer for whom Quarry had been trying to obtain the Tarot card? Someone working for him?

Maybe Quarry's death had nothing to do with the theft of the card. Maybe Quarry was mixed up in something else, something totally unrelated, and it was this that had gotten him killed.

Possibly. But he was the second person who'd been in La Cienega last Saturday who'd been murdered. Both murdered within a week of each other. Quite a coincidence. I didn't much care for coincidences.

Neither, of course, did Hernandez and Green. Which is why they were so fond of me at the moment.

The door opened and Hernandez entered. He shut it behind him, crossed the floor, sat down once more against the desk. He looked at me. He nodded thoughtfully. "No prints on the ice pick. Not even smears. How'd you manage that? You weren't wearing gloves."

"No prints on the weapon," I said. "No witnesses. No motive. All you've got is my proximity to the victim. The attorney general won't touch that, Hernandez, and you know it."

He turned to Green. "*Proximity*. Did you catch that?"

Green nodded.

I said to Hernandez, "Could I ask a question?"

Hernandez grinned and held out his big hands. "Hey. That's what we're here for." He turned to Green. "Right?"

Green nodded. "To protect and serve."

I said, "You people swept the fireplaces and checked the drains at the house in La Cienega. Did you find anything?"

"Yeah, we did, as a matter of fact." He turned to Green. "Should I tell him?"

Green shrugged.

Hernandez said, "We found traces of burnt leather in the fireplace in Bernardi's room."

"And you think it's from the binder that held the Tarot card."

"It occurred to us, yeah."

"Aren't you supposed to notify the defense lawyer of the evidence you find?"

He shrugged. "Didn't get the report till this morning."

"Were there traces of anything else?"

"Like what?"

"Like paint. From the Tarot card."

"Nope. But, ya know, funny you should ask. We *did* find traces of blood in the drain. It matches Bouvier's. It doesn't match Bernardi's." He grinned. "Doesn't look good for your client, huh?"

"Bernardi's room was empty after he left the house. Anyone could've planted that evidence."

"The skinny Anglo guy?"

I shrugged. "The house was unlocked."

Hernandez nodded. He narrowed his eyes. "It could've been rubber cement." He turned to Green. "Remember that guy in Taos last year?" To me: "Burglar. Coated his hands with rubber cement, let it dry. No prints. Thing is, he tore off the cement outside the house, left patches of the stuff lying on the ground. Perfect prints on the patches. We got him." He nodded. "You could've used rubber cement."

"Anyone see me peeling rubber cement off my fingers?"

He grinned. "This guy. The skinny Anglo. If he's the one killed Quarry, how'd he know Quarry would be here?"

"The same way I did. His friends all knew that Quarry hung out here. He thought the steam was good for his emphysema."

"Who told you that?"

"Brad Freefall."

"And who told our skinny little anglo friend?"

"Beats me. Maybe you should ask around. Ask his friends if they know him. Ask his wife."

"Thanks for the advice. We did. She doesn't. Oh yeah, I almost forgot. She wants to talk to you. The wife."

"Good. I'd like to talk to her."

"You don't mind if we tag along, right?"

"Do I have a choice?"

He turned to Green. "Does he have a choice?"

"Not that I can see," said Green.

ANOTHER STATE CRUISER was parked in front of Quarry's house, and, inside it, a trooper sat writing something on a clipboard. Green and Hernandez nodded to him as they passed. I followed them up the front steps. Hernandez knocked on the door, which was opened by still another trooper.

Green greeted him with a nod. "Ortega. How is she?"

Ortega shrugged. "She seems pretty broke up. She called a friend to come and stay with her. Hasn't shown up yet."

"You get anything?"

"He didn't have any enemies, she says. She doesn't recognize the description of the man the attendant saw. She says she had a phone call, someone asking for him, at approximately one-thirty. Just after the private detective showed up." He glanced at me, but kept his curiosity from rising to the surface of his face.

Hernandez nodded. "Okay. Wait with Slawson in the car."

"Right. She's in the living room."

We made room for him, and the trooper climbed down the steps. I followed Green and Hernandez inside.

Her head bowed and her hands in her lap, where they held a crumpled cotton handkerchief, Sierra Quarry sat alone at the end of a long sofa upholstered in a floral pattern. Lace curtains were open at the window. The smell of wood smoke floated from an expensive metal stove in the corner. The room was small, furnished with embroidered antique chairs and a heavy antique cherrywood coffee table.

Hernandez said, "Mrs. Quarry?"

She looked up. Her beautiful face was ravaged. Her mouth was slack, her nose was crimson. Most of her mascara was gone, probably smeared onto the handkerchief, but some still remained, blurred bruises in the puffy flesh around her red-rimmed eyes. The pale skin along her cheeks was mottled now, and the cheeks seemed more hollow, as if anguish had been eating away at her flesh.

"Mrs. Quarry, I'm Agent Hernandez of the state police. This is Agent Green. I guess you've already met Croft."

She looked at me as though she hadn't noticed, till now, that I was there. Then, slowly, narrowing her eyes, she stood up. Her hand was trembling and for a moment I wondered whether she meant to strike me. She reached out tentatively and plucked with thin quavering fingers at the sleeve of my jacket. "You were there?" she asked me, and her voice was quivering as badly as her fingers. "When he...when it happened?"

"Yes."

"He wasn't... Did he suffer? Leonard was such a baby about pain." She cocked her head slightly and tried for a smile; it came off a grimace. "He seemed so big and strong, but he was really just like a little boy. He—" She stopped, and tears were rolling down her face. She said, "He didn't, did he? He didn't suffer?"

A gazelle, in the final embrace of the lion, will suddenly stop struggling and relax into what looks like an almost blissful acceptance. Human beings, brought back to life by modern medicine, report that death is a soothing experience, an opening onto peace. Only the dead know for certain, and they aren't telling.

But she didn't need speculation. She needed comfort. "No," I told her. "It was very quick."

She bit at her lower lip. Tears welled up in her eyes again and rolled slowly down her cheeks.

Hernandez touched her lightly on the shoulder. "Maybe you should sit down, Mrs. Quarry."

Sniffing, she sat back down. She lowered her head and dabbed at her eyes with the handkerchief.

Hernandez sat down beside her. Green and I remained standing. Maybe we shared the sense that becoming comfortable would be an affront to her grief. Just being there, it suddenly seemed to me, was an affront to her grief.

Hernandez said gently, "The other officers probably told you, Mrs. Quarry, that it's important for us to get as much information as we can. I know this has been a terrible shock to you, but in order to find the person who did this, we've gotta ask you some more questions."

She nodded. Her head still bowed, she plucked at the edge of the handkerchief.

"Officer Ortega says you received a phone call?"

She nodded.

"When was that?" Hernandez asked her.

She swallowed. Without raising her head, she said, "Just after... just after Mr. Croft was here." She plucked some more at the handkerchief.

"Did he give a name?"

She shook her head.

"Did you recognize the voice?"

Again, she shook her head.

I said, "Mrs. Quarry?"

Hernandez turned a glare toward me but said nothing. The woman raised her head. "Yes?"

"Your husband was trying to buy a Tarot card from Eliza Remington. Do you know the name of the man he was trying to buy it for?"

She frowned. "The man?"

"Wasn't your husband acting as an agent for someone else?"

She was still frowning, puzzled. She looked at Hernandez, looked back at me. "I don't understand. Leonard wanted the card for himself."

Like most cops, Hernandez didn't like to see information, any information, go public. He turned to Green and jerked his head in my direction. "Drive him back to the springs."

"Then what?" Green asked him.

Hernandez waved a hand. "Take him around back and shoot him."

Green said, "We're not supposed to do that anymore."

"Oh yeah." He looked at me. "Beat it. We'll be in touch."

"Call me," I said. "We'll do lunch."

THE HERMIT.

IT WAS A bizarre building for northern New Mexico, where private homes seldom grow above two stories tall and usually give up at one. It was a bizarre building for anywhere. It was a tower, flat-roofed, three stories, frame and brown shingle, built on the square and perhaps only twenty feet wide. At each story, two small double-hung windows, trimmed in darker brown, peered out at the half mile of driveway, twin ruts running in a straight line across the damp flat caliche. Three miles outside the tiny town of Mesa Roja, it stood at the base of another tower, a broad column of reddish brown rock climbing up from the barren plateau to rise seventy or eighty feet above the wooden structure. Out here the snow had melted and the only thing in sight for miles was dead scrub grass and an occasional small piñon, twisted over the years by wind into a gnarled green claw. The sun was sinking toward the gray hills in the west and its light was thinning out, dissipating into the brown sprawling emptiness.

I parked beside an old blue Karman Ghia blotched with gray primer, got out of the station wagon, followed the footpath, knocked on the door. It opened immediately, as though Peter Jones had been standing on the other side of it all day, waiting for me.

He was too tall to have been the man seen by Paco at the hot springs—an inch or two taller than I was, which made him six foot three or so. Slim, his shoulders square, he wore a black cotton turtleneck sweater with the sleeves pulled up along his forearms, black denim pants, and black cowboy boots. He was probably in his late thirties. His longish hair was a dark, shiny black, parted on the left and dusted at the temples with gray. His face was one of those pale, brooding, handsome faces that show up in Gothic novels, pasted onto the heads of intense young men who spend their days staring off tragically at the moors. Dark, deep brown eyes over angular cheekbones, a forceful nose, a wide sensitive mouth. But his smile surprised me—it was easy and open, almost boyish, and it was about as far from tragic as a smile can be.

"Sorry I'm late," I told him. It was four-thirty now. Our appointment had been for four o'clock, and at four, just before I left Agua Caliente, I'd called him and told him I'd been delayed. I hadn't explained that it was the state police who had delayed me, or why.

He grinned. "No problem. I wasn't going anywhere."

He led me inside. Inside was a single square space that served as kitchen and living room. The kitchen was an old gas stove and a small porcelain sink. The living room was a black futon sofa, a rectangular pinewood coffee table, and a black canvas director's chair. The walls were white and undecorated, the floor was wood and uncarpeted. At the northeast corner, a wrought iron stairway, narrow and spindly, circled up to the second floor. A motel room in the middle of Siberia would've been more festive. A monk's cell in the middle of Siberia would've been more festive.

Sitting down in the director's chair, he offered me the sofa. I took it.

"Interesting house," I told him.

He grinned. "The House on Haunted Hill," he said. "It's not mine. I'm watching it for a friend. He built it himself."

"Why'd he build it out here?"

He jerked his thumb back over his shoulder. "The pile of rocks behind us. Mesa Roja. The Indians around here, the old ones, used to believe it was a power point. An energy focus. Jim, the guy who built the house, liked the idea. And he thought that if he built the house so that it resembled the Mesa, it would pick up some of the energy."

"Has it worked?"

He grinned. "No more and no less than any other kind of house, probably." He frowned suddenly. "Looks like I'm not much of a host. Can I get you something? Tea? A glass of water?"

"No thanks."

He put his arms along the arms of the chair. "Okay. What can I do for you?"

I said, "You slept with Justine Bouvier last Saturday night, down in La Cienega. Did she leave the room that night?"

He blinked in surprise and then, grinning, he shook his head. "You don't mess around."

"You testified to the police that the two of you slept together."

He nodded. "Sure. And if you know that, you probably know that I testified that she *didn't* leave the room."

"And you're going to stick with that?"

He shrugged. "It's the truth."

"How long have you and Justine Bouvier been involved?"

His face flushed. Anger, possibly. Shame, possibly. "I don't think that's any of your business."

"You told the police a year."

"So why ask?" he said. Then he frowned again. "Hold on. You don't think that Justine killed her husband?"

"Someone did. I don't think it was Giacomo Bernardi."

He took a breath, let it out. He shook his head. "No," he said. "Neither do I. I can't see Giacomo doing something like that. But sometimes people can surprise you." He frowned. "How *is* Giacomo anyway?"

It occurred to me that he was the first person to ask me this. Even Brad Freefall and Sylvia Morningstar, both of whom claimed to be his friend, hadn't bothered.

"He's okay," I said. "Not very happy about being in jail."

"That's understandable. Especially if you're innocent of what you're being accused of. But so is Justine. She was with me all night. And why would she want to kill Quentin?"

"Money?"

"She already had all she needed."

"But maybe not all she wanted."

He smiled. "I don't think that's a distinction that Justine makes."

"And maybe life would be a lot simpler without a husband around."

"How? He never interfered with her. She lived exactly the way she wanted to." He put his hands together, fingers interlocked, and leaned slightly forward. "Look. Have you met Justine?"

I nodded.

"And you really think she could kill someone?"

I shrugged. "Sometimes people can surprise you."

He smiled. He looked at me and narrowed his eyes. "What did you think of her?"

"You want an honest answer?"

He shrugged, smiling, and sat back. "If you've got one."

"I think she's a user," I said. "I think she uses men to give herself a sense that she's in control. To give herself a sense that she's alive."

He nodded calmly. "Empowerment. Sure." Then he smiled. "She got to you too, huh?"

I frowned, momentarily irritated, and then I smiled. "Yeah," I said.

He laughed. "I can hear it in your voice." He laughed again and sat back. Grinning, he asked me, "Have you met Veronica yet? Veronica Chang?"

"No."

"Veronica makes Justine look like Shirley Temple. She's a Saku master—you know what that is?"

I shook my head.

"Saku is terrific," he said, "it's supposed to be an ancient Brazilian technique, something used by the Indians in the Amazon. You put your hands over John Smith and you concentrate on your ancient Brazilian Indian symbols, and you cure John of whatever ails him." He grinned. "Ever heard of Brazilian Indians practicing a technique like that?"

"No."

"Neither have they."

I smiled. "But I'm not an anthropologist."

"Neither was Horst Beuller, the guy who invented Saku. He discovered it in a vision."

"Good for him."

"And you might think," he said, "that it'd take you a while to learn how to pull this off, all this terrific healing."

"I might, yeah."

He smiled. "Uh-uh. It'll take you three hours and cost you a hundred and fifty bucks. Cheap at twice the price. And, bingo, you're a first-degree Saku practitioner. Then, if you want, you can become a second-degree Saku practitioner. You get a whole new set of ancient Brazilian Indian symbols. That'll cost you another three hours and three hundred bucks. And then, if you really want to go for the big time, you can spend ten grand and become a Saku master. The cute thing is, once you become a Saku master, you can give classes in first-and second-degree Saku, and each class can hold up to fifty people at a time. Figure it out. Fifty people at a hundred and fifty dollars apiece. That's seventy-five hundred bucks for three hours' work. Fifteen thousand bucks for the second-degree class."

"Who appoints the masters?"

"Another master."

I nodded. "A pyramid."

"Like Amway." He grinned. "Only Amway is more spiritual." He leaned slightly forward again. "The thing is, okay, it's a scam, but Veronica is for real. She's got something. A force. A power. She'd have it if she'd never heard of Saku."

I nodded. "I've heard that she was involved with Justine."

He blinked again. And then he smiled. "I've heard that, too."

"Is she still involved with her?"

He shrugged. "You'd have to ask them."

I nodded, and he suddenly grinned again. He said, "Must be weird for you, talking to all these crazies."

I smiled. "Now and then."

He laughed and sat back. "They're all sick. All these people, New Agers, Seekers, call 'em whatever you want. I include myself, naturally. It's a sickness of the soul, and a sense that there's something out there that can heal it. If we get lucky, we finally figure out that there isn't anything out there at all, and there isn't anything in here"—he pointed to his chest—"and that that's just perfect."

I nodded some more and he grinned. "And some of us don't get lucky. And we get involved with crap like Saku. It's another kind of empowerment. And power is the wet dream of the powerless."

"What's spiritual alchemy, by the way?"

He smiled. "Just another brand of lunacy. It's a meditation technique, visualizing certain areas of the body that correspond to the chakras. You know about chakras?"

What I'd known about chakras was that sooner or later in this investigation I'd stumble over some. "Vaguely," I said.

He grinned. "None of this is helping you very much, is it?"

"Nope."

He laughed. "Who have you talked to so far?"

"Justine. Brad Freefall. Sylvia Morningstar. Leonard Quarry and his wife."

He nodded. "I like Brad and Sylvia." He grinned. "What'd you think of Leonard?"

"We didn't get along very well."

He grinned again. "Not many people get along with Leonard."

"Not many will. Not now. He's dead."

He blinked, and then he frowned. "What?"

"Someone put an ice pick through his heart. A couple of hours ago."

He sat still for a moment, staring at me. Finally he said, "You like doing that. Catching people off guard."

"I don't necessarily like it. But sometimes it's useful."

He stared at me some more. "Manipulative, you mean."

"That, too," I admitted. "But I've got a job to do."

He frowned. "Nice job."

"Sometimes."

"You could've told me before, about Leonard."

"Yeah."

He nodded. He continued to stare at me. "You don't trust anyone, do you?"

"No one involved in a case."

His eyes narrowed. "How do you sleep at night?"

"On my back."

He nodded sadly. He said, "I don't think I'd want to be you."

"I don't have much choice in the matter."

He nodded, slowly, faintly. He looked away and took a deep breath and let it out. His shoulders seemed to slump.

I said, "Any idea who might want to kill him?"

He shook his head, and then turned back to me. "Why was he killed?" he asked me. "Do you know why?"

"If I knew why, I'd know who."

He looked away again. He took another deep breath, let it out. He said, as much to himself as to me, "Christ. This is really a mess."

He ran his hand through his hair and then looked at me. "How did it happen?"

I told him. I asked him if the tanned, thin Anglo sounded like someone he knew.

"It's not much of a description," he said.

"I know."

"It could be anyone."

"But not anyone who was at La Cienega last Saturday night. And that bothers me. I've been working on the assumption that the person who killed Quentin Bouvier was one of the people there, at the house. This guy wasn't."

"Your assumption was wrong."

"Maybe. Let's forget Quarry for a minute. Was there anyone in La Cienega that night who might've had a reason to kill Quentin Bouvier?"

"As far as I know, no one. Including Giacomo. The police asked me the same thing."

"What do you think of the idea that Bernardi stole the card?"

"Not much. Giacomo's not a thief." He frowned again. "You think this is all about the Tarot card? Quentin's death? Leonard's death?"

"Leonard's I'm not sure about. But Quentin's—I think so, yeah."

He shook his head. "It's such a shame."

"A shame?"

"A shame, yeah, because it's a violation of what the cards are all about. For me, the Tarot is a kind of graphic representation of a spiritual pathway. Like the old woodcuts done by the alchemists. It's a guide to the sacred. The Tarot suits—the wand, the sword, the cup, the pentangle—they're the Grail Hollows. And what's the search for the Grail if not the search for the holy? The other uses for the cards, divination, magic, they may've come first, but I think that at some point someone got hold of the cards and reorganized them as a kind of handbook to enlightenment."

"I heard a theory recently," I said. "Bernardi hung Bouvier because Bouvier was a traitor to the cause of White Magic."

He smiled sourly. "I can tell you where you heard that theory. From Bennett Hadley. He expounded it to me. Bennett's good at expounding."

"What do you think of the theory?"

"I think it sucks. Bennett should stick to writing books."

"What do you think of Bennett?"

"I like Bennett. He sees himself as a kind of observer, above the fray. But in his own way, he's just as screwed up as the rest of us. Writing books like his, cataloguing experience, that's a kind of self-empowerment, too. The cataloguing puts you in control of the experiences, even if you've never had them yourself. Especially if you've never had them yourself."

"What do you think of Carl Buffalo?"

He looked at me. "You want to know about all of them, right? All the people who were in La Cienega."

"Yeah."

He shook his head. "Even if I suspected that one of them was a murderer, I wouldn't tell you that. I could be wrong. And if I knew anything about any of them that wasn't common knowledge, then revealing it would be a violation of trust."

"Look," I said. "It seems to me that there are two possibilities here. First, one of you, one of the people at the Freefall place last Saturday night, killed Quentin Bouvier. Second, none of you did. If Leonard Quarry's murder is connected in some way to Bouvier's, then maybe the second possibility is true. Maybe it *was* this guy, this brown skinny Anglo. Or maybe he was working for, or with, one of you. I don't know. But if one of you did kill Quentin Bouvier, then there's nothing to stop him from killing again."

"Him? You're convinced it was a man? Then why ask about Justine?"

"I'm not convinced of anything. I don't know anything. Except that by not cooperating, you may be protecting a murderer."

He sat back and folded his hands across his lap. He nodded. "You're good at this."

"Yeah?"

Another nod. "First you tell me you don't trust anyone. But by telling me that, you imply that you trust *me* enough to reveal the truth. Then you start to work on my guilt." Another nod. "You've got a job to do, right?"

"Yeah."

He shrugged. "Sorry. I can't help you. If I knew that one of us was a killer, I'd go to the police and tell them. But you admit it yourself—Quentin could've been killed by the same man who killed Leonard. It sounds to me like he's the one you should be looking for."

"I don't know where to find him. I know where the rest of you are."

"I'm sorry," he said. "I can't help you."

SITTING AT THE kitchen table, cutting salt pork into small squares, I said, "This Anglo guy bothers me."

"Understandably," Rita said. She sat across the kitchen table from me, dicing carrots. Her head was lowered and her long black hair leaned forward, off her shoulders. She wore a lavender blouse, open at the throat.

"He just suddenly turns up out of the blue and ice-picks Leonard Quarry."

She nodded. "So you said."

"Who the hell is he?"

"I don't know."

"And how did he get the ice pick into the resting room without anyone seeing it?"

"I can think of one way."

I stopped cutting and looked up. "How?"

Rita didn't stop cutting, didn't look up. "I haven't been to Agua Caliente for years. Do people still carry jugs of drinking water into the pool?"

"Yeah..." And then I understood. "They're translucent. And the handle of the ice pick was clear plastic. The only thing that'd show up would be the shaft of the pick. Maybe not even that."

"And who takes a careful look at a gallon jug?" She diced some more carrots.

"When you want the ice pick," I said, "all you've got to do is pour out some water till the pick pops out along with it. There are drains all over the floor in the resting room, and water everywhere. No one would've noticed more of it."

She looked up, smiled. "I'm not saying that's the way it was done. But it's one of the ways it could've been."

"But how'd he get past the attendant?"

"There's only one attendant, you said."

"Right."

"And he leaves whenever someone comes into the building and buzzes to enter the locker room. He goes into the locker room and checks to make sure they've got a ticket."

"Right."

"Can you see the resting room from the showers?"

"It's all one big room." I nodded. "Right. The Anglo guy waits in the shower till the attendant leaves, makes sure that there are no witnesses, then runs up and stabs Quarry. If there's any blood on his hands, he can run back to the shower to wash it off. Very neat. But he'd still have only a minute or so to pull the whole thing off."

"How long does it take to stick an ice pick into someone?"

"But how did he know that Quarry would be there just then?"

"You said that Quarry used the pool fairly often."

"Yeah, but not necessarily at any regular time. Even if the Anglo knew that Quarry went there fairly often, how'd he know that Quarry would be there today, at two o'clock?"

"Had the attendant ever seen the Anglo before?"

"He said he wasn't sure. He said the guy looked familiar, but he couldn't swear that he'd seen him there, at the pool. I got the impression that he really doesn't pay much attention to the people coming and going."

Rita shrugged. "So perhaps the Anglo had been there before, without finding Quarry. But this time, on what became his final attempt, he did."

"He'd still be taking a couple of big chances."

"Which?"

"Quarry was underneath a sheet. His face wasn't visible. The Anglo couldn't be sure that the fat man on the table was Quarry."

"You said that Quarry was monumentally fat. Was the Anglo likely to mistake someone else for him, even if he *was* covered by a sheet?"

"But you'd think that he'd want to be sure."

"If he'd been waiting outside in a car, watching the entrance, he would've seen Quarry enter the building. And he would've seen everyone else enter it. He would've known that the man on the table was Quarry."

I nodded. "And he waits in the car long enough to be fairly sure that Quarry will be out of the pool and lying on the resting table. Okay. I can buy that, I guess. But there's something else."

"What?"

"If he'd been there before, he had to know that the attendant would see him. He had to give the attendant his ticket. The attendant could identify him later."

"Not identify him. Recognize him. And that would only be dangerous if he were caught, sometime later."

"Yeah, but he can't have been certain that he wouldn't be caught."

"Even if he were, no one actually saw him stab Quarry."

"But if the police can establish a connection between him and Quarry. If they can establish a motive."

"That still might not be enough for a conviction. Or even for a trial."

I shook my head. "I don't know, Rita. It all sounds a little iffy to me. Why kill him there, at the hot springs? Why not kill him somewhere else, somewhere private?"

"I don't know." She smiled. "But I'm sure you'll find out. You *are* missing something, however."

"And what might that be?"

"Which month is this?"

I frowned, narrowing my eyes. "You're going to go didactic on me, aren't you?"

She laughed. "Which month."

I sighed. "February. Dear."

"And how did the attendant describe the Anglo?"

"Medium height. No scars. Very tanned." I frowned. "Oh shit," I said.

Rita laughed.

I said, "He was tanned and this is the middle of winter."

Smiling, she said, "Very good, Joshua."

"So he wasn't from here. Or he's been using a tanning salon."

"Or perhaps he wasn't tanned at all. Perhaps he was wearing—"

"Dye. Body dye, skin dye, whatever. Misdirection. The cops are looking for somebody who just got back from Antigua, and he goes home and washes the stuff off." I frowned again. "But wouldn't it come off in the shower?"

"Not necessarily. There are some theatrical dyes, oil based, that aren't water soluble."

I nodded. "I've got to see Hernandez tomorrow, to sign my statement. I'll mention all this to him."

She smiled. "I'm sure he'll be grateful for your help. Are you finished with the salt pork?"

"Not yet."

Both of us went back to work. Rita was dealing with the parsley now. After a moment, I had another thought. I looked up. "What about Quarry and the card?"

"What about them?" She continued chopping.

"Quarry's wife seems to think that he wanted that card for himself. The card went for two hundred thousand dollars. I wouldn't have said, judging by the house he lived in, that he had that kind of money."

"He didn't," she said, chopping carefully away.

I frowned. "Have you run an asset search on him?"

"Mmm-hmm."

"And are you going to share the results with me?"

She looked up and smiled. "Not including the house, if he cashed in everything he owned, he could probably come up with fifty thousand dollars."

"Max?"

"Max."

"And including the house?"

"Twenty thousand in equity."

"What about inventory? He's a dealer. Maybe he's got a bunch of stuff tucked away. Ancient Aztec treasures. The Maltese Falcon."

"I doubt that." She went back to her parsley. "His bank statements show a small but steady increase each year since he arrived in New Mexico. Nothing dramatic."

"When did he arrive?"

"Seven years ago."

"From where?"

"San Francisco. Where did you put the shallots?"

"There in the bag. Next to the sugar. He had to know he couldn't pick up the card for fifty thousand. Or even seventy thousand."

She nodded. "Presumably." She plucked a shallot from the bag, examined it.

"So he was lying to his wife?"

"Or she was lying to you." Delicately, she cut the root end from the shallot.

"She was pretty ragged when she told me—she'd just learned that her husband was dead."

She pulled the two cloves of shallot apart. She nodded. "You believe her."

"Yeah."

She began to slice the shallot. "Then you'll have to determine why he lied to her. Are you done with the salt pork?"

"This is an art, Rita. Art can't be rushed."

"No, of course not. In the meantime, I'll do the chicken."

She stood, walked around the table, lifted the plate that held the chicken, and walked with it back to her seat. She sat down, glanced up at me. "What are you grinning at?"

"You. When are we going to walk from here down to the Plaza?"

While she'd been paralyzed, Rita had refused to leave the house. She would leave it, she'd told me, when she could walk down to the Plaza. She was leaving it now, nearly every day, but we still hadn't done the walk to the Plaza. I wanted to do it, as a kind of ritual, a formal end to a difficult period.

"Soon," she said.

"Sunday."

She smiled. "Maybe."

"Maybe." I cut some more cubes of salt pork. "The computer tell you anything about Bennett Hadley?"

"He wasn't in the army and he wasn't in Vietnam."

"Oh yeah? He told Brad Freefall that he was."

"So you said."

"Any kind of police record?"

"No."

"You have his medical record?"

"Not yet."

"What about Brad Freefall?"

"A marijuana bust in Venice, California, in 1965. Charges were dropped."

"Peter Jones?"

"Nothing."

"I wish he'd been a bit more forthcoming. I would've liked to know what he thought about the rest of them."

"Why?"

"He seems to be almost normal."

She smiled. "A spiritual alchemist who slept with the murder victim's wife?"

"Normal by comparison. I liked him."

"Maybe the two of you can take in a ballgame someday. Beer and peanuts, nudging each other as the bimbettes walk by."

I smiled. "I don't think he's very fond of me. The computer have anything on the others?"

"Nothing very helpful."

"Anything on the ones I haven't talked to? Veronica Chang?"

"Not really. Chang and her brother were in San Francisco at the same time Leonard Quarry was, but I can't find any connection between them."

"They were both members of the occult community," I said.

"San Francisco has a large occult community. It's possible they never met."

"This is done. The salt pork."

"So's the chicken. You're talking to Veronica Chang to-morrow?"

"Yeah."

"Watch out for the brother. He was arrested for assault. Twice. Where'd you put the wine?"

JUSTICE.

THERE WERE NO squat naked Indians skulking across the sunny lawn. There were no brightly colored jungle birds eyeing me from the bare branches of the big oak tree beside the driveway. There was no exotic flute music trilling from the windows of the low, stately brick building, no throbbing jungle drums. It was an old one-story house on East Marcy, a house that had probably been sitting here for a hundred years, quietly watching the seasons and the people come and go. It was a house that could have been owned by a doctor or a dentist or a successful real estate broker, or by any other professional who could afford to drop something like half a million dollars on a place to bunk. There was nothing about the building, or about the neatly landscaped grounds, both of them hidden from the street by a tall and carefully pruned hedge of evergreens, which suggested that the occupant was a master of an ancient Brazilian healing technique, genuine or otherwise.

The man who opened the front door was Asian, slender, about six feet tall, with shiny slicked-back black hair and a dark impassive handsome face that revealed nothing at all,

including his age, which might have been anywhere from
thirty to forty-five. He wore a loose pale blue silk shirt,
pleated gray slacks of tropical weight wool, gray silk socks
and gleaming black leather slip-on shoes that looked as sleek
as ballet slippers. Hanging from a gold link chain around his
taut neck was a small gold charm that resembled a stylized
bird in flight. Maybe it was an ancient Brazilian healing
symbol. Maybe it wasn't. This was the brother, presumably.

I introduced myself and, without a word or any change of
expression, he gestured for me to enter. I entered. He shut
the door and gestured for me to follow. I followed. He
moved well. Lightly, hips forward, shoulders back, as re-
laxed within his body as a panther.

We padded across a carpeted living room that held expensive but probably uncomfortable furniture, shiny
chrome and nubby beige upholstery. On the wall were two
or three framed examples of what some people like to think
of as Southwest Art—rugged landscapes through which
weary Navajos plodded, looking to the left, looking to the
right. Every pitcher tells a story, ladies and gentlemen.

I followed him into a kind of enclosed porch off the living room: vigas and latillas overhead, red Mexican tile un-
derfoot, at the opposite wall a set of French windows
leading out onto a patio and the rear lawn. The furniture in
here was Taos stuff, oversized and boxy, plump colorful
cushions in heavy dark-wood frames. A single Navajo rug,
an extremely good one, lay on the floor. Nice things, all of
them, but there was nothing here that in Santa Fe would
seem remotely exotic. Except, of course, for the woman sitting across the room. Veronica Chang.

She sat at the far corner of the long sofa. Because she was
so tiny, about the same height as Sally Durrell, she should
have disappeared against the sofa's bulk. She didn't. She
wasn't beautiful in the way that movie stars and multi-
million-dollar models are beautiful. For me, that kind of
beauty, the perfect features assembled in perfect symmetry
around a perfectly shaped face, has always seemed vacant
and brittle, like a porcelain mask. Veronica Chang's black,

almond-shaped eyes were a shade too large to be classically beautiful. Her red mouth was a shade too broad, a shade too lush. Her cheekbones were a shade too feline. Her breasts, beneath a bright purple long-sleeved leotard top, outlined by the two straight lengths of glossy black hair, were perhaps a shade too voluptuous for her slender frame.

Not classically beautiful, maybe. But I remembered what Brad Freefall had said. He had been right. She was drop-dead gorgeous. I wondered how she had lived in Santa Fe for five years without my ever having seen her. I knew that if I had seen her, I would have remembered her.

She was smiling at me. "Mr. Croft," she said. "Please. Come and have some tea." She patted the cushion beside her.

Okay by me.

I turned to thank the brother and saw that he was gone.

He moved very well.

I crossed the room and circled the coffee table, where an ornate silver tray held a bone china tea service—a graceful pot, a small pitcher, a sugar bowl, a pair of delicate cups and saucers. I unzipped my leather jacket, sat down.

Up close, I saw that her olive skin was flawless, not a wrinkle or a pore visible anywhere. Except for the lipstick, she wore no makeup. Her perfume was something floral, as subtle and as fresh as the scent of a crushed petal. Sitting beside her, on this side of the coffee table, I learned that what she wore below the top of the leotard was merely the bottom of the leotard. And, above it and beneath it, nothing else. A pair of East Indian sandals sat together on the floor beneath the table, patiently waiting to embrace her tiny feet.

She poured tea into one of the cups. "Milk? Sugar?" Her language was unaccented and her voice was soft. I hadn't spoken since I'd entered the house. I wondered now if I would stutter. Or spill drool down the front of my shirt. "Sugar," I said.

She smiled. "Normally, it would be very bad for you. One teaspoon or two?"

"Two. Normally?"

Delicately, she spooned the sugar into my cup. Like her brother, she moved well. She handed me the cup and saucer and she smiled again. "I've treated this sugar to remove the toxins. It's quite safe now."

"Treated it how?"

"Saku." She poured herself some tea. "The healing tradition in which I work."

"Ah."

She put two spoonfuls into her own cup, raised cup and saucer, sat back against the wooden arm of the sofa, and smiled at me. "Cheers," she said, and lifted the cup from the saucer. She was left-handed.

"Cheers," I said. I sipped at the tea. "How do you go about removing the toxins from sugar?"

"Meditation." She lowered the cup and saucer to her lap. "Saku meditation. It can remove the toxins from any substance."

"I see," I said. From Jack Daniel's? From Drano?

"But you came to talk about the death of Quentin Bouvier," she said.

"And the death of Leonard Quarry. You know that he was killed yesterday?"

She nodded, her face solemn. "Yes. Sierra called me yesterday evening. She mentioned your name."

"I was there when it happened."

"She told me. How painful that must have been for you."

Not as painful as it had been for Leonard Quarry. "How's Mrs. Quarry doing?"

"She is grief-stricken, of course. But Sierra has an inner strength surprising in one who seems so fragile. She will be fine, I believe."

"Good." I sipped at my tea. "Miss Chang, you were at that get-together last Saturday night, at Brad Freefall's and Sylvia Morningstar's house in La Cienega. I've read all the statements made by the people who were there, and most of them agree that at dinner, you asked Leonard Quarry how he felt about not being able to obtain that Tarot card. The card that Quentin Bouvier had just purchased from Eliza Remington."

She nodded calmly. "Yes." Her large black eyes looked directly into mine, and her gaze seemed to penetrate through cornea and pupil and plunge directly into the center of my mind.

It's a trick. A stage magician once explained it to me. You look toward someone's eyes, but you focus your own eyes a few inches beyond theirs. It can be impressive, even when you know how it's done. Up until now, despite what Peter Jones had told me about Saku, despite her talk of removing toxins, I'd been giving Veronica Chang the benefit of the doubt. Her being spectacularly beautiful and only a few feet away in a skintight purple leotard had nothing to do with my tolerance, of course. But from this point on, I was fairly well persuaded that she was a fraud.

"How did you know that Quarry wanted the card?" I asked her.

"Quentin told me."

"When?"

"The week before, I believe. While the two of them were still negotiating with Eliza."

"And why would Quentin tell you?"

She smiled. "Quentin and I were close friends. He often discussed things with me."

"What did he say about the card?"

She shrugged her small shoulders. "Merely that both of them wanted it, he and Leonard. And that he had managed to outbid Leonard for it."

"Did he say why he wanted it?"

"He planned to use it in his rituals."

"What kind of rituals?"

She shrugged. "I couldn't say. The magical side of Quentin's life didn't interest me."

"Why not?"

"I have no interest in magic."

"Did Quentin say how much Leonard had bid?"

She took a sip of tea. "One hundred and seventy-five thousand dollars."

"Quarry didn't have one hundred and seventy-five thousand dollars."

"He was merely a middleman, Quentin told me. He was bidding for someone else."

"His wife says that Quarry wanted the card for himself."

"He may well have. But, as you say, he couldn't have afforded it. Obviously he was bidding for a third party."

"Do you know who that might be?"

"No. Will you be talking to Eliza Remington?"

"This afternoon."

"She might know."

"Assuming he was bidding for someone else, why would he tell his wife differently?"

She smiled again. "I have no idea. Leonard and I seldom spoke with each other."

"Why not?"

"I found him rather an unpleasant man. A mercenary man."

"How so?"

"His only real concern was making money."

I glanced around the expensively furnished room. It wasn't as swank as Justine Bouvier's reproduction of ancient Luxor, but it was hardly a hovel. I didn't have to say what went through my mind: she anticipated me. She was smiling when I looked back at her. She said, "Yes, I make money, Mr. Croft. But this is America, is it not? And here, the making of money is neither a crime nor a sin. And I make money from my work, by providing a method of healing and by teaching others how to provide it. I spent many years in training to learn how to do so. And many years before that, seeking the spiritual path that was right for me."

"Whereas Leonard Quarry...?"

"Whereas Leonard Quarry bought things low and sold them high. He contributed nothing to society, nothing to humanity. He was a leech. It is a kind of karmic justice that he's been removed."

"What about Quentin Bouvier?"

She frowned slightly. "What about him?"

"Was his removal a kind of karmic justice?"

"All karma is just, Mr. Croft. Whatever happens was destined to happen."

"So it's okay for someone to hang Bouvier from the rafters."

"Of course not," she said softly, without heat. "The person responsible has incurred a terrible karmic debt, which sooner or later must be paid."

"But it was his karma that led him to kill Bouvier."

"To act as the instrument, yes, that paid some karmic debt owed by Quentin."

Impressive stuff, this karma. "All right," I said. "Giacomo Bernardi. In your opinion, could he have killed Quentin Bouvier?"

"In my opinion, anyone is capable of killing."

Given the proper karma, no doubt. "Do you think that Bernardi was capable of killing Bouvier last Saturday night?"

Once again she shrugged lightly. "Who am I to say?"

"And Leonard Quarry? Do you know of anyone who might want to kill him?"

"I imagine that many people might have wanted to." Pretty much what Leonard Quarry had said about Quentin Bouvier.

"Anyone in particular?" I asked her.

"None that I know of."

I sipped my tea. "You said that you were a close friend of Quentin Bouvier's."

She nodded lightly. "Yes."

"How close a friend?"

She smiled. "How do you mean?"

"I think you know what I mean, Miss Chang. Were you and Quentin lovers?"

She smiled again. "Surely, Mr. Croft, that is none of your business."

"My business is finding the person who killed Quentin Bouvier. And to do that, I have to learn as much as I can about the people who were in La Cienega last Saturday night."

She did her focusing trick again and gave me another small smile. "You are entitled, of course, to learn whatever you can. Or to attempt to. But you will learn nothing about this particular subject from me."

"You're denying that you and Quentin were lovers?"

"I neither deny nor affirm it. I merely refuse to answer the question."

"Miss Chang. It doesn't bother you that Giacomo Bernardi is in jail right now for a crime he didn't commit?"

She smiled, shrugged lightly. "The police believe he committed it."

"I think the police are wrong."

"If it is Giacomo's karma to remain in jail, he will remain in jail. If it is his karma to be released, he will be released."

"And meanwhile everybody sits around on his backside sipping tea?"

Pointedly, smiling, she took a sip of tea. "If that is his karma," she said.

I said, "Did Quentin know that you and Justine had been lovers?"

She lowered the cup to the saucer in her lap and sighed. "Mr. Croft, you grow tiresome. It is time, I think, for you to leave." She looked toward the doorway. "Please show Mr. Croft out, Paul."

I followed her glance, saw her brother standing just inside the entrance to the room, arms folded across his chest. He did move very well—he had appeared without me hearing a thing. And he had appeared, so far as I could tell, without being signaled by his sister. Maybe she actually did possess some strange mysterious power of the East. Or maybe, all along, Paul had been loitering just around the corner.

I set my cup and saucer on the silver tray, turned to her, and smiled. "Thanks for the tea."

She said nothing, merely looked up at me with her faint smile in a very attractive demonstration of inscrutability. Paul had glided across the room and now stood beside me, his hands hanging loosely at his sides. He, too, said nothing. I unfolded myself from the sofa, nodded to Veronica Chang, and started walking toward the door. Paul fell in behind me. I didn't much care for that. I didn't want him behind me.

The passage through the house was uneventful. At the front door, he came around in front of me, opened it, and gestured for me to leave. I left. He came along behind me, pulling, the door shut after him. I didn't much care for that, either.

We were halfway across the lawn, him still behind me, when he tapped me on the shoulder.

I knew that I could've been wrong about his intentions. Maybe he only wanted to ask me who I liked in tonight's Lakers game. Maybe he wanted to discuss quantum physics. If I were wrong, what I was about to do would make me look more than a little like a fool. But I'd looked like fool before. And I'd been sucker-punched before. On the whole, I preferred to look like a fool.

Instead of turning around, and to the right, which is what most of us do when we're tapped on the right shoulder, I feinted to the right and then I sank into a crouch as I wheeled around to my left. I hadn't been wrong. Probably he'd waited until we got outside because he didn't want my blood spattered all over the designer furniture.

His right arm went whistling through the space that was supposed to be occupied by my head.

Karate or one of the other martial arts, Brad Freefall had said. Paul was Korean, so probably his hobby of choice was tae kwon do, the Korean brand of karate. Mostly footwork, leg thrusts and round-house kicks. Long-distance stuff—you needed room to bring your feet to bear. If he was using tae kwon do, he'd be backing up soon, to give himself enough space to create a potential circle of action. I wouldn't be able to do any damage unless I could get inside the circle.

But at the moment I was already inside the circle. And most of these martial-art types share a serious flaw. They've never really been hurt. They learn how to take falls, they learn how to parry thrusts. They seldom experience sudden, excruciating pain. Administering it is an excellent way to get their attention.

It's strange how elastic time can become in certain situations. All of this went through my head in something like a millisecond as I whirled down into my crouch and saw that he was off balance his right side toward me. It took only one more millisecond to slam my fist, all the momentum of my spin behind it, into his stomach, just below the arch of rib cage.

I'd been wrong about his ability to deal with sudden pain. He dealt with it very well. A good solid punch to the solar plexus will leave the average person—will leave me—doubled up and out of action for a day or two. Paul merely gasped and began to backpedal, probably looking for enough room to use his feet.

I didn't think that this was a good idea. I went with him, and, as we danced across the grass, I feinted a left. He parried with a swipe of his right arm and I jabbed a straight right at the side of his exposed neck.

He took that punch very well, too. It hurt him, I believe it hurt him badly, but he only blinked. Then he remembered that he had fists and he began whipping them at me, left and right. I stayed inside, riding it out, taking it on shoulder and upper arm. And then he grabbed my arms and butted me, his forehead smacking against my cheekbone. My teeth clacked together.

There was no pain, not yet, but the shock jarred me for a moment and that was time enough for Paul to spring back and twist into a sudden skillful spin, his left foot sailing toward my head. I staggered away, but he followed through, landed on his left foot, swiftly pivoted and twirled, slashed up his right foot in a smooth continuation of the attack. I backed away from that one, too, and he did it again, landed on the right foot, pivoted, swung around with his left foot, all in one fluid motion, quick, graceful, lethal, just the way they do it in the movies.

I outweighed him by about fifty pounds. He may have had the momentum, but I had the mass. I stepped inside the arc of the swing, blocked his upper leg with my right forearm. He had quite a bit of momentum. I staggered with the force of it. But when he began his next move—a leap off the right foot to jackknife it at my face as he went down, prepared to roll away—I smashed my right fist, as hard as I could, down into his crotch.

Unless he was wearing a plastic cup, that would slow him down a bit.

He wasn't.

His right leg buckled and I stood back and he crashed to the grass on his back. The breath left him in a single explosive rush and he rolled onto his side and curled up, clutching with both hands at his groin.

The entire thing had probably taken no more than a minute, maybe two minutes at the most, but I was panting and the chamois shirt beneath my leather windbreaker was soaked with sweat. I realized that I was standing in a kind of stoop, my back hunched over. I straightened it, sucked in some air. My cheek was throbbing. I reached up and touched it. Tender, and my fingers came away red and slick with blood. He'd broken the skin. I looked around the lawn. But when I glanced toward the house, I saw that Veronica Chang was standing beyond the picture window, her arms crossed beneath her breasts, her face expressionless. I nodded and I turned and left.

"WHAT HAPPENED TO YOU?" Hernandez asked me, glancing at the bandage on my cheek.

"I was watching MTV. I got carried away."

"In an ambulance?"

He was behind his desk, his black boots perched on its top. Standard cop office, tile floors, cement block walls, fluorescent lighting. Agent Green was off somewhere, probably polishing up new nightclub material for the two of them.

I said, "You've got a statement for me to sign?"

He swung his feet off the desk, pulled his chair closer to it, lifted a manila folder. He tossed it across the desktop. "Initial each page. Sign it at the end."

I picked up the folder. "Okay if I sit down?"

He waved a hand toward an empty chair. "Taxpayers' money."

I sat down, opened the folder, read through the statement, initialed each page. Hernandez watched me without saying a word. I signed the last page, closed the folder.

Hernandez said, "Anything you want to add? A confession, maybe?"

"My partner came up with a way for the Anglo guy to get the ice pick into the resting room."

Hernandez sat back, smiling faintly, and put his arms along the arms of the chair. "Do tell."

I told him.

He nodded. "That the way you did it? Inside a gallon jug?"

"She also pointed out something about the guy that I hadn't noticed."

"Jeez," he said. "You didn't notice something?"

"His tan. It's February. Where'd he get it?"

Hernandez shook his head in mock admiration. "Now why didn't I think of that?"

I nodded. "You did, in other words."

"Amazing, isn't it? We've had troopers hitting the tanning salons in Santa Fe and Albuquerque since this morning."

"He could've been wearing a skin dye."

"Jeez. You think of everything."

"Did you learn anything at the tanning salons?"

He smiled again, hooked his thumbs over his belt. "I know you're not going to believe this, you being so helpful and such a hotshot and all, but my superiors, they don't want me to tell you. They're funny that way. I begged them, I really did. I said, hey, this guy is a *sleuth*. He can solve the whole damn case for us."

"I wouldn't do that. I wouldn't want to put a blot on your record."

"You're already a blot on my record."

But he said it without any real conviction, more from force of habit, I think, than anything else. I smiled. "You still like Giacomo Bernardi for the Quentin Bouvier killing?"

"Three little words. Means, motive, opportunity."

"And you don't think that Leonard Quarry's death was related somehow?"

"Your Anglo friend wasn't on the guest list down there."

"It doesn't strike you as a coincidence? Two people go to the same party, both of them get killed within a week?"

He shrugged. "Coincidences happen."

"I don't think that Bernardi killed Bouvier."

He mimed surprise: mouth open, eyebrows raised. "Jeez, why didn't you say so? I'll call C.C.A., have them turn him loose."

"And he couldn't have killed Quarry. He was in jail at the time."

"Now I've got two little words for you."

"Merry Christmas?"

"Fuck off. You're working for the public defender's on the Bouvier thing. You're entitled to ask about that. I don't have to tell you anything more than the law requires, but you're entitled to ask. You're not entitled to ask anything about the Quarry killing. They're two separate cases."

"What if I can prove they're not?"

He shrugged. "Then maybe we'll renegotiate. In the meantime..."

"Fuck off?"

He nodded. "Like I said."

IT WAS ONE O'CLOCK when I reached the office, carrying a takeout lunch from the Burrito Factory. Rita was out. A note on my desk told me that she'd be back by three. I ate my carne adovado. I called Sally Durrell, told her what I'd learned and what I hadn't, then wrote up my formal reports for her. I called Carl Buffalo. A woman, the same woman that I'd spoken to before, told me that he was still up in the mountains. She said that he was due back tomorrow. I called Carol Masters, the film actress turned channeler. Her machine told me, as it had before, that she was out of town. I wondered whether she knew that a burglar would be delighted with that piece of information. I called Ernie Beller, a friend who ran a used car lot on Cerrillos Road. Ernie was in. He probably didn't know who killed Quentin Bouvier, so I didn't ask him. He did know about cars, however, and he said he had a late-model Jeep Cherokee available, "almost cherry," that he was practically giving away. I told him I'd stop by tomorrow.

At two-thirty, I left for my next appointment.

TEMPERANCE.

"I NEVER DRINK alcohol," she said. "Not even a glass of sherry. It clouds the mind." She spoke with a clipped, no-nonsense Yankee accent that had been softened by years of Southwest living, but not very much softened.

I smiled. "My mind is usually so cloudy that another cumulus or two doesn't make much difference."

"All the more reason not to befuddle yourself." She smiled. "But try one of the almond cookies. They go well with the tea. I made them myself."

The cookies, all perfectly rounded, all exactly the same thickness, had obviously not been made by hand. If she'd baked them, she was moonlighting for Stella d'Oro.

We were sitting in the parlor of the house. The furniture was colonial, the chairs and the loveseat garnished along their backs with lace antimacassars. The curtains were also lace, and the rug on the dark hardwood floor was a kind of patchwork quilt. The walls were covered with floral wallpaper, the white background slightly yellowish now, the colors slightly faded. The one painting in the room showed a quaintly decrepit covered wooden bridge set against a billow of trees wrapped in brilliant autumn tints, reds and golds and coppers. The air was threaded with the scent of lavender sachet. If it hadn't been for the view through the window, a panorama of Santa Fe and the brown hills to the south, I might've thought that I'd been whisked magically away to New England, and the late nineteenth century.

It was a house I'd noticed many times before from the car as I drove along the northern sweep of Paseo de Peralta. Poised at the top of the ridge, it stood out from the two large and showy adobes that flanked it. It was probably the only house in Santa Fe built to a mock Tudor design, beam-and-plaster exterior walls, a mansard roof, and I'd often wondered who owned it. Now I knew. It occurred to me, once again, that these New Age people had staked out some nifty real estate for themselves.

I leaned forward from the loveseat and plucked up a cookie. I sat back, bit into it. Stella D'Oro.

Eliza Remington took a sip of tea from a Wedgwood cup. As Veronica Chang had done, earlier today, she kept the saucer in her lap. "Now let me see," she said, cocking her head and eyeing me speculatively through her rimless rectangular glasses. "You'd be an Aries."

"That's right."

"On the cusp of Pisces, I'd say. A few days off. The twenty-second of March? Twenty-third?"

I smiled. "The twenty-third."

She smiled, obviously pleased with herself.

If Bennett Hadley had been telling the truth, and she had access to a computer database, it wouldn't have taken her long to discover my birthday.

Her blue-rinsed hair was permed into tight wiry waves. Her hands were peppered with liver spots. She was in her late sixties or early seventies, about five foot five, thin and angular and somewhat stooped. But she was still very spry. Her movements were quick and decisive; her voice was strong. The blue eyes behind her rectangular rimless spectacles were clear. She wore black sensible walking shoes with thick soles and flat heels, black stockings, and a black dress festooned with small yellow fleurs-de-lis. At her throat, perhaps to hide her neck, she wore a yellow silk scarf. She had most likely never been beautiful: her chin and her nose were too forceful for that. But she had probably always been formidable, and time and experience had molded character into the lines and hollows of her face, and an expression that seemed to shift between alertness and a private amusement.

She said, "Your moon's in Sagittarius?"

"In Seattle, for all I know."

She laughed, nearly spilling the saucer from her lap. She caught it with one hand before it slid to the floor—good reflexes—and she looked up at me, smiling broadly. Her teeth all seemed to be her own. "Not a believer, huh?"

"I'm afraid not."

She leaned slightly forward. "Pardon?"

"No," I said, "I'm not."

She sat back, shrugged amiably. "Well, some are, some aren't. For those that are, astrology can provide a real solace."

"I'm sure it can."

She grinned. "No need to be polite. If you think I'm a crazy old bag, that's fine with me. I'll get by. Always have. Did Paul Chang do that to your face?"

I smiled. "You've been talking to his sister?"

She returned the smile. "She phoned me about an hour ago. Wanted to know if I'd talked to you yet. Told me you'd beaten Paul up."

"I wouldn't put it that way, exactly."

"Paul's supposed to be good at that karate of his."

"I imagine he is."

"What'd you do? Fight dirty?"

"Paul probably thinks so."

She smiled. "Good. Never liked him. Nasty, I always thought. Veronica says he's furious at you."

"You and Veronica are good friends?"

"Wouldn't go so far as to say that. We know each other. We talk from time to time. She told me to warn you."

"Warn me about what?"

"Paul. He's looking for you."

"She told you to tell me that?"

She smiled. "You must've made quite an impression on Veronica."

"She kept it well concealed."

"She wants you to call her."

Interesting. "All right," I said. "Thanks."

She nodded toward the tray on the coffee table. "Have another almond cookie."

I took one.

"So," she said. "You told me over the phone you wanted to know about my Tarot card."

"That's right."

"Why?"

"It's missing. Quentin Bouvier and Leonard Quarry, the two people who wanted it, are dead." I finished the almond cookie, sipped some tea.

She nodded. "Heard about Leonard yesterday. And Quentin, of course—I was there when it happened. But the card didn't kill 'em."

"No, but I'd still like to know something about it."

She nodded, sipped at her tea. "You know anything at all about Tarot cards?"

People kept asking me that question. "Justine Bouvier thinks they came from Egypt. Bennett Hadley says they came from Italy. Peter Jones thinks they're a kind of pictorial guide to enlightenment."

She smiled, raised her eyebrows. "Talked to Peter, did you?" She nodded. "I like that boy. Sharp. Serious without being an asshole about it. You know what I mean?"

"I think so, yeah."

Her blue eyes narrowed behind her spectacles. "It bother you, my talking straight out?"

"Not especially."

Again she leaned slightly forward. "Come again?"

"Not especially."

She sat back and nodded. "Not that it'd make any difference." She smiled. "One of the advantages of endurance. I'm a colorful old lady these days. Used to be a loudmouthed bitch."

I smiled.

She took a sip from her teacup. "Justine, now, she's an idiot. Learned everything she knew from Quentin, and outside of that magic mumbo jumbo of his, Quentin was a complete ignoramus."

"What about Bennett Hadley?"

She frowned, puzzled. "You're feeling badly?"

"Bennett Hadley," I said. "What do you think about him?"

"Bennett's an asshole," she said comfortably. "Without being serious, although God knows he thinks he is. He's right, though, about Italy. That's where the cards came from. Started as a game. *Trionfi.* Triumphs. Which is where we get the word *trumps.* They weren't called *Tarrochi* until later. Back in the fifteenth century, they were a pretty hot item among the wealthy. Lot of the rich old farts back then, they commissioned a deck for themselves. Charles the Sixth of France had one done. And so did Pope Alexander the Sixth—Rodrigo Borgia. The Borgia Deck. That's the deck we're talking about. Painted by Pinturicchio, one of Rodrigo's favorites. Famous for the gilt work in his paintings, Pinturicchio. Anyway, Rodrigo gave the deck to his daughter, Lucrezia—you know Lucrezia?"

"Only by reputation."

She blinked, apparently puzzled once again. "Constipation?"

I smiled. "I know of Lucrezia Borgia only by reputation." I was beginning to wonder if she was actually hard of hearing or whether she was putting me on.

She narrowed her eyes again. "She wasn't a poisoner, you know. Lots of people believe that old story about her killing off her husbands. Horseshit."

I nodded. "If you say so."

"Damn right I say so. It's the truth." She frowned, vaguely looked around the room, looked back at me. "Where was I?"

"Rodrigo gave the deck to Lucrezia."

She nodded. "As a wedding present. When she married Alfonso d'Este, the Duke of Ferrara. Her third husband, that one was. She passed it on to their son, Ercole, when he got married. The deck was split up sometime after that. Fifty or sixty years later, half of it, including the Death card, turned up in France.''

"How'd that happen?"

"Who knows? Ercole's wife was Renee, the daughter of Louis the Twelfth, the French king. Maybe she had something to do with it. But the French were all over Italy during the fifteenth and sixteenth centuries. They wanted Milan, Ravenna, Florence, most of the Italian towns. Folks today think that the people in the Renaissance, they just sat around and listened to lute music, ate squab all day. Horseshit. Half the time, they were out killing each other. The other half, they were getting killed.''

She frowned again, looked off at the far well.

"The Death card was in France," I prompted her.

Another frown. "His head in his *pants?*"

"The Death card. It was in France."

"I know that," she snapped at me. "I haven't gotten senile yet. And it was with the rest of the deck, the first twelve trumps. The Bourbons had them. Henry the Fourth, Louis the Thirteenth, that whole sorry bunch. The Death card disappeared sometime around 1774. Stolen from the royal palace.''

"By whom?"

"Cagliostro is a good bet. You know Cagliostro?"

"A magician?"

"No," she said. "He was a magician. Or so he claimed. Claimed to be two hundred years old, too. Horseshit, of course. But he was there at the time, and he was suspected. Next place it showed up was Switzerland.''

"In 1776. Court de Begelin mentioned it."

She smiled. "Done your homework, eh? Good." She nodded. "And de Begelin knew Cagliostro, which fits in with the theory that Cagliostro was the thief. Anyway, from then on, it didn't show up much. Once in 1886, as I recall. Eliphas Levi claimed he'd seen it. Probably had. He described it well enough.''

I said, "From what I understand, the last person to see it was Aleister Crowley. Sometime around the turn of the century."

She nodded.

"So where did it go from there?" I asked her.

A blink, a frown. "What chair?"

"Where did the card go after Crowley had it?"

She smiled, evidently pleased with herself once again. "To my great-grandfather."

"How?"

She grinned. "He stole it. He was one of Crowley's disciples. He and his wife both were. Kirby and Loretta Knight. You know that Crowley's specialty was sex magic? He was going to rule the world with his penis." She smiled. "Lot of men make the same mistake. But usually not on so big a scale." The smile twisted slightly at the corner of her mouth. "Of course, I've heard that Crowley had reasons to think big along those lines."

I smiled.

"He never got to rule the world," she said, "but he probably had a pretty good time trying. At one time or another, he jumped all his women disciples. Couple of the men, too. And an occasional passerby. Kirby, though, he finally got tired of Crowley jumping Loretta—I never *did* hear how Loretta felt about it—and so he dragged her away and went back to Devon. This all happened in Sicily in a town called Cefalu, where Crowley had a retreat. But before Kirby left, he took the card."

"How did Crowley feel about that?"

"Oh, he called up all the demons of hell and sent them after Kirby. Kirby was supposed to die in agony and torment, his body ripped apart, his soul blown to smithereens."

"And?"

"And nothing. Kirby lived another thirty years and died in his sleep. He outlived Crowley."

I smiled again. "Why didn't Crowley report the theft of the card? Use legal means to get it back?"

"Probably because he didn't own it legally himself. Legally, I suppose, it belonged to the French government. Anyway, Kirby gave the card to his son, Walter, my grandfather, and Walter gave it to Charles, *his* son. My uncle. In Devon. Charles gave it to my cousin, Adam. Adam gave it to me, mailed it to me."

"Why?"

"Because he was dying. Heart. He needed the money. He told me we'd split whatever I could get. This was six months ago."

"*Was* dying, you said?"

"He passed away in December."

"I'm sorry."

"No need to be. He was a fool. He could've sold the thing years ago, at auction, and made himself some real money. Waited till the last minute instead. A fool."

"Why didn't you sell it at auction after he died? Your cousin was gone. You would've made more money."

"I'd already opened up negotiations with Leonard and Quentin. Couldn't go back on my word, could I?"

"What does the card look like?" I'd gotten a rough description of it from Giacomo Bernardi, but Eliza Remington had actually possessed the thing.

"Oversize," she said. "About three inches by seven. It's got gilt along the edges, framing it. Shows a skeleton in a long black robe, holding a scythe. Death, of course. He's standing in a field littered with skulls. One of the skulls is a bull's skull—the bull, that was the Borgia family emblem. All the cards in the Borgia Deck have a bull on them somewhere."

I finished my tea, leaned forward, set the cup and saucer on the coffee table. "Sierra Quarry told me that her husband wanted the card for himself, that he wasn't bidding on behalf of someone else."

She frowned impatiently. "Sierra's an idiot. What she knows about money wouldn't fill a gnat's asshole. Leonard never told her anything about his business."

"So he *was* bidding for someone else?"

"Course he was. Leonard didn't have two dimes to rub together."

"For whom?"

She shrugged. "Haven't got the faintest idea. But listen, if you think Leonard's death had anything to do with my Tarot card, you're way off track. I talked to Sierra. From what she says, Leonard was killed by someone she never heard of."

"The question is why."

Still another puzzled frown. "You want to get high?"

I smiled. She'd gone a long time without mishearing me. I was fairly certain now that her deafness was a sham, either a private entertainment or a kind of camouflage. Maybe both. "Why was Leonard killed?"

"How the hell would I know? Leonard was usually involved in two or three deals at a time. I wouldn't be surprised if now and then he got himself involved in something a bit shady. Maybe someone got pissed off at him. Wouldn't take much to get pissed off at Leonard."

"He was killed within a week of the murder of Quentin Bouvier."

She frowned again. "Giacomo didn't kill Quentin because of that damn card."

"You think Giacomo's guilty?"

"Guilty as sin."

"Why?" I sipped some tea.

"He's had it in for Quentin for years now. Quentin was seeing some little girl that Giacomo had the hots for. Some little hippie girl. Moonbeam was her name. No. Starlight." She waved her hand impatiently. "Can't remember. One of those damn silly hippie names. *Starbright!* That was it. Starbright. Idiotic name, if you ask me. Anyway, Quentin dumped her and the brainless little thing went and killed herself."

"How?"

"Tied a nylon stocking around her neck, climbed upon a chair, tied the other end to some kind of hook in the ceiling. One of those things designed to hold a lamp? And then she jumped off the chair, boom, and that's all she wrote."

"WHY DIDN'T YOU tell me about this girl?" I asked him.

He shrugged. "This happen many years ago."

"Three years ago."

He shrugged again, as though his point had just been proved.

Still in his baggy orange cotton pants and sagging T-shirt, Giacomo Bernardi once again sat opposite me across the small Formica table in the interview room of the Detention Center. His fleshy jowls were still stubbly with whiskers, but probably he had the kind of beard that grew back in while he was rinsing his razor. The puffiness at his right eyelid had gone down slightly, and the bruise beneath his right cheekbone had turned a lovely saffron yellow.

"Back then," I said, "after it happened, did the police talk to you?"

He nodded. "Yeah, they talk to me. They know I know Starbright. A friend of hers, she tell them."

"And since you've been arrested, have the state police mentioned it?"

"I no talk to the state police."

"But they talked to you. Have they mentioned the girl?"

He nodded, still lodged within that dull and seemingly impenetrable stolidity. "Yeah, they mention."

"How?" I could imagine, but I wanted to hear it.

"They say, maybe I kill Bouvier this way, with the muffler, because of Starbright. Revenge, they say."

"They didn't say this in front of Sally Durrell." If Sally had known about the girl, she'd have told me.

He shook his head. "No. Before she come here. When I wouldn't talk to them, they say this."

I nodded. "Why didn't you tell Sally about it? About the girl, about the cops asking?"

He shrugged. "Not important. It happen many years ago."

He was beginning to seem almost willfully stupid. "Giacomo," I said patiently. "The prosecution lawyer is bound to use the information."

He shook his head, slowly, stubbornly. "I no kill her."

"Doesn't matter. If you thought that Quentin Bouvier was in some way responsible for her suicide, that gives you another reason to kill him."

He raised his eyebrows slightly, the first sign of animation I'd seen from him. "Three years ago, it happen. If I want revenge, why wait so long?"

"The D.A. will say that you were waiting for the right opportunity."

Once again, with the same sluggish stubbornness, he shook his head. "I no kill him."

"Who else knows about the girl?"

"Who you mean?"

"The people who were down in La Cienega last Saturday night. How many of them knew about the girl in Albuquerque?"

He shrugged. "No one know."

"Quentin Bouvier knew. Elizá Remington knew. She said that you went to Quentin's house a few days after her suicide."

He frowned. "How she know that?"

"Bouvier was a client of hers. She did his charts. He told her about you."

He nodded. "I was upset when I go there. About Starbright, you know? She's a good girl and he treats her bad. So she kills herself. I want to talk to him. Tell him what I think. He laughs at me." He shrugged. "A scumbag."

"Who else knew?"

"No one know."

"Quentin's wife, Justine?"

He shrugged. "Maybe he tell her." He frowned. "Why you ask?"

"Look, Giacomo, I believe you. I don't think you killed Quentin Bouvier. But someone did. And whoever it was, he tried to make it look like you were the murderer. If all he wanted to do was kill Bouvier, he could've just hit him again, harder, with that piece of quartz. But he went to the trouble of getting your scarf from your room, when it was possible that anyone could start wandering around the hallway and see him, and then he used the scarf to haul

Bouvier up the rafter. If he *knew* that you'd been involved in an earlier case involving a hanging, that might've made him more likely to think of using the scarf. So who else knew?"

"I tell you. No one."

"Giacomo, how could they *not* know? This is a small town."

Another shrug. "People in Santa Fe, they don't care what happens in Albuquerque."

To some extent that was true. A good many of the Santa Fe locals, insular and smug, tended to think of Albuquerque as an overlarge truck stop. "But this was the death of a young girl. A suicide. And it involved not only you, but Quentin Bouvier."

Another shrug. "Maybe he tells somebody about her. Not me. And no one never asks."

"Three years ago," I said, "you were going back and forth between Santa Fe and Albuquerque on a regular basis?"

"Not regular. Sometimes. Sometimes I'm there for some weeks or a month, maybe, then I come back. I stay with friends, do readings."

"Where'd you meet this girl? Starbright?"

"A psychic fair. You know? At the Hotel Hilton."

"She was involved with Bouvier then?"

He nodded. "Yeah."

"And you became involved with her?"

He frowned. "You mean to sleep with her? No, no." He shook his head firmly. "She's a good girl. I like her. She tells me about Bouvier, how he treats her. What he does. Rituals, you know. Sexual things. She's ashamed. I'm concerned, huh? I'm worried for her. She's a good girl. And then Bouvier, he tells her to go away, stay away. He don't want her no more. And she's unhappy. I tell her, is better without him, for her. But she's unhappy. And so she kills herself. And so, later, I go to Bouvier. I told you."

He frowned at me. "Why these questions, huh?"

"I don't know. I'm just trying to make sense of all this. How did you get along with the rest of the people in La Cienega?"

"Okay." He shrugged. "Yeah, I get along okay. I know them for years, you know?"

"You got along okay with Leonard Quarry?"

"Sure. He's dead, huh? I read it in the papers."

"He's dead, yes."

"Who kills him?"

"I don't know. Do you know an Anglo man, thin, medium height, black hair?"

He shrugged. "I know many people. Many like that."

"Any of them who might have something to do with Leonard Quarry?"

He shook his head, frowned. "This is the one who kills Quarry?"

"I think so. I have to go, Giacomo. Is there anything I can bring you, the next time I come? Books? Magazines?"

He shook his head. "What I want," he said, "is a drink."

"Me too," I told him.

WHEEL of FORTUNE.

"HELLO?"

"Miss Chang?"

"Ah, Mr. Croft. I am very glad you called. You've spoken with Eliza, then?"

"Yes. She said you wanted to talk to me?"

"Yes, I did. You haven't seen my brother, have you?"

"Not since this morning."

"Neither have I. He left shortly after you did. He is very angry with you, Mr. Croft."

"Is he."

"Yes. His pride was hurt. No one has ever defeated him in that way. Physically, I mean. Are you all right?"

"I'm fine."

"I'm very sorry for what happened. It's all my fault, I realize. Sometimes Paul takes it upon himself to...interfere. He believes that he is helping me, protecting me. This morning, I think he felt that I was angry at you, and he decided to act as his sister's keeper."

"That was very fraternal of him."

"I should have anticipated him and tried to stop it. I really am terribly sorry. And I did want to let you know that he might be looking for you."

She hadn't seemed terribly sorry when she was standing on the other side of the window, watching me leave her front lawn. But, as Peter Jones had said, sometimes people can surprise you. "I appreciate that," I said.

She said, "I wonder if we could try again."

"Try which again?"

"Talking. I know that I wasn't very helpful this morning. Could we make another attempt?"

"Of course."

"But I don't think, under the circumstances, that it would be a good idea for you to come here again. Could you meet me somewhere?"

"Where?"

"Do you know the Big Trees Lodge?"

"Up by the ski basin?"

"Yes. It's usually quiet there at night. We could meet for a drink at the bar tonight. My treat."

"Fine," I said. "What time?"

"I have some errands to run in the early part of the evening. Would nine o'clock be all right with you?"

"Nine o'clock would be fine."

"Good. Nine, then. I look forward to it. Goodbye."

"Goodbye."

She hung up, and the sound of a dial tone spilled from the speaker phone and filled the office. I leaned across the desk, pushed the button. The dial tone abruptly died.

"She has a sexy voice," Rita said.

"You think so?"

Sitting in the swivel chair behind her desk, arms folded, Rita smiled. "Yes. And I think she's aware that it's sexy."

She was wearing a pale lavender turtleneck sweater and a small strand of pearls. Against the light pastel of the cashmere, the black of her hair looked at once deeper and more luminous than usual.

"Holy smokes," I said, and raised my eyebrows. "You think I'm being set up?"

"What do *you* think?"

"I think she's a very nice person. I think she genuinely feels terrible about the way she treated me this morning. I think she wants to make up for it by buying me expensive drinks and giving me everything I need."

She smiled again. "Everything you need? Are you planning to bill Sally for this?"

"Everything I need to break the case."

She nodded. "So you'll be taking your gun along?"

"Yeah," I said.

She knew that there wasn't much else I could do. No one had actually threatened me. Possibly Veronica Chang was trying to set me up; but possibly she wasn't. And probably she possessed information that would be useful. I needed to talk to her. All I could do was act like a Boy Scout, and be prepared.

I LEFT RITA AT her computer terminal and went next door to my office and called Sally Durrell to tell her about Giacomo Bernardi and the young woman in Albuquerque.

"Shit," she said.

"Is that one of those technical legal terms?"

"Why didn't he tell me?"

"It probably just slipped his mind. What there is of it."

"Very funny, Joshua. That's all I need right now. Bad jokes."

"You don't get Robin Williams for fifteen bucks an hour, counselor. Isn't the D.A.'s office supposed to provide you with full disclosure of their evidence?"

"Jim Baca is the prosecutor. He can get cute. He may be doing that now. I'll find out. Anything else?"

"Nothing so far. I still think that Quarry's death is connected to Bouvier's, but I don't know how to prove it. Rita had an idea, and I'm going to check it out."

"What idea?"

"I told you this morning that the guy who killed Quarry, the guy that I *think* killed Quarry, had a heavy tan?"

"Yes. You said the state police were inquiring at the tanning salons."

"And I told you about the possibility of skin dye?"

"Yes."

"So Rita thinks it might be a good idea to check with Quarry's friends and relations, see if they knew anyone connected to Quarry who was involved in the theater."

Only a brief moment passed before she said, "Stage makeup."

"Yeah."

"You know, Joshua, it's possible that this man's tan is genuine. That he flew into New Mexico from somewhere like the Caribbean, and then flew out again, after he killed Quarry."

"Sure it's possible. But that would probably mean that he's a contract killer, and so far I haven't seen anything to indicate that."

"Someone sent by the man for whom Quarry was bidding on the card?"

"Maybe. If he exists. But even if he does, it wasn't Quarry's fault that he lost out on the bidding. And Sally, I've got no way of checking arrivals and departures at the Albuquerque airport. The police can, but I can't. This is something I *can* check on."

A pause, and then: "It's worth looking into, I suppose." She sounded dubious.

"It won't take much time. A few phone calls. And I don't have much else to look into."

"I know, Joshua. I know you're doing the best you can. But you have to bear in mind that my interests here revolve only around the defense of Giacomo Bernardi for the murder of Quentin Bouvier. What if you and Rita are wrong? What if Quarry's death has nothing to do with Bouvier's?"

"Then I'll be wasting your fifteen dollars an hour. Maybe you'd better try hiring Robin Williams."

She laughed. "All right, Joshua. Keep me informed."

WHEN I TELEPHONED the Freefall-Morningstar house, Brad answered. "Crystal Center."

"Hello, Brad. This is Joshua Croft."

"Hey, man, what the hell is going on here? I heard that Leonard got killed. The state cops were here. A couple of troopers."

"What did they want?"

"They wanted to know if anyone who knew Leonard was into theater. Actors, stagehands, like that."

So the state police were following the same trail. Hernandez had told me this morning that he didn't believe that Quarry's and Bouvier's deaths were related. But a couple of state troopers talking to Brad didn't necessarily mean that Hernandez had been lying to me. Brad had known both men. The state police were investigating both cases.

"And what did you tell them?" I asked Brad.

"I told them no, man. I don't know anyone like that. Except for Carol Masters, and they couldn't care less about her. How come they want to know?"

"They didn't tell you?"

"Not a thing, man. Typical cop mentality. They told me they were the ones asking the questions."

I explained to him what had happened, told him about the heavily tanned man who had probably killed Quarry.

"No, man, no. I don't know anyone like that. Could this guy be the one who killed Quentin, too?"

"I don't know. One more thing, Brad."

"What?"

"A young woman, a friend of Giacomo's, killed herself a few years ago, down in Albuquerque. Did you know anything about that?"

"Killed herself? A friend of Giacomo's?"

"Yeah."

"No, man. I didn't know. Why'd she do that?"

"I'm not sure. Thanks for the help."

I CALLED Bennett Hadley and received pretty much the same responses: the state police had asked him about theatrical people who'd known Quarry, and, other than Carol Masters, he'd been unable to come up with any. Like Brad, Hadley wanted to know if the tanned Anglo man could have killed Quentin Bouvier. I told him I didn't know. He didn't know, or said he didn't, about the suicide of Starbright in Albuquerque. I called Peter Jones. No answer. Called Justine Bouvier. Got her machine, asked her to call me. I tried Eliza Remington, found her and received, once again, the same responses. Called Sierra Quarry. Apologized for bothering her, asked her how she was. She was all right, she said. But she didn't sound all right: she sounded lost. I asked her about a theatrical connection to her husband. Except for Carol Masters, she didn't know of one. Like the others, she had been questioned about it by the police. Like the others, she wanted to know why the police were interested. I explained.

"Oh," she said in her soft, solemn voice. "But why are *you* interested, Mr. Croft? The state policeman, Mr. Hernandez, told me that Leonard's death probably had nothing to do with the death of Mr. Bouvier."

"I think that Hernandez is wrong, Mrs. Quarry. The state police are committed to the idea that Giacomo Bernardi killed Quentin Bouvier. And since Giacomo's in prison, so far as they're concerned the two deaths can't be related. I think they are."

She sighed slowly and I could hear her sadness over the phone line. "I don't know that it makes any difference."

"I think it does. And Mrs. Quarry? I'm pretty good at this. Sometimes I can do things, go places, that the police can't. There's a possibility that if they can't find the man who killed your husband, then maybe I will. I just wanted you to know that I'll be trying."

Another sigh. "All right, Mr. Croft. Thank you for your concern."

"Mrs. Quarry?"

"Yes?"

"Are you sure that your husband was bidding on that Tarot card for himself?"

"That's what he told me. I . . ."

"What, Mrs. Quarry?"

Another sigh. "I don't know, Mr. Croft. Leonard never really talked to me about his business. I'm sorry, but I'm not very good with money, it's just something that never interested me, and Leonard knew that. And now, well, I've been talking to everyone, all our friends, and they all say that Leonard couldn't have afforded it for himself. And the police, too, they say the same thing. They must be right, all of them. But I just don't know. He never told me about anyone else. He never mentioned anything about anyone else."

"And he *did* tell you that he wanted the card for himself?"

"Well, yes. I mean, I was sure he did. But he couldn't have afforded it, could he? So why would he have said that?"

"I don't know yet. To your knowledge, had he been involved in any other deals recently?"

"Oh dear. The police asked the same question. I really don't know, Mr. Croft. I'm sorry, I'd like to help you, but I honestly don't know."

"All right. Just one more question. Did you ever hear of a young woman named Starbright? She lived in Albuquerque and she was a friend of Giacomo Bernardi's. She committed suicide a few years ago."

"How awful. Starbright was her name? No. No, I don't think so, Mr. Croft. Is it important?"

"I don't know, Mrs. Quarry. Thank you."

THE AIR WAS CLEAR and mild; bright stars crowded the black sky. Back in town, most of the snow had melted away, but up here in the mountains, beyond the tall caped forms of the conifers, the pale silent trunks of the aspens, it still sheeted the steep slopes, a cool white blaze in the beams of my headlights.

There weren't many cars on the Ski Basin Road, and none of them, it seemed, contained Paul Chang. A pair of headlights did stay behind me all the way, about two hundred yards back, but never moved any closer. When I reached the Big Trees Lodge, at ten minutes to nine, I parked the station wagon and twisted myself around in the seat to watch the road through the rear window. I saw that the headlights belonged to a gray Chevy pickup, about ten years old. It drove by the restaurant's parking lot without a hesitation. I couldn't see the driver.

I got out of the Subaru, closed the door, locked it. There were only four or five other cars in the parking lot at the base of the big A-frame building. A slow night. I climbed up the wooden steps. I hadn't climbed them for a couple of years.

Every five years or so, some ambitious would-be restaurateur decides that the Big Trees Lodge offers more promise than it's ever actually kept before. He buys the place, refurbishes it, hires a new staff, puts some ads in the *Reporter* and the *New Mexican*, and then sits back and waits for the tourists and their money to roll in. The tourists who've come for the skiing roll right on by, up to the big lodge at the ski basin, and the other tourists seldom drive the ten miles required to get there from town. Neither do many of the locals. Sooner or later, the owner cuts back on the staff, hires a less imaginative chef. The tourists don't care, but the few locals who have been coming, stop coming. Usually, five years after he buys it, he sells it.

Just now the restaurant was about midway into its cycle. It still did some dinner business on the weekend and occasionally some lunch business during the week, but not much of anything on a weekday night.

Inside, there were two couples sitting on opposite sides of the room at small, candlelit tables. The bar, a low-ceilinged space separated from the dining area, was empty, and so were the booths that ran down the opposite wall. I perched myself on a Naugahyde stool and ordered a weak Jack Daniel's and water.

The bartender, Sabrina, was a tall, thin, blond woman who'd been born and raised in Santa Fe. I'd seen her around town, as a cocktail waitress or a bartender, in one bar or another since I arrived here myself. Tonight she passed the time by gossiping to me about the local luminaries: who was divorcing whom, who was marrying whom, who was drinking more these days, who was drinking not at all.

She told me about a Santa Fe politician who'd come into the bar, two weeks before, with his new girlfriend. ("I swear,

Joshua, half the people we get here, we get them because they're screwing around and they figure this place is so dead they won't get caught.'') The two of them had sat at the far booth. Fifteen minutes later, the politician's wife had come in with her new boyfriend, and they'd sat down two booths away.

Sabrina took a drag from her cigarette, exhaled. "Louise was on that night—the cocktail waitress—and she was so nervous she could hardly carry her tray."

Nothing had happened, she said, for half an hour. "A *half* an hour Louise and I are watching them, waiting for one of them to spot the other. And then Bill and the girl get up, and they're walking out, and *just* as they go by the other booth, Bill smacks his hand down on the girl's butt and gives it a great big squeeze. And then he looks over—his hand is still on her butt—and he sees Maria. And Maria sees him and in less than a second she's out of that booth. She climbs right up onto the table and *jumps* on him and she grabs at his hair—that nice white hair of his—and she starts pulling it out by the roots. She's got her legs wrapped around him and he's staggering all over the bar, reeling around, and she keeps shouting, '*This* is your Property Tax Commission, you son of a bitch?'''

I laughed. "Poor Bill."

"Poor Bill nothing. He's been cheating on her since the day he got married. I heard he chippied one of the brides-maids in the hallway closet." She sucked on her cigarette, exhaled. "Like they say. What goes around, comes around."

I nodded. "It's all karma."

She frowned at me. "You're not going Hindu on me, are you, Joshua?"

"It's all karma, Sabrina. You can't escape the stuff. We're all trapped on this big wheel, going round and round. If you kill somebody, that's karma. If you get killed, that's karma. If you don't believe in karma, that's karma. If you decide to run away from your karma, *that's* karma."

"Karma does it all, huh?"

"Absolutely."

"Then what are *we* hanging around here for?"

I shrugged. "It's our karma."

She laughed.

"But what happened to Bill and Maria?" I asked her.

Behind Sabrina, on the back counter, the telephone rang. She frowned. "One second," she told me, and then turned to pick it up. "Bar."

I looked at my watch. Twenty minutes after nine. Veronica Chang was late.

When I looked back up, Sabrina was holding out the cordless telephone receiver in her right hand, her left over the mouthpiece. "It's for you, Swami. A woman."

I took the phone. "Hello?"

It was Veronica Chang, calling to apologize and to tell me that something important had come up, that she couldn't get here tonight. She asked if I'd call her tomorrow to reschedule. I said I would, and she apologized some more and then hung up.

I turned off the telephone and handed it to Sabrina. She was smiling. "You got stood up," she said.

"Apparently."

"Serves you right for cheating on Rita."

I shook my head. "Business meeting."

She smiled. "Right."

Bartenders seldom believe the best of people. They seldom see it.

"So what happened to Bill and Maria?" I asked her.

"Oh yeah." She replaced the phone in its cradle, then turned back to me, leaning her elbows on the bar. "A couple of the waiters came in from the dining room, and finally they were able to get the two of them separated and quieted down." She tapped her cigarette into the ashtray. "Bill took her home. Never even looked at the girl. She just stood there the whole time, watching."

"How'd she get home?"

"Maria's boyfriend took her." She shrugged. "Maybe they'll live happily ever after."

I nodded. "Karma."

She smiled. "Another drink?"

I shook my head. "Gotta go. It's—"

"Right, yeah. Karma."

ABOUT A MILE DOWN the road, and maybe sixty yards behind me, the headlights picked me up again.

To my occasionally paranoid eyes, at any rate, they seemed to be the same headlights that had followed me from town. But if it was Paul Chang, why hadn't he tried something on the way up?

I could think of one answer to that, and I didn't much like it.

On the way up, the Subaru and I had been on the mountain side of the road: anyone wanting to run us off the road might think that the trees and the bank of the hill would cushion our arrival.

Heading back into town, we were on the cliff side of the road. For the next four or five miles, the right edge of the highway ran along the edge of the mountain, which sometimes sloped gently downward beneath the weight of its towering black ponderosas, but more often simply plunged straight into the valley, a drop invisible from the car. The only barrier was a line of flimsy retaining posts, each set with a small round plastic reflector that peered at me like a single unblinking eye.

I looked into the rearview mirror. The headlights hadn't moved up. Maybe it wasn't the same car.

There was a glow ahead, through the trees. It became a beam of light swaying through the treetops and then it became another pair of headlights. They grew larger and then the car whooshed by and I watched in the mirror as its taillights diminished and finally vanished behind the glare of the car following me.

Which began to move up now, closing the distance between us.

In New Mexico, except in a bar or restaurant, and so long as it's visible, you're allowed to keep a gun on your person. You're also allowed to keep one in your car. Some enterprising souls, true Sons of the Pioneers, do both. I reached down under the seat and retrieved mine, a .38 Smith & Wesson. The Model 42, five shots maximum, but I keep an empty chamber beneath the shrouded hammer. I'm not usually attacked by more than four people at a time.

I wedged the butt down between the cushion of the passenger seat and the seat back, so the thing wouldn't get lost.

Up ahead, a bright yellow diamond-shaped sign indicated that the road would soon start acting like a snake.

There was no glow down there, no car approaching. I tapped my brakes, suggesting to the driver behind me that I was about to slow the Subaru, and then I downshifted into third and hit the gas, swinging wide to the left lane just before I slipped into the right-hand turn. The tires whined in protest, the engine coughed, but the station wagon held the asphalt. I shifted into fourth and the car shot toward the next curve.

The headlights found the rearview mirror and then, on the straight, they began to grow larger.

It was possible, of course, that the car behind me was being driven by some idiot who was guilty only of recklessness and pride, and who'd been insulted by my attempt to outrun him in a puny Japanese wagon. In which case, by trying to stay ahead of him, I'd just be making things worse.

It was possible. I could worry about it later.

Next curve winding left. No glow, no cars coming. Downshift into third, slide into the turn. The steering wheel fighting me, the wagon's rear end fading off to the right. Hold it steady, ease up on the pedal, get the road back beneath all four tires. Clutch, stick, gas.

Another cough from the engine.

Hang in there, kid. Pull through this and I'll buy you some nice new oil. I was only kidding about the new car.

The headlights stayed behind me all the way, disappearing on the turns and reappearing after them, slightly farther back at first, and then moving closer on the straights.

At last the curves ended and the road ran straight for maybe half a mile. The Subaru was running flat-out but the headlights kept getting larger in the mirror.

Let's see what he has in mind.

What choice do we have?

The headlights filled the mirror. He was less than twenty feet away.

If he hit me from the rear, rammed me hard enough at the left rear bumper, he could cause me some serious trouble.

He moved out into the oncoming lane and lumbered up alongside me. I sent off a silent prayer of thanks to Hollywood, which has encouraged a belief in this sort of nonsense. Out of the corner of my eye I saw the hood of the truck—it was the gray Chevy pickup—and when the driver pulled even with me I risked a quick glance. Saw only a vague featureless shape in the grayness. Ski mask?

Just as the cab of the truck ran ahead of me, I slammed on the Subaru's brakes. Thrown forward, bracing myself stiff-armed against the wheel, I watched the truck lurch into the right lane. The driver, perhaps half expecting the crunch of mass slamming into mass, nearly lost control. The truck wobbled, swayed from left to right a moment, right to left, and then at last straightened out.

But by then I'd stopped the Subaru, cut the ignition, whipped up the emergency brake, snatched the .38 from the passenger seat, opened the door, jumped out, and braced both forearms against the top of the window, the pistol aimed at his gate.

I hadn't been able to read his license plate; the light was out.

The truck raced away, down the hill, its red taillights shrinking, shrinking, and then disappearing around a bend. The sound of its engine slowly faded into the silence of the trees.

I let out a breath and turned and sagged down into the seat, my feet still on the road, my arms on my thighs, the Smith dangling loosely in my right hand. I was soaked with sweat.

It didn't *have* to be someone trying to kill me. It could have been some local cowboy, annoyed that I wouldn't let him overtake and pass.

But he'd cut back into the right lane while I was supposed to be in it.

Maybe he was drunk. Maybe he misjudged the lane change.

I didn't really believe that the driver had been a drunken cowboy. But I was trying to persuade my body that I did, because my body was absolutely horrified at the thought that someone might set out, deliberately, to end our existence.

It was a drunken cowboy.

It was someone who wanted to *kill* us.

Both of us realized, simultaneously, that the station wagon and I were sitting in the middle of the right lane of the highway. Where another drunken cowboy, coming down from the ski basin, *would* very likely kill us.

I swung my legs into the car, pulled the door shut. Wedged the pistol down against the cushion again. Put the stick in neutral. Turned on the ignition. Fastened the seat belt. Released the emergency brake. Checked the rearview mirror. Took another deep breath. And then set off down the road, slowly, driving like a rickety old man.

He wanted to kill us!

Shut up. We're still alive. Drive.

He got me just at the end of the straight, where the road arched off to the left. I went back up there later, and I worked it out. He must have spun around, turned off his lights, driven back to the turn, parked it. He must have left the truck, its engine running, and bolted back to the road to watch for my approach. Probably he saw the car sitting there, immobile. Probably he saw it start moving. Then he must have run back to the truck, climbed in, and waited till the brightening glow from my headlights told him that the time was right.

From my left, suddenly, a pair of headlights flared brilliant white, blinding me as they rushed directly toward the car. I jerked the wheel to the right, knew instantly that this was a mistake, felt the Subaru stagger as it snapped the retaining post. The car lifted itself off the road and then it tilted to the right and then the right front wheel slammed down onto something and then the car was spinning over, left to right, and it seemed to keep spinning forever, over and over, like a Ferris wheel in hell.

THE CHARIOT.

"THIS BABY'S GOT everything," Ernie told me. "Look at this. You got your AM, you got your FM, you got your C.D., you got your cassette. You got your amp, you got your graphics equalizer. You got speakers like you wouldn't believe. Monsters. What kinda music you listen to, Josh?"

"Lawrence Welk."

"The accordion guy? Yeah? Well, I tell you, Josh, it's amazing, a system like this. You're sitting in the car and it's like you're actually sitting *inside* Lawrence Welk's accordion."

One of life's cherished dreams fulfilled.

The car in which we sat, me in the driver's seat, Ernie to my right, was a three-year-old Jeep Cherokee. Ernie was my height, bulkier in the shoulders, chest, and stomach. White haired and white bearded, he was wearing a gray down jacket that made him look like the Michelin man, and he and the coat were stuffed into the bucket seat like a pillow into a shoebox. Even though the seat was shoved all the way back, the interior of the car seemed cramped.

"Look at this," Ernie said. "You got your air. You go
your cruise control. You got your rear window wiper, yo
got your rear window heater. This baby's got it all."

"How big is the engine, Ernie?"

"Four liters. Hey it's not a Maserati. We're not talkin
Formula One here. But this baby can move. In two-wheel
it'll keep up with just about anything on the road. In four
wheel, it'll take you up and down the craters of the moon
And power? *Whoa!* The winch? Up front? You hook tha
sucker to the Empire State Building and you turn it on, and
I bet you that damn building comes down on top of you."

A new dream to cherish.

"Does it run?" I asked him.

"Does it *run?* Josh, this baby runs like a goddamn sew
ing machine. Go ahead. Turn it on."

I reached forward, winced, turned on the ignition, winced
again.

"You okay, Josh? You're looking a little peaked."

"I'm okay."

"Rough night last night, huh?"

"Kind of."

I DIDN'T PASS OUT while the Subaru was careening throug
the air. I noted with a mild, detached interest everything tha
happened. Centrifugal force ripping at my body, pulling m
in every direction at once. The insane spin of the car as i
wheeled through the air on its horizontal axis, left to right
The series of deafening crashes as it rolled. The final cras
as it hit something, punching my left side against the door
knocking my breath away.

It became clear to me, after a while, that Movement ha
stopped.

But the engine was still running. How could that be?

I watched my hand reach out, reach out, out, out, to th
end of the known universe, and turn off the ignition. Tha
was good, I remember thinking. But the dashboard light
were off now. Was that good? I didn't know.

It was good, yes, because now I could smell gasoline.
Don't light any matches, I told myself. Idiot. You don't have
any matches. You don't smoke.

Something was strange here.

I realized that I was upside down.

That wasn't so good...

If I was upside down, let me see, if I was upside down,
then the road should be that way, to my right. Does that
make sense? Sure, the road was off to my right, so all I had
to do was get out of the car and walk in that direction.
Which would be left, then. Or would it? Left or right?
Which was right? He got left because he couldn't tell right
from left. Right from wrong. Left, right, left, right, company *halt*...

Why am I not breathing well?

Because you're upside down, you idiot. The seat belt
harness is digging into your chest.

Well, that's not good. Maybe I should do something...

What if I can't do anything! What if I'm paralyzed?

Check it out. Right arm. Okay. Left arm. Okay. Right leg.
Okay. Left leg. Okay.

Nothing broken. No blood. Everything's fine.

Except that I'm upside down.

With both hands I reached up and felt for the roof. It
seemed much closer to my head than it was supposed to be,
only an inch or so away. And it was lumpy in strange places,
and there was something scattered all over it—clicking,
clattering chips of something.

Glass. A window must have shattered. I reached out to
check the window to my left. My hand went through empty
air until it hit cold damp snow. I realized, abruptly, that I
felt cold and damp myself.

I looked at the windshield. It was still there, but in the
faint glow of starlight on snow I saw that it was cobwebbed
with fractures.

Time to get out of here.

Okay. Here's the plan. You brace yourself with your left
elbow against the roof. Get to the seat belt with your right

hand. Tuck in your head. Unbuckle the belt. Then, like a
stone, you fall.

Before I could put all this into operation, a bright light
started flickering at me, off to my right.

"Hey. *Hey,* you okay in there?"

Paul Chang?

I reached over to the passenger seat, groped around for
the gun.

It wasn't there.

"Hey, mister," came the voice. Suddenly a flashlight
beam lanced through the passenger window, directly into my
eyes. "You okay in there?"

The passenger window was gone, too.

"Yeah," I said. "Could you get that light out of my
eyes?"

He did, whoever he was.

"Thank God," he said. "I thought you were a goner. I
saw that truck coming at you and then you went off the road
and started cartwheeling. *Jesus!* You are one lucky man,
mister."

"Where's the truck?"

"The sonovabitch took off. I couldn't believe it! Just
backed up and turned around and headed down the hill. The
sonovabitch! I never saw anything like it! He came right *at*
you, *deliberately!*

My head, saturated with down-rushing blood, felt as big
as a basketball. "You think—"

"What's this world coming to? Jesus, mister, your car is
totaled!" There was a kind of awe in his voice, almost re-
ligious.

"You think you could come around and help me get out
of here?" I said.

"I don't think you should move, mister. That's what they
say. You don't move an accident victim. I already called the
cops on the car phone and they're on their way. Be here any
minute. An ambulance, too. Judy, that's the wife, she's up
there waiting. She'll send them right down."

As though she'd heard her name mentioned, a woman called out from somewhere far away, *"Roger? Are you all right down there?"*

"I'm fine, hon!" the man called out. "He's okay, I think!"

"Roger," I said.

The flashlight blinded me. I shut my eyes and turned away. I realized that my neck hurt.

The beam swung off my face. "Sorry," he said.

"Roger, it's probably become pretty obvious to you by now that I'm upside down. This isn't my normal position, Roger. I'd like to get back to my normal position. Do you think you could help me do that?"

"I don't know, mister. You're not supposed to move the victim."

"Fine, Roger. I'll do it myself."

"Wait wait wait. Hold on. I'll see what I can do."

I watched through the crazed windshield as the beam of the flashlight, occasionally revealing Roger's upside down legs and feet, slid and slipped across the upside down snow. And then Roger was outside my window, his head and shoulders a black silhouette against the gray. I still couldn't see his face.

"Jesus," he said, "your car's a wreck. I hope you've got insurance."

"Are you going to help me, Roger?"

"You're sure you want to do this?" he asked me.

"Yeah. I'm going to open the door."

"Hey. Hold on. *Wait.* I smell gas." He stood up. I could see only his lower legs against the pale gray snow.

"Is there any gasoline by the door?" I asked his legs.

The flashlight beam wobbled. "I don't see any," his legs said. They didn't sound entirely convinced.

"Okay." I pulled the door handle. Nothing.

"It's jammed," I told Roger.

"Why don't we just leave it until the cops come. They've got tools. They've got that Jaws of Life deal."

"Can you pull on the door, Roger?"

"I don't know, mister."

"My name is Croft, Roger. Joshua Croft. I'm perfectly okay. I'm fine. Just pull on the door for me. I'll push from this side."

"I don't think this is a good idea. You've been in an accident. You're a victim."

The woman's voice came again: *"Roger, what are you doing?"*

"Everything's okay, hon!" he called out. "The guy wants to get out of the car!"

"Then get him out of the goddamn car! It's freezing up here!"

He muttered something under his breath.

"Roger?" I said.

His head and shoulders were back in the window. "What?" A note of impatience in his voice now. I think that he was reappraising the concept of the good Samaritan.

"Pull on the door, Roger," I said.

"Awright, awright." Under his breath: *"Shit."*

"You got it?" I asked him.

"Yeah, yeah, I got it." Very slightly, the car rocked.

"Won't open," he said.

I sighed. "I wasn't ready, Roger. Wait a second." I braced my knees against the dashboard, my feet against the ceiling-floor, my right hand against the passenger seat. "Okay. Let's try it on the count of three. One, two, *three.*"

With a sickening metallic crunch, the door swung open.

"IT WAS JUST LUCK, I guess," said Roger, walking beside me. "I mean, we haven't been up to the Big Trees in ten, twelve years. It was Judy's idea. Jesus, we didn't expect anything like this."

"Me neither," I said.

"Yeah, well, sure. Of course not. And you're really okay?"

"I'm fine."

We walked up the incline, the soles of my boots slippery against the snow. My body was beginning to stiffen up, joints going grainy, ligaments tightening. I felt very cold, very shaky. I paid close attention to the beam of Roger's flashlight as it spotlit the lumps and ridges in the snow along my path. I didn't want to fall down. I wasn't sure that I'd be able to get up.

"Why would someone do a thing like that?" Roger asked me. "Come at you like that? *Deliberately?*"

"It's a cruel world, Roger."

"Yeah, but *deliberately*..."

We reached the top. I could make out, against the backdrop of roadway and forest illuminated by the headlights, a figure standing beside the car, wrapped in a bulky coat, hands buried deeply in the pockets.

Roger said, "This is Judy, my wife."

The flashlight beam lit up the wincing, displeased face of a middle-aged woman. *"Roger!"*

"Sorry," he said. "And this is, um."

"Joshua Croft," I said. "Hello. I want to thank you, both of you, for..."

"Hey," said Roger, "are you okay?"

I didn't actually faint, although I admit it might've looked as though I did. I simply decided that I was tired of standing up and being conscious, and so I toppled to the ground.

EVERYONE KEPT TELLING ME that I was a lucky man. The paramedics did, when I came to, inside the ambulance as it raced toward town. The head nurse did, in the emergency ward at St. Vincent's. The X-ray attendant did, as he walked beside my gurney on the way to his radioactive lair.

They wouldn't let me get off the gurney. They wouldn't let me make a phone call.

"Just relax," everyone kept telling me. "You'll be fine."

"I've got to make a phone call."

"Relax."

For some reason, I've never been able to relax in an emergency ward, surrounded by people in various states of dismemberment.

"Nothing is broken," the doctor told me, after he received the X-ray results. He was a small slender man, East Indian, probably Pakistani, with large brown eyes and a small slender mustache. We were in a small examining room and I had finally been allowed to sit up. I was perched on the examining table. Getting upright had taken me less than an hour. "You have many contusions on your left side, oh my yes, many many contusions, eh? And, yes, a serious strain, here, you see, along the neck. Painful, eh? You will need to wear a collar for a time, most probably. But nothing is broken, nothing at all. You are a very lucky man, yes indeed."

"A collar? What kind of collar?"

"A foam collar, to provide the support, you see. It will reduce tension to the neck."

"Great," I said. "Can I get my collar and go home now?"

He giggled. "Oh no, no no no. Not as yet, you see. We will be keeping you for observation, you see. Overnight. Because, you see, there is always a danger, in situations of this sort, of the bleeding inside the skull.

"Subdural hematoma."

"Ah yes, excellent, you understand, do you? Excellent!"

"Could I make a phone call?"

He frowned. "Not as yet, I am afraid, no. There is a policeman wishing to speak to you, you see. He seems quite a nice chap. If you are too tired, of course, I can ask him to postpone this discussion."

"After I talk to the cop, can I make a phone call."

"We shall see, yes?"

"HELLO, HECTOR."

He nodded. "Josh."

Sergeant Hector Ramirez worked the Violent Crimes Unit of the Santa Fe Police Department. A weightlifter, he was under six feet tall and he weighed about two twenty. His neck, thrusting up from the collar of his black trench coat, was as big around as my thigh. Beneath the trench coat he wore a gray three-piece suit, a tattersall shirt, a blue silk tie. "You come here often?" he said.

"Whenever I can," I said. "It's the smell of disinfectant. It drives me wild."

He ran his hand down over his Frito Bandido mustache. "They tell me you're going to live."

"Yeah. But they won't say for how long."

Hector smiled grimly. "Not very long, you keep getting run off the road like that. How you feeling?"

"I'm okay. But what brings you here, Hector? You working Traffic these days?"

He shook his head. "I was at my desk when Gonzalez told me you'd taken a tumble. The officers in the cruiser called in your name. The witnesses said the guy in the truck took off after he ran at you. That right?"

"I saw him run at me. I didn't see him take off."

"Any idea who it might've been?"

It didn't seem to me that I owed Paul Chang or his sister anything. I told Hector about meeting the lovely Miss Chang that morning, about the fight with Paul, the two phone calls from Veronica, the race down the highway.

When I finished, Hector said, "But you couldn't identify the driver of the other car as Paul Chang?"

"No. I didn't see his face. And the license plate was out. But it was a gray Chevy pickup. Fairly big. Three-quarter ton. Maybe ten years old."

He nodded. "Are you working on anything else right now?"

"No."

"Can you think of anyone besides Paul Chang who might want to see you splattered down the mountainside?"

"No one, Hector. I'm beloved by all and sundry."

"By sundry, maybe, but not by all. You're sure that the vehicle that came at you was the same truck that'd passed you?"

"I told you, I didn't actually see the vehicle. The headlights blinded me. Roger, the witness, the guy who helped me out of the car, he told me that it'd been a truck. Speaking of which, do you people have his address?"

"The officers do."

"Could I get it from them? I'd like to thank him."

He nodded.

"And my gun," I said. "It's in my car somewhere."

He shook his head. "Sanchez, one of the officers, found it. You know, Josh, it was a good thing for you that Roger Morrison came along when he did. You're—"

"Hector, please don't tell me that I'm a lucky man. My car is totaled. I feel like I spent my summer vacation inside an Osterizer. The doctor tells me that probably I'll need one of those collars that make you look like you've got a goiter. I don't feel very lucky right now."

He nodded. "Well, think about this. Whoever was in that truck, he probably drove away because he saw Morrison's car. If the car hadn't shown up, he might've left the truck and come down to make sure you were out of action."

I hadn't considered that.

"Maybe," I said. "Listen, Hector. They haven't let me use a phone. Could you call Rita for me and tell her what's going on?"

"I already did. She's waiting outside." He smiled. "Want me to send her in?"

SMILING, SHE CAME ACROSS the room. Her walk seemed perfectly normal; unless you were looking for the faint limp, you wouldn't notice it.

Gently, almost tentatively, she put her arms around my shoulders and her face against mine, cheek to cheek. I held her. Carefully, because the muscles along my left side were sore, from my calf all the way up to my ear. I could smell the perfume she used and the lingering scent of shampoo in her hair. She felt as soft as a cloud, something I could sink into, and disappear.

"Hi," she said. Her breath was warm against my neck.

"Hi."

"I'm glad you're all right."

"Thanks." My voice sounded a bit scratchy. Damage from the accident, no doubt. I cleared it. "So am I. It's good to see you."

She kissed my cheek. "Nothing's broken, the doctor told me."

"They want to keep me overnight."

"Naturally."

"I feel fine."

"Joshua?"

"Hmmm?"

"Shut up."

I smiled. We stayed like that for a time, neither one of us moving or saying, anything. Finally she said, "Are you really all right?"

I nodded. "I had a couple of bad moments there. But I'm okay now. A little stiff."

She looked back, looked at me. Concern had tightened the corners of her big dark eyes. "They said you fainted."

"I was just resting for a while."

"Joshua?"

"Shut up?"

"Yes."

I don't know why it happened then, or why it hadn't happened before. Maybe it had been waiting, like some beast of prey, to catch me off guard, to jump at me when finally I felt safe, wrapped in Rita's arms and the warmth and the smells of her. But suddenly it was there: the headlights flaring as the big truck rushed at the Subaru, the sickening sensation as the station wagon soared off the road and began to roll, the disorientation, the feeling of helplessness, the crashes coming like explosions as the car and I cartwheeled crazily down the slope...

My body started to shake and I could feel sweat popping from every pore of my body.

Rita moved closer, held me. I couldn't get my breath.

She stood back. "You'd better lie down."

"I feel stupid," I said, but I let her help me get my legs up onto the table, let her ease my head and shoulders down to the pillow.

My teeth were chattering. "This is dumb," I said.

Rita had found a blanket somewhere and now she draped it over me. "You're in shock," she said. She tucked the blanket around my shoulder, sat beside me, wiped lightly at my forehead with the fingertips of her right hand.

"Shit," I said. I took another deep breath. "Why now?"

"Because you're so dense that it takes you forever to realize that you nearly got yourself killed."

"Oh," I said. "Thanks."

She leaned forward, kissed me lightly on the lips, sat back. "I'll get the doctor."

"No, wait." I brought my hand from under the blanket, found hers. "Stay here. I feel better now. And he's not going to be able to do anything. Give me a couple of aspirins. Tell me to call him in the morning."

She shook her head and smiled. She squeezed my hand. "Sometimes you're infuriating, Joshua. You've built up this persona for yourself. Tough guy. Wiseass. Never at a loss for the glib response."

I smiled. Weakly. "Justine Bouvier tells me I'm wearing emotional armor."

"I hate to say it, but she's right."

"Maybe I should get in touch with my inner child."

She smiled. "Maybe you should develop an outer adult."

"Great. Kick me when I'm down."

She smiled. She put the palm of her left hand against my cheek. "I'm glad you're all right. When Hector called and told me you were in here, I was frantic."

"I have a hard time picturing you frantic, Rita."

"You're very important to me, Joshua."

"Oh yeah? Prove it."

Smiling again, she leaned forward...

And the doctor apparently took this as an invitation for him to return. He bustled back into the room, rubbing his hands together. Rita sat up.

"Ah well, Mr. Croft," said the doctor, "we've found you a most wonderful room."

THE NEXT MORNING at eight o'clock, after they released me, Rita drove me home. It was when she was pulling her old diesel Mercedes into my driveway that she told me she was going down to Albuquerque.

"Albuquerque?" I said. "Why?" To look at her, I had to turn my entire body toward her. My body was as stiff as a plank and the collar at my neck, foam or not, felt like a shackle.

"I need to talk to some people down there." She was wearing her long blue coat, a white turtleneck, a black skirt, slender black leather boots.

"What people?" I said. "About what?"

She smiled. "You sound like my mother, Joshua."

"This is something you're working on?"

"Partly, yes. Don't worry. I should be back tomorrow."

"Tomorrow?"

"I'll call you tonight. You stay in bed."

"I've got to find someone who can get the car down from the Ski Basin."

"I called Pedro." One of her cousins. "He'll rent a tow truck and take care of it."

"I need to deal with the insurance people."

"I called them. They're sending someone up there to meet Pedro. You get to bed. And leave the collar on."

"Damn thing itches."

"Joshua, stop whining. If you don't leave the collar on, your neck won't get better."

"Especially if you keep being a pain in it. Why are you going to Albuquerque?"

"I'll tell you later." She opened her purse, reached in, pulled out a revolver, handed it to me. My .38. I'd completely forgotten about it. "Here," she said. "Hector gave it to me last night."

I took it and she leaned across the seat to kiss me. "Get to bed," she said.

When Rita didn't want to talk, she wouldn't.

Back inside my house, I took a long shower, as hot as I could stand it, trying to loosen up muscles that had set like cement. I dressed, which didn't take much longer than a lifetime or two, and then I stuck the collar into my belt, at the back, beneath my leather jacket. I felt that it might not inspire confidence in my driving skills.

I slipped the Smith & Wesson into my jacket pocket, which made it a concealed weapon. If I had to use it on Paul Chang, I'd worry about the legality later.

I called for a taxi. When it arrived, I told the driver where to take me.

"YOU WANT ME to crank this baby up?" Ernie asked me, tapping the stereo. We were driving along Agui Fria, toward the airport. The car handled well. It may not have been a Maserati, but, after the Subaru, it felt like one.

"That's okay," I told him.

"You gotta hear this system, Josh." He picked up a black plastic box set between the bucket seats, set it on his lap, began to rummage through it. "No Lawrence Welk."

"Damn."

He rummaged some more. "Who's been screwing around in here? Someone copped my Neil Diamond tape."

"Damn."

"What about Megadeath? Ever heard of them? They any good?"

"Think I'll pass, Ernie."

"So what do you want to hear?"

"Nothing."

"Right. Okay." He sat back. "So what do you think of the Jeep?"

"I'll take it," I told him.

VIII

STRENGTH

I FILLED OUT the paperwork with Ernie, wrote him a check for the down payment, and drove the Cherokee off the lot. I liked the car, liked it very much, but I didn't have the strength, or the nimbleness, to sit there and fondle the dashboard, as I might've done in different circumstances. I drove a few blocks away, down Cerrillos Road, then pulled over to the side and tugged the foam collar free from behind me. I had barely the strength and the nimbleness to do that. I wrapped the collar around my neck, pushed the Velcro closure together. I swung the rearview mirror around to admire myself. I did look like I'd grown a goiter.

I waited for a break in the traffic, pulled back onto the road, and drove downtown. I parked the car in the lot behind our building and then, moving with the grace and agility of Robbie the Robot, I shuffled to the office.

Inside, I hung my coat on the rack, arranged some things on the desk, and then sat down stiffly in the swivel chair. I took a deep breath and gave some very serious thought to going home and falling into bed. But the light on the answering machine was flashing. Duty called. Mine not to reason why. I leaned forward, slowly, and tapped the Play button.

There was a message from Hector Ramirez, asking me to call him at home, but not before ten o'clock this morning. I looked at my watch. Ten minutes to ten.

There was a curt message from Veronica Chang, asking me to call her as soon as I could.

And finally there was a message from Rita: "Joshua, I knew you wouldn't stay home. Sometimes you really are annoying. I'll talk to you tonight."

I smiled.

And then I wondered, once again, what she was planning to do down in Albuquerque. This was the first time she'd left Santa Fe since Martinez's bullet had put her in a wheelchair.

It couldn't have been anything to do with the Bernardi case; there, the only connection to Albuquerque was the suicide of Starbright, Bernardi's hippie friend, and that had happened three years ago. Maybe some case *she* was working on?

But most of Rita's work involved the computer, searching databases. If she needed someone to do fieldwork, why hadn't she asked me?

Because I was busy?

Maybe. Never mind. Find out later today, when she calls.

I called Roger Morrison's number, got his wife, and thanked them for coming to my rescue the night before. I called Larry Porter at the insurance company and picked up some coverage for the new car. He suggested that it would be a good idea for me to take better care of the Jeep than I'd taken of the Subaru. I thanked him for his sage advice.

Then I dialed Veronica Chang's number.

"Hello?"

"This is Joshua Croft. You wanted to talk to me?"

"What was the idea," she said, "of sending that big dumb policeman to my house last night?" She sounded considerably less cordial than she'd sounded yesterday. That was fine with me. I felt considerably less cordial than I'd felt yesterday.

"I didn't send anyone to your house," I said.

"That big Hispanic cop," she snapped. "Gonzalez, Ramirez, whatever his name was. You gave him my name."

"Where was your brother last night, Miss Chang? Between nine-thirty and ten?"

"That is none of your goddamn business. I may have to talk to the police, but I certainly don't have to talk to you."

Suddenly I was listening to the drone of a dial tone. I decided that I preferred it to the snarl of Veronica Chang. But I couldn't listen to it all day.

I looked at my watch. Ten. I dialed Hector's home number.

The phone was picked up and there was a brief silence on the line before I heard Hector's voice, raspy with sleep: "Ramirez."

"Morning, Hector."

Another brief silence. "Shit."

"I know how you feel."

"Shit."

"You left a message for me to call you."

"Shit."

"Didn't quite catch that, Hector. Come again?"

"Hold on a second."

I waited. I heard a muffled cough. After a moment, Hector said, "God. Mornings don't get any easier. Okay. Veronica Chang. I saw her last night."

"She told me."

"Her and her brother. Paul. She admits she made an appointment with you. Admits she canceled it. Her brother says he was with her from nine o'clock on. At their house. She corroborates that."

"Does he own a gray Chevy pickup?"

"If he does, it's not registered with Motor Vehicles."

"Hector, he's the only person with a motive."

"Maybe so. He's also got an alibi."

"Okay, Hector. Thanks. Go back to sleep."

"I'll send someone to talk to the neighbors today. See if they saw anything last night."

"Thanks. Bye."

"Yeah."

I sat back. Slowly.

If Veronica Chang and her brother had set me up, and it
seemed to me that they must have, then it made sense for her
to alibi him. But I'd probably never be able to prove she was
lying. And I didn't expect the Changs' neighbors to be
helpful—the hedge around the Changs' house would make
comings and goings invisible, at least to anyone on their side
of the street.

If I could locate the gray Chevy pickup, prove that Paul
Chang had access to it . . .

Later, maybe. Right now I had to worry about Giacomo
Bernardi. I reached into my inside jacket pocket, pulled out
my notebook, flipped through it till I came to the page with
the list of people who'd attended the soiree in La Cienega
last Saturday. So far, the only people I hadn't talked to were
Carl Buffalo and Carol Masters. I sat forward, slowly, and
dialed Carl Buffalo's number.

He was home.

THE ADDRESS was off Agua Fria, not far from Alto Street,
where Sally Durrell had once lived. It was a mixed neighborhood of tidy frame houses owned, for the most part, by
Hispanic families, and of plump ersatz adobes owned, for
the most part, by Anglos.

On the right side of the street, the houses sat along a small
bluff that fell gently to the Santa Fe River, a body of water
that would've been called, almost anywhere else, a brook.
A thin trickle in the fall, slightly more ambitious in the
spring when it caught some of the mountain runoff, it ambled between deep banks through the town and divided it,
roughly, into north and south. Sometimes, at its peak in
early summer, the Fish and Game Department dumped
several tons of bewildered fingerling trout into the current.
They fought their way past the empty soda bottles and the
limp condoms and the ranks of eager adolescent anglers
until, miles away to the east, they were flushed into the wide
brown Rio Grande. Occasionally I wished that I were trav-

eling along with them. Occasionally, like today, I felt that I had been.

Carl Buffalo's yard was surrounded by a thick, low adobe wall painted the color of a Snickers bar. Over the top of the wall I could see the house, a free-form single-story adobe painted the same color as the wall and shaped, roughly, like a pair of large buckets that were attempting to breed. I drove the Jeep through the gate into the gravel driveway, parked it, stepped out, noted the solid-sounding slam as I swung the door shut.

Nice car. Let Paul Chang try to run me down while I was driving *that*.

The yard was unkempt. Brown grass, uncut all summer, buried beneath the snow until recently, lay flat and sodden against the uneven ground. I followed the cement walkway to the front step. Above the door hung another steer skull, nearly identical to the one that had hung above Leonard Quarry's front door. It was a fairly popular decorative item here in New Mexico; Georgia O'Keeffe and her paintings have a lot to answer for. But maybe, in some other dimension, steers are painting pictures of Georgia O'Keeffe's skull.

I opened the screen door, rang the doorbell.

The man who opened the door was about five feet ten inches tall, and almost as wide. He was stripped to the waist and he was decked out, elaborately, with muscle tissue. One of those bodybuilders who went more for definition than for power, sculpting each muscle into a flashy, precisely delineated mass, he reminded me of a Native American Arnold Schwarzenegger. Dangling on a leather thong and hanging between his swollen pectorals, like a dead mouse between a pair of cantaloupes, was a deerskin medicine pouch. His features—brown eyes, snub nose, small thin mouth, lantern jaw—looked no more Native American than my own. But I could tell he was a Native American because his long, straight black hair was held in place with a beaded band, and because he wore fringed suede pants, beaded leather moccasins, and, on his wrist, a gold Rolex, just like the one Sitting Bull used to wear.

But certainly, he couldn't have been the thin Anglo man who'd been seen by Pablo at Agua Caliente.

"Croft?" he said.

"Yeah. Carl Buffalo?" Silly question.

He nodded, held out his hand, took mine, tried to flatten it. Failed, stood back. "Come on in."

I walked into a billow of Brut cologne.

Personally, I thought that the Indian motif was maybe just a tad overdone in the living room. On the white walls hung bows and arrows and quivers, war lances and shields. The furniture—some chairs, a long sofa—was draped with deerskins. Crowded onto the shelves of the bookcase to my right was a collection of Navajo and Pueblo pottery: bowls, plates, statuettes. Under the glass top of the long wooden coffee table was a ceremonial Navajo sand painting—a fake; the real ones, I knew, were destroyed at the end of the ceremony for which they were constructed. An enormous buffalo hide, complete with legs, tail, and huge shaggy head, lay sprawled out along the wooden floor, as though its former occupant had just toppled from the roof of a ten-story building and landed there in a splatter.

"What happened to your neck?" Carl Buffalo asked me.

"I was water-skiing."

He frowned, puzzled. "There's no water-skiing around here."

I smiled. "I was misinformed."

He frowned again.

"May I sit down?" I asked him.

"Yeah, yeah, sure. Anywhere." He frowned once more, probably still attempting to work out the skiing accident.

I sat in one of the chairs; he sat at the end of the sofa.

I told him, "I've been trying to reach you for a while."

He nodded. "I was with one of my groups, up in the mountains."

"Must be fairly cold up there, this time of year."

"A warrior learns to endure."

He delivered this as though he had a lot more pithy epigrams stored away. I managed, just barely, to keep my eye-

alls from rolling around in their sockets. "What kind of
eople go up there with you?"

He shrugged his enormous shoulders. "Doctors. Poets.
Businessmen. Anyone, right? Anyone who wants to learn
he ancient skills. Anyone who wants to get back their forgotten warrior tradition."

"Forgotten?"

"Modern Man," he said, "has lost his connection to
Nature, and to the Great Spirit. What I do, I show the men
n my groups how to do their own Vision Quest, so they can
ind their personal totem animal, right? That way, see, they
an learn about their own personal intimate involvement in
he natural world. We're all part of it, right?—each and
very one of us, but sometimes we lose sight of that basic
act."

"Right," I said, and nodded. "So how's business?"

He shook his head. "This isn't a business. Not for me.
This is part of a sacred shamanistic tradition that goes back
o the dawn of time."

"Sure. I was just wondering how much you charge for
hese trips."

He frowned again. "It's all in my brochure. But you said
over the phone you wanted to talk about Giacomo."

"Yeah." A shaman with a brochure. Neat. "What do you
hink of Giacomo?"

"I've seen him around, here and there, right? I wouldn't
say I really know him very good."

"You were at La Cienega last Saturday night. Were you
surprised when you learned that Quentin Bouvier had been
killed?"

"A warrior is never surprised. He understands that everything that happens is the will of the Great Spirit."

My eyeballs were beginning to cramp. "So you weren't
surprised, either, when Giacomo was arrested for the murder."

He shrugged. "It happened, right? So the Great Spirt
must've willed it."

I nodded. "Sort of like karma."

He frowned as he thought about this. I could sense th
effort involved. "Well, karma, the idea of karma, that isn
really a part of my own personal tradition, right? But I'v
studied it, naturally, and sure, you could say it's somethin
like the will of the Great Spirit." He nodded sagely. "Ther
are many paths to the top of the mountain."

And a lot of jerks along the way. I nodded again. "Ho
long were you involved with Justine Bouvier?"

The warrior tradition must have briefly slipped his minc
because he blinked at me for a few moments and then h
said, "Huh?"

"I understand that you and Justine were an item a fe
years back. I wanted to know for how long."

His face was petulant, which made it look a bit sill
perched atop all that beef. "Who told you that?" he aske
me.

"Just something I heard."

He shook his head. "Justine and me, we're friends. W
been friends for a long time, right? Quentin and me wer
friends too."

"Sure. But for a while there, weren't you and Justine a b
more than that?"

He frowned once more, and then he narrowed his eyes, a
though he were trying to figure out what kind of trick I wa
playing. "What's all this got to do with Giacomo?"

I went through the spiel that by now had become stan
dard: if Giacomo didn't kill Bouvier, then someone else dic
In order to discover who that might be, I needed to know a
much as possible about everyone who was present in L
Cienega last Saturday night.

"Wait a minute," he said. "Hold on there. You sayin
you think I had something to do with all that? With Quen
tin getting killed?"

"I'm saying that I've got to learn everything I can."

"Yeah, well, you're way off base there. Justine and I wer
only friends, right? I don't care *what* you heard. And lis
ten, I resent the implication."

"Which implication?"

"That Justine and me, um, that her and me were something besides friends."

"I thought maybe you resented the implication that you were involved in Bouvier's death."

"That one too!" His face was flushed. "I resent that one too. I told you, Quentin was a friend of mine, right?" He frowned again. "What are you trying to do?"

"Like I said. I'm trying to find out who killed Quentin Bouvier."

"Yeah, well I didn't."

"Who do you think did?"

"How the hell would I know? Giacomo, probably, right? Cops think he did. And he never liked Quentin."

"Why?"

"He just never did. He told me."

"Ever heard of a girl called Starbright?"

"Who?"

I repeated the name.

"Who's she?" he asked me.

"A girl who committed suicide down in Albuquerque."

"Why?"

"Because Quentin Bouvier dumped her."

"When was this?"

"A few years ago. Did you know her, know about her?"

"Uh-uh. No."

"How well did you know Leonard Quarry?"

Once again, his face flushed. "I never killed *him*, neither."

"I know that, Carl. How well did you know him?"

"Not hardly at all."

"He wasn't a friend?"

"No way."

"Do you know anybody who'd have a reason to kill both Bouvier and Quarry?"

"No." He frowned. "Kill both of them? The same guy? But the cops, they told me it had to be somebody else killed Leonard."

"Which cops?"

"State cops. They were asking me about Leonard yesterday."

"Asking about any of Leonard's friends who had an interest in the theater?"

"Yeah, right."

"Do you know any?"

"No. Carol Masters, maybe. But I hardly knew Leonard, right? I told you."

"Okay. Why don't you run me through what happened last Saturday night."

He frowned again. "I already told the cops all about that."

"I know. But the sooner I get your testimony, the sooner we can wrap this up."

He considered that. Finally he nodded. "You want me to start at the beginning, right?"

"That would be nice."

He leaned forward, lifted a leather pouch from the coffee table, opened it, pulled out some rolling paper. "You smoke?"

"No. Thanks."

"This is special stuff," he said. He took a pinch of brown shreds from the pouch, began to dribble them along a curled sheet of paper. "Natural tobacco, no additives, mixed with real kinnikinnick."

"Yeah?"

He licked the edge of the paper, rolled the cigarette. "Kinnikinnick, that's Indian tobacco."

"Uh-huh."

He stood up and then he held the cigarette with a certain amount of drama to the south, then the west, then the north, then the east. Having completed the circle, he slipped his hand into the pocket of his suede pants, pulled out a gold Dunhill lighter, sat down, lighted the cigarette. He snapped the lighter shut and placed it on the table, so I could admire it at my leisure, presumably. Exhaling, he said, "That's one of the problems of Modern Man, right? He's lost his rituals."

I nodded, trying to imagine serious chain-smokers going through this particular ritual whenever they lit up. Half of them would collapse before they reached their morning coffee.

It occurred to me—had been occurring to me since I arrived here—that Carl was about as genuine, Indian-wise, as the sand painting on his coffee table. I knew some Indians who smoked, and none of them, and certainly not in front of an Anglo, would make a production out of it.

"Okay," he said. He sat back, crossed his leg, left ankle over right knee. The fringes of his leggings flapped. "I got there, at Brad and Sylvia's at about five, I guess . . ."

After the gaudy overture, the opera was something of an anticlimax. Nothing he told me contradicted anything that he'd originally told the police in his statement, or anything that anyone else had already told me.

From the way he spoke of them, I got the sense that Carl felt a bit uneasy about most of the other New Age folks. He was a not-very-bright guy, I thought, who had stumbled onto a pretty good scam for himself, this shaman thing, and who wasn't certain how the others reacted to it, or to him. The role he was playing required him to pretend a wise and compassionate acceptance of them all, but I felt that he had been truly comfortable only with Brad Freefall and Sylvia Morningstar. Brad because he, too, was something less than a genius; Sylvia, because she was so relentlessly nonjudgmental about everything and everyone.

He had heard nothing, seen nothing, sensed nothing that might help me determine who had killed Quentin Bouvier.

When he was finished, I closed my notebook, slipped it into my jacket pocket, and rose from the chair. "Okay," I said. "Thanks for your time."

He stood up. "So I'll get you one of my brochures, right?"

"Great."

Maybe, stalking across the forest glen with his happy band of poets and proctologists, he moved as silently as a shade. Here he just lumbered off, his moccasins thumping against the floor.

He came thumping back after only a moment or two, and handed me a slim brochure printed on heavyweight paper. I glanced at the bold type on the cover. "Discover the Warrior Within," I was advised. I decided to read the rest of it later. Next year, maybe.

"Thanks again, Carl," I told him as he walked me to the door.

He nodded solemnly. "May the Great Spirit be with you."

"Thanks," I said. "Happy Trails."

BACK AT THE OFFICE, I hung up my coat again and rearranged things on the desk. There were more messages on the machine. Rita had called at twelve-thirty, fifteen minutes before I arrived. Her message said that she'd call back in half an hour. Justine Bouvier had called, returning my call of yesterday. What with one thing and another, I'd forgotten that I'd called her.

I dialed her number.

"Joshua," she said, her voice lilting. "How *are* you?"

"Fine. And you?"

"As well as can be expected, I suppose. I've been thinking about you, you know."

"I've been thinking about you. I wanted to ask you something."

"Yes? Please *do*."

"Did you know any of Leonard Quarry's friends? Any of them who might be involved in theater work?"

I heard her sigh. "*God,* Joshua, I was hoping for something a teeny weeny bit less dull from *you*. I've been talking to the dreary old police about the same thing for *ages*."

"The cops tend to get dreary when someone's been stabbed with an ice pick."

"I heard that you were actually *there,* darling. When it happened."

Darling?

"And who told you that?" I asked her.

"I honestly can't remember. But you'll have to tell me *all* about it, all the horrifying details."

"You sound pretty broken up about all this, Justine."

"Well, it's a shame, naturally, and I do feel sorry for poor Sierra. But then I've always felt sorry for poor Sierra." She laughed lightly, musically. "And I'm not the sort of person, Joshua, who makes believe she's grieving when she's not. I'm no hypocrite."

"I can see that."

"Besides, Leonard's gone to a better place. And he's definitely improved this one." She laughed again.

"And what did you tell them, Justine? The police. When they asked about theater friends of Leonard's."

"I told them I haven't the faintest idea who Leonard knew. And I really couldn't care less."

"All right. Thanks."

"When are you coming up here again, darling? I'd *love* to do your past-life regression for you."

"Sorry, Justine. Right now I'm still fairly busy with my current life."

"You've got to learn to loosen up, Joshua. Get rid of some of that armor you carry around."

"Yeah. Pawn it, maybe."

She laughed. "Well, don't forget to give me a jingle."

"Right."

"Bye now."

"Goodbye, Justine."

As I hung up, I realized that I hadn't yet asked Peter Jones about Leonard Quarry's theatrical connections. Probably, like all the others, he would know of none. But I still had to speak with him.

I was going through my notebook, looking for his phone number, when the door to my office opened and Paul Chang stepped in, holding a large automatic in his right hand.

THE DEVIL .

I KNOW a few people who claim to feel an enormous affection for the M-1911 Colt .45 automatic. They mention, and sometimes keep mentioning, its reliability and accuracy, its size, its weight. But the feature they most esteem is what they call, with a certain relish, its stopping power. One slug in the arm or anywhere else, they like to say, and a guy goes down, and he stays down.

The slug in question is nearly half an inch wide and weighs nearly half an ounce. Propelled from its casing, it moves more slowly than the .38 or the nine-millimeter, but it carries quite a bit of momentum.

While I'm not personally fond of automatics and the maintenance they require, I'm prepared to admit that the government Colt, when its big muzzle is aimed at my head, does get my attention.

"Hello, Paul," I said. "Nice gun."

He shut the door behind him and leaned against it. "Asshole," he said.

I realized that this was the first time I'd hear his voice.

Yesterday, when I met him, he hadn't spoken a word. Like his sister's voice, his was low and nicely modulated.

He was wearing black leather gloves, a black leather jacket with its collar up, a black silk scarf, a black silk shirt, black twill trousers, black socks, black slip-on shoes. The Contemporary Ninja look.

"What can I do for you?" I asked him. My voice was nicely modulated, too, but it may have been higher than normal by an octave or two.

"Get up," he said. "You're coming with me."

I sat forward in the swivel chair, put my hands on the desk. "Have you thought this out, Paul?" The important thing, it seemed to me, was to keep jabbering away until something distracted him. I glanced at the phone, willed it to ring.

"Get up," he said.

"Why?"

"Because if you don't, I'll kill you where you sit."

"Why should I care where you kill me?"

His eyes narrowed. "Get up."

"Are we going to be using the car?"

"I'm not going to tell you again. Get up."

"Because if we are, maybe you should start thinking about who's going to drive. If you're the driver, you won't be able to hold the gun. If I drive, how are you going to stop me from piling into a dump truck and taking you with me?"

He took a step toward me and cocked the pistol's hammer. His hand was trembling, the gun barrel wavering slightly. "Shut your fucking mouth. And get up out of that chair."

The phone rang. He turned toward it. I shot him. He shot back.

"YOU'RE LUCKY," Hector Ramirez told me.

"Yeah."

"And you were smart for a change, putting the gun where you could reach it."

I shrugged weakly. "He tried to kill me yesterday. I didn't want to give him a second chance."

"Where'd you have it?"

I was sitting in one of the client chairs, Hector was sitting in the other. I jerked my head toward the desk. "Behind the box of Kleenex."

He nodded. "How are you feeling?"

I shook my head. "Just great, Hector. Just fucking great."

"The paramedics said he's probably going to pull through."

"Yeah."

The paramedics had left; and so, after taking my statement, had the uniformed cops. Hector, who was supposed to be off duty today, had arrived sometime in the middle of all the excitement, cops asking me questions, paramedics sliding Paul Chang onto a gurney and hooking him up to an I.V. Everyone, or so it seemed, had been furiously talking into walkie-talkies while they bustled about. One of the paramedics had been in the ambulance with me last night, when I was carted down from the sky basin. He had looked at me today as though I were Charlie Manson.

I felt a bit like Charlie Manson.

Over by the doorway, the hardwood floor was puddled black with blood. Black footprints crisscrossed the room, some of them smeared, some of them as distinct as if they'd been painted there with a stencil.

"Self-defense, Josh," Hector said. "Him or you."

"Yeah."

"He fired at you. If he'd hit you, you'd be the one in the ambulance."

I looked over to the wall behind my desk. At approximately chest level, Paul Chang's slug had pocked a ragged hole in the plaster. One of the uniforms had used a penknife to pry it out of the adobe beyond.

"Yeah," I said.

Hector said nothing.

The telephone rang.

It had been Rita calling before, when the ringing phone had distracted Paul Chang. I hadn't answered it because I was busy kicking the Colt away from the doorway, where he'd dropped it when he crumpled to the floor. I'd heard her voice coming through the answering machine as I ripped clumps of Kleenex from the box and stuffed them into Chang's wounds, one just above his hip on the right side, the other in his right shoulder. I couldn't recall shooting at him twice. I had been moving when I fired, heading for the floor.

Lying there, he had been in shock, his eyelids fluttering. I had mumbled the entire time I worked on him, calling him a stupid shit, telling him that everything was going to be fine, calling him a stupid shit again. Probably, even if he'd been able to understand me, I wouldn't have made much sense.

The phone was still ringing. I got up, shuffled over to the desk, lifted the receiver. "Hello?"

"Joshua?" Rita. "You sound strange."

"Yeah. Well, there's been kind of an accident here."

"What kind of an accident?"

"Paul Chang. I kind of shot him." I giggled. It sounded inappropriate, even to me.

After a moment Rita said, "You're all right?"

"Just swell. Hunky dory. Never felt better."

"Is anyone there with you?"

"Hector."

Another brief pause. "Joshua? May I talk to him?"

"Yeah, sure." I held out the phone to Hector. "Lovely Rita."

Hector stood, crossed the room, took the phone. "Hello, Rita."

I circled the desk, sat down in the swivel chair, slumped myself against the backrest.

"Yeah," Hector spoke into the phone. "He's fine... No... Yeah... They say he'll live... I don't know. Not well... No, nothing like that... Yeah... Yeah, I will... I will, Rita, I promise... Okay, I'll tell him... You too. Okay. Later."

He hung up. "Okay," he said to me. "Let's go."

I looked up at him. "Where?"

"I'm taking you home."

"Jesus Christ, Hector. I shot the guy, nearly killed him. If nothing else, I fired a gun inside the city limits. Don't I at least get a ticket?"

"You were on your own property, protecting yourself. All the evidence corroborates your story. We've got his gun, we've got the slug he fired. We've got your statement. Anything comes up, I'll let you know. Meanwhile, I promised Rita I'd drive you home. She'll get there as soon as she can. An hour or two, she said. Let's go."

I shook my head. "I can't, Hector. Got to clean that up." I nodded to the doorway, to the smeared puddle of blood.

"Rita said you'd say that. She's calling the service. They'll take care of it. Come on. I'll drive you."

"We'll take my car?"

He shook his head. "Mine. Yours will be fine where it is."

Suddenly I was too tired to argue about it. Too tired to argue about anything.

HECTOR AND I didn't speak much as he drove me home. But in my driveway, just as he stopped the car, he turned to me. "Joshua," he said. "I know how you feel."

I nodded. He probably did. But somehow that didn't seem to matter much.

He said, "There are a few things you should remember. First of all, he's still alive."

"So far."

"Second, like I said before, if you hadn't nailed him, you'd probably be dead right now."

I shook my head. "We don't know that, Hector. He wanted to take me somewhere. I hurt him pretty badly yesterday. Maybe all he wanted was another shot at the title."

"If he didn't plan to use the gun, he should never have pulled it."

I shook my head. "I keep seeing his face. He looked so goddamned *surprised*."

"He wasn't the one who was supposed to get shot." He reached out, squeezed my arm, released it. "Don't punish yourself, Josh. And listen. Call me if you want to talk."

I looked at him. He had been something like a friend for a long time now, as much like a friend as any cop could be to a private investigator. He was big and he was genuinely tough and he looked about as sensitive as a set of brass knuckles. I knew that there were cops—not many of them, thank God—who wouldn't be at all bothered by the idea of shooting someone. And who would never understand why I'd be bothered by the idea of shooting someone.

There were things I wanted to tell him, but they were things that didn't easily come out of male vocal cords. Out of my vocal cords, anyway. What I said was, ''Thanks, Hector.''

I WANDERED AROUND the house for a while, aimlessly, moving things, picking them up, setting them down. I'd been sleeping at Rita's almost every night for the past month or so, coming here only for a change of clothes. The rooms felt unused and abandoned. So did I.

When I looked at my watch, I saw that it was already three o'clock. Paul Chang had entered my office just before one. Time flies when you're having fun.

I went into the kitchen, found the Jack Daniel's, built a drink, carried it into the living room, sat down. Tasted the drink. Noticed, on the folded-back cuff of my denim shirt, a large dark brown smear.

I put the drink on the coffee table. I stood up, ripped the shirt off, tossed it across the room, stalked into the bathroom, and was extremely sick.

IT SEEMED LIKE A long time that I sat there on the sofa, drinking, thinking.

I had killed two human beings in my life, a pair of thugs from El Paso. They had tortured and killed a defenseless old man; and, at the time, on a dusty mountainside in Arizona, they had been trying very hard to kill me. If any two people had ever deserved to die, I believe that they had. But I still had dreams about them. Bad dreams.

When medieval cartographers drew the Atlantic Ocean, they often scrawled a notation across the blank unknown area beyond the Azores: *Here be monsters.* Today's cartographers could, with more accuracy, scrawl it across the entire globe. The monsters are everywhere now. They are ruthless and they are unredeemable. Captured, imprisoned, they are almost certainly not going to be rehabilitated. Whatever lethal combination of gene and scene created them, they are damaged beyond repair.

I can understand the arguments for capital punishment. I can understand the thirst for revenge. An eye for an eye, a tooth for a tooth. Destroy the destroyer. It's pretty basic stuff.

But, maybe because the thirst is so basic, I tend to distrust it. Too often, I suspect, what we wish to destroy is just a handy screen onto which we project the psychic ghosts shaped by the bitterness and the brutality we've all suffered, our own private devils and demons. You can sometimes see this on the faces of those ghouls who stand vigil outside the prison when an execution is about to take place. What shows in their eyes, in the set of their mouths, isn't compassion for the prisoner's victims, but lust for the blood of the prisoner. When we destroy the destroyer, murder the murderer, collectively we reduce ourselves to his level.

Was Paul Chang a monster? I didn't know. Did he deserve to die? I wasn't equipped to provide an answer. I didn't think that anyone was.

If someone were threatening Rita's life, without a moment's thought I would do everything I could to stop him. Paul Chang had threatened mine, and without a moment's thought I had stopped him. No doubt, in a similar situation, I would do so again.

But that didn't mean that I had to like it. And it didn't mean that I could forget what I'd done. Over and over as I sat there that afternoon, I saw the look on Paul Chang's face as the slugs from the .38 slammed into his flesh. Saw the red blood seeping down the lining of his leather jacket and soaking into the carpet . . .

THE DOORBELL RANG at four-thirty. With an effort—alcohol and exhaustion and damaged muscles slowed me down—I stood up and walked to the door. For all I knew, the person standing outside could be Veronica Chang, come to finish what her brother had started. I didn't even bother to peer through the peephole.

It was Rita. She stood there for a moment, looking at me. Then she said merely, "Joshua." Her voice was soft.

"Hey, Rita. Come on in."

She came in. Over the outfit she had been wearing this morning, she wore now a different coat, tan leather, three-quarter length.

"New coat?" I said.

She nodded, her face solemn.

"Nice," I said.

"Thank you." She started to take it off, and I moved to help her.

"Here," I said, and slipped it from her shoulders. She turned to face me, her large dark eyes staring up at me, and I stood there holding the coat, looking down at her.

She put the palm of her right hand against my cheek. "Joshua," she said. Her face was even more solemn now, almost tragic.

I tried a smile. It wouldn't stay in place. I took a deep breath, let it out. "Jesus, Rita," I said. "It's been a hell of a day."

Her hand slipped from my cheek to the back of my neck and I bent down toward her as her left hand came around to my back, and then I was tightly up against her, breathing the familiar smell of her hair and the new-leather smell of her coat, and I was sobbing like a baby.

Maybe I believed, at least at the beginning, that I was crying for Paul Chang and what I'd done to him. But grief, for good or for ill, finally isn't concerned with other people. In the end, we all cry for ourselves.

Rita and I didn't talk for a long time. I couldn't have talked if I'd wanted to.

I don't know how we got into the bedroom. I don't remember. But somehow we did, and then somehow, after a time, we were joined together once again in that miracle which, perhaps out of terror at its mysteries, we often make banal and commonplace: two isolate beings stripped of their day-to-day identities, their masks, their costumes, as naked before each other as sacrificial victims, or as gods.

"JOSHUA?"

"Hmmm?"

"Have you called the hospital?"

"No," I said.

We were lying on my bed, me on my back, Rita on her side, her head on my shoulder, her hand on my chest.

"Shall I call?" she asked.

"They won't tell you anything."

"Hector may know what's happening."

"Yeah."

"Will he be home?"

"Probably."

"Shall I?"

I breathed in deeply. Breathed out deeply. Nodded. "Yeah."

She turned slightly, kissed my arm, then gracefully rolled away to reach the phone on the nightstand. Supporting herself on her elbow, she picked up the receiver, dialed the number. I turned to her, reached out my left hand and ran my index finger lightly down the knuckles of her spine. At the small of her back, just to the right of the delicate ridge of bone, was the round puckered white scar left by the bullet that had left her paralyzed for nearly three years. Another inch over, and Rita would still be in the wheelchair today, would be in it forever . . .

"Hello, Hector . . . Yes . . . He's fine . . . Yes. Have you heard anything? . . . Good . . . *Good* . . . Thank you, Hector . . . Yes. You, too . . . Soon, yes. Bye."

She hung up the phone, rolled back to me. "You heard?"

"Yeah. He's all right?"

"He's stabilized. Serious but not critical. No major organs damaged. Barring complications, he'll be fine."

I let out another breath. I nodded. "Okay. Thanks." Kissed her forehead. "And thanks for coming here. Thanks for being here."

She smiled. "What are friends for?"

I kissed her again.

She put her head against my shoulder once again. "It doesn't make much sense, does it?"

"Which?"

"Paul Chang, trying to kill you."

I shrugged. "Maybe he wasn't. This time. Maybe this time, like I told Hector, he wanted the two of us to go off somewhere for a rematch. But I don't think that was what he had in mind last night."

"If that was Paul Chang last night, driving the truck."

"Who else could it have been?"

"You'd rather it was Paul Chang, wouldn't you?"

"Yeah."

"Shooting him would seem more justified."

"Yeah."

"He had a gun, Joshua."

"I know."

"You had to operate on the assumption that he was prepared to use it. And he did."

"Yeah."

She turned and kissed my shoulder again. "Do you want to take some time off?"

"Can't. Not now." I turned to her. "What did you have in mind?"

"Cancun."

"Cancun?" I grinned. "You're serious?"

She smiled. "For a week or so. You're always talking about lying on the beach down there. Let's do it."

"Yeah?"

Another smile. "Yeah."

I kissed her forehead. "Okay. Cancun. A week. That's a good idea. That's a very good idea. But I've got to wrap this up first."

"Yes." Her hand moved down my chest, down my stomach. "A man's got to do what a man's got to do."

"Bet your ass."

She laughed softly against my neck. "You're such a fraud."

"Oh yeah? How?"

"You know how. It's what I was talking about last night, in the hospital. You like to act so tough and self-reliant—"

"And you think I'm not?"

"Self-absorbed, perhaps."

"Self-absorbed? Hey—"

"When you're working on something. You *are*, Joshua. And I don't believe, basically, that it's a bad thing. Although it's sometimes a little difficult to live with. Joshua, you know that I think you're a good man. And a lot more sensitive than you like to pretend."

"It's important to be sensitive. All the chicks really dig it. *Ouch!*"

Her laughter was less soft. It was a lewd chuckle, low in her throat.

"Shit," I said. "You shouldn't do that, Rita. You could cause a serious sexual malfunction."

Another chuckle. "Let's see if I have, shall we?"

"SO JUST WHY did you go down to Albuquerque?" I asked her. Both of us were lying on our backs now. Idly, slowly, I was stroking her thigh with the back of my hand.

"Some things I had to take care of," she said.

"Business?"

"Some of it."

"What was the rest?"

"A candlelit tryst with a wealthy Italian count."

"Oh." I turned toward her. "Does he have a sister? A countette?"

She smiled. "Do you really want to know my major reason for going down there?"

"Yeah."

"Clothes."

"Clothes?"

"Clothes. Joshua, I haven't been shopping for over three years."

"Maria went shopping for you." Maria had been her housekeeper and companion. "And I could've gone. Anytime. All you had to do was ask." I realized, as soon as I heard the words, how silly they sounded.

So, evidently, did Rita. She laughed. "Joshua, your idea of shopping is running into K-Mart and grabbing a pair of jeans."

"Excuse me? Are you suggesting that I'm less than sartorially splendid at all times?"

"Of course not. Right now, in fact, I think you look very dashing. And I think that, generally, you pull off the Urban Cowboy look rather well. It's just that I'd rather shop for myself. And I badly needed some new things."

"Urban Cowboy? That leather jacket of mine is an Armani."

She laughed again. "Was I saying something earlier about your being self-absorbed?"

"I don't know. I wasn't listening."

Another laugh.

"Why Albuquerque?" I asked her.

"There are more stores down there, and the prices are better. And it was *fun,* Joshua. I went to Coronado Mall. Do you know how many stores there are in Coronado Mall?"

"Three?"

"Hundreds. It was a true adventure in shopping."

I rolled over, up onto my elbow, to look at her. I smiled. "This is a side of you I've never seen before, Rita."

She smiled. "I imagine that you'll see more of it."

"I bought something today, too, as a matter of fact."

"What?"

"A car. A Jeep Cherokee."

She frowned. "I didn't see it outside."

"It's down in the lot behind the office. Hector drove me home."

Smiling, she put her hand on my shoulder. "Poor Joshua. You haven't had much of a chance to play with it, have you?"

"I'll play with it later."

"It's a nice car?"

"It's a sweetheart."

Another smile. "Aren't you being a bit fickle? The Subaru isn't even in its grave yet."

"Guy's gotta have a car. Oh damn," I said suddenly.

She looked at me, frowned. "What?"

"What an idiot I am. You had to come back from Albuquerque. Because of me."

She smiled. "I don't regret it."

With my right hand, I brushed the hair from her forehead. "You can go back down there again. Tomorrow."

She smiled again. "I plan to."

XVII

THE STAR.

"MY GOODNESS. What on earth happened to your neck?"

"An automobile accident."

"How terrible."

Carol Masters lightly put a hand, heavy with ornate rings, to her own neck. Both the hand and the neck were thin and corded, their skin leathery. Her bright shiny red fingernails were long enough and sharp enough to slice luncheon meat. Several pounds of jewelry were draped around the neck, links of gold and silver and beads of coral and turquoise. Whenever she moved, she clicked and clattered slightly, like a pocketful of change.

It was Saturday morning. Rita had returned to Albuquerque, and Carol Masters had returned to New Mexico from Alpha Centauri, or wherever she'd been hiding. I had called her from my house and she had agreed to see me, so I had taken a taxi down to the office, picked up the Jeep, and driven out here. We were standing in the doorway of her home in Tesuque, a small town a few miles north of Santa Fe.

"Are you quite all right?" she asked me.

"Fine, thanks."

"Well, please, do come in."

I followed her and the clicking of change and a trail of Giorgio perfume into a huge living room that had me blinking against its glare. Sunlight splashed through the wide picture window and swirled around the furniture. Everything in here was blinding white: the enormous sectional leather couch, the massive enameled wooden coffee table, four or five plump leather chairs, the walls, an acre or two of carpet with pile so thick you could lose small children in its depths. The only color in the room was provided by Carol Masters herself, and by a full-length oil portrait of a young Carol Masters standing tall and proud in a diaphanous pink nightgown at the base of an ornate curving staircase. The staircase must have been specially constructed, because Carol Masters, no matter what sort of pride she might possess, was no taller than the average ten-year-old girl.

"Won't you have a seat," she said, smiling.

I thanked her and sat down in one of the chairs. She lowered herself to the sofa, where she sat politely smiling, her back upright, her knees together, her fingers interlaced on her lap.

"A real private dick," she said to me, smiling again. "A *shamus*. How *exciting*."

I smiled. "For whom?"

She laughed. "Well, for me of course. I've never met one before."

She wore a red silk caftan with long flowing sleeves and a hem that reached to her gold sandals. I knew that she was, officially, nearly seventy years old, and it seemed to me that she hadn't given up a single one of those years without a struggle. Her hair, a confusion of wild curls, was the same bright red shade as her fingernails and her lipstick, but it glistened with highlights of something that might have been purple. Her eyebrows were thick dark arches that looked as though they were attached with Elmer's glue. Perhaps they had been. Certainly the thick black lashes below the half-moons of green eye shadow were unreal: I imagined, whenever she fluttered them, that I could feel a faint breeze.

Her skin was white, as though it had never seen the sun, and it was tight against the fine bones of her skull, as though someone had grabbed a handful of it at the back of her neck and tied it off with a rubber band.

But buried beneath the cartoonish makeup and the drumtaut skin was a face that had once been exceptionally beautiful. Her nose was small and delicately shaped. Her mouth was wide, the generous lips sculpted. Her best feature was her eyes, which were large and bright green and alert, and they watched me with a kind of avid amusement.

"But this is all such a terrible thing, isn't it?" she said. "First Quentin and now Leonard Quarry. I came to New Mexico, you know, because the vibrations here were so loving. So peaceful. It's a holy place, don't you think? Santa Fe in particular. A sacred spot. And now, suddenly, there's all this violence everywhere. Hangings and stabbings and whatnot. It's just horrible." She shivered theatrically, but there was a faint gleam in the green eyes. I got the feeling that she didn't entirely disapprove of anything, including stories of violence, that might brighten up her day.

I said, "The police have talked to you, then, about Leonard Quarry?"

"Oh yes. This morning. They only left about an hour ago." She smiled happily. She had enjoyed their visit, evidently.

"They asked you whether Leonard knew anyone involved in the theater?"

"Yes. I didn't quite understand why. And they never said."

"The man who killed Leonard may have been wearing theatrical makeup."

The eyebrows lifted themselves, a pair of caterpillars doing push-ups. "Really? Why on earth would he do a thing like that?"

"A disguise."

"Oh." She nodded. "Yes, of course. How clever of him. And how dull of me not to realize. But why would he want to off Leonard?'' She smiled, pleased with herself. ''Isn't that the way they say it now? *Off?*''

I smiled. ''Sometimes, yes. I don't know.''

''Aside from the obvious reasons for killing him, of course.''

''The obvious reasons?''

She smiled. ''Did you ever meet Leonard?''

''Once.''

''Then you must've seen that he was an absolutely *dreadful* man. Rude and hateful. I can't imagine how that lovely girl could stand living with him. You've met Sierra?''

''Yes.''

''She's a dear, isn't she? An absolute dear.'' She shook her head, which made her beads and bangles rattle. ''And Leonard was such a boor.'' As though hearing herself speak ill of the dead, she frowned, took a deep breath, and then smiled ruefully. ''Araxys keeps telling me that I'm much too judgmental.''

''Araxys,'' I said.

''Yes. I'm a channeler, did you know?''

I nodded. ''I'd heard something about it, yes.''

''Araxys is the entity I channel. He's a being who exists on Alpha Centauri.''

I nodded. ''Doesn't Alpha Centauri have a surface temperature of something like eighty million degrees?''

She laughed and her jewelry tinkled. ''I couldn't begin to tell you. Science was never my strong suit, you know. All those numbers and laws and tables and such. But I'm sure it's very hot, Alpha Centauri. Stars *are*, usually, aren't they? But you see, Araxys has transcended matter. He exists as pure mind. Heat doesn't bother him, any more than the terrible coldness of space.''

''He hangs out on Alpha Centauri because he likes the neighborhood?''

She laughed again. She pointed a finger at me. The red fingernail looked lethal. ''You're very naughty. I can tell. You're a tiny bit skeptical about these things, aren't you? Confess now.''

''A tiny bit.''

She smiled and sat back. "Well, at least you're not like one of those awful reporters. They pretend to believe everything you say and then they go off and write things that make you look like an absolute idiot. I've never liked them, not even years ago, when I was in Hollywood."

She said the word *Hollywood* with a calculated casualness. I nodded toward the portrait behind her. "That was painted then, wasn't it?"

She turned to look at the painting. "Yes. Many years ago, of course. That was me in one of my favorite roles. Clara, in *The Marshal Takes a Wife.*"

I nodded. "Good movie. Randolph Scott as the marshal, Robert Ryan as Doc Holliday."

She looked back at me, fluttering those immense lashes in surprise. "You've seen it?"

"Sure." Years ago, and I could barely remember it. But I'd stopped at the library to take a quick look through a film guide. "I think it was one of the best things you did."

Smiling, she narrowed her eyes and, once again, she aimed her fingernail at me. "You really are naughty. And unfortunately, I've always had a fondness for naughty men." Another smile. "So how can I help you?"

I smiled. "As I said over the phone, I'm working for the public defender who's handling Giacomo Bernardi's case. She doesn't think he's guilty. Neither do I."

She nodded. "Neither does Araxys."

"Oh?"

"No, not at all. He left me a note about it. I thought that Giacomo was guilty, I admit it. It seemed so obvious at the time, didn't it? That silly Tarot card was missing, and so was Giacomo, and he'd had that nasty argument with Quentin the night before, all that screaming and shouting and carrying on. It reminded me of the scene in *Red Beauty* where Scott Brady starts shouting at Lyle Bettger—do you remember?"

"Ah. No. I'm sorry." Araxys had left her a note?

"*I'm* the one who should be sorry—I wish I'd never done that piece of trash. Disgusting right-wing nonsense. I was supposed to be the beautiful foreign correspondent who's

actually a Communist spy, and Scott was the steely-eyed
F.B.I. agent. That's what the script said. *Steely-eyed.* Scott
nearly made himself ill trying to get his eyes to look steely.
We fell in love, of course, he and I. In the film, that is. In
real life we hardly spoke to each other. He was a bit of a
moron, I always thought. And he was married, of course.''
She brightened. ''Which goes to prove my point, doesn't
it?''

Which point, I wondered.

She said, ''Lyle played my cell leader, Bronski. Or Kron-
ski. I can't recall.'' She frowned. ''Do you suppose that the
Communists really had cells, the way everyone said they
did?''

''I don't know,'' I told her. I had the sense that I was los-
ing control of this conversation. I said, ''I wonder if we
could go back for a minute. To the police asking about
Leonard Quarry's theatrical connections?''

''He didn't have any,'' she said. ''None at all. I doubt that
Leonard even knew what a theater was. He was an absolute
philistine.''

''And do you have any contacts in the theatrical world
these days?''

''None at all, thank goodness. I still receive an occa-
sional Christmas card from one or two friends out on the
Coast, but that's my only contact with that world. I've left
all of it behind me.'' She blinked and then she smiled.
''Surely you don't think that *I* had anything to do with
Leonard's death?''

''No. But it was a question I had to ask.''

She nodded. ''The police think that Leonard's death had
nothing to do with Quentin's, you know.''

''I think they're wrong.''

''Well, of *course* they are,'' she said, indignant. ''That's
exactly what I told them. But they're just...dumb flat-
foots, aren't they?'' She smiled brightly, pleased with herself, I think, for having found the proper phrase. ''First
Quentin, then Leonard. Just like John Carradine and Mike
Mazurka in *Haunted Holiday.*'' She leaned toward me con-

spiratorially, and her voice dropped to a stage whisper. "Who's next, do you think?"

"No one, with any luck."

"Disasters always happen in threes," she said. I wasn't sure whether she spoke out of conviction or hope.

"About the deaths, Miss Masters. Can you think of anyone who might have a reason to kill Bouvier and Quarry?"

She sat back. "You know, I've thought and thought about it, really I have, and I can't, honestly. If someone wanted to kill those two because they were so obnoxious, then both of them would've been dead years ago. Don't you think? What we want here is a *motive*, isn't it?"

I smiled. "Yes. So far I haven't found one. And now that I've met you, I've talked to all the people who attended the get-together at Brad Freefall and Sylvia Morningstar's last Saturday."

She nodded shrewdly. "It has to be one of us, doesn't it?"

I nodded. "I thought so. I'd still like to think so. But from his description, the man who killed Leonard Quarry wasn't at the get-together."

"Yes, but he could've been a gunsel, couldn't he? Hired muscle. A gun for hire." She was having a good time, using the dated slang with obvious enjoyment. "If you could track him down and lean on him, make him squeal..."

I smiled again. "Maybe. Miss Masters, did you ever hear of a young woman called Starbright? She lived in Albuquerque."

She blinked. It was hard to miss one of her blinks. "Starbright? What kind of a name is that?"

"You've never heard of her?" I asked.

"I would've remembered." She shook her head again, more in dismay than in denial. "Starbright. Goodness." She looked at me shrewdly. "Why do you ask? Was she someone's moll?"

"Apparently she was involved with Bouvier at one time."

"Oh. Well, no. I'm sorry, but I never heard of her."

"She committed suicide a few years ago."

"Oh. How awful. It's such a tragedy, suicide, isn't it? Such a waste. Araxys says that the people who commit suicide are turning their backs on love."

"Speaking of love," I said, "do you happen to know if Bouvier or Quarry were involved with anyone besides their wives?"

"Oh, I don't follow gossip anymore." She smiled. "I used to, hundreds of years ago, but that was back in the days when I was causing it. I *have* heard that Quentin was a terrible cad, but then Justine, his wife, is hardly Florence Nightingale. Or so I'm told. But as for Leonard, I can't imagine *anyone* getting involved with him."

I nodded.

Time to go. I had enjoyed talking with the woman, but it seemed clear that she knew nothing useful. I closed my notebook. "Okay, Miss Masters. Thanks very much for your help."

Her green eyes widened and her thick black eyebrows lifted. "Oh, are we all done? Don't you want to hear what Araxys has to say?"

"Thanks, but I really should be getting—"

"Oh, I know you don't believe in any of it. I don't blame you at all. *I* didn't believe it myself, not at the beginning. Fifteen years ago, that was, and I can still remember how I felt. Disbelieving. And *frightened*. I was playing with a Ouija board when it first happened, a gift from a very dear friend of mine. All of a sudden, Araxys started spelling out messages to me. There I was, all alone, out on the balcony of my darling little apartment. I was *stunned*. Why should some celestial being be bothering little Carol Masters? But he explained that I'd been chosen, despite my...well, my obvious limitations."

She smiled sweetly. "I haven't been terribly *good*, I must admit. Not when I was younger. I always had a terrible weakness for, oh, let's call it adventure, shall we?" She smiled again. "That sounds so much *nicer,* doesn't it? But Araxys told me that none of that mattered. And he explained how I could go into a trance state, so he could take over. It was very strange at first, believe me, all of it. Bizarre. I've always been a person who had both feet on the ground, and this was just *too much*. But finally, you know, all I could feel was gratitude. For the wonder of it, the absolute wonder of it. And I've never stopped feeling that. It's been a way for me to help people, people from all walks of life with all sorts of terrible problems. And right now I feel that I've done so little to help you. And you seem like such a nice man.'' She smiled. ''Even if you are naughty.''

I smiled. ''I thought that Araxys had already spoken to you about the murder.''

''Oh no. Not spoken, no. I'd been on the phone with someone one night, talking about Quentin's death, and I'd been saying *beastly* things about Giacomo. The next morning, when I woke up, the note was there, by my bed. He does that, sometimes, leaves sweet little notes for me. He uses my hand to write them, while I'm asleep.''

''You haven't asked him about Bouvier's murder?''

''No.'' She glanced around, as though Araxys might be lurking somewhere in the room. Lowering her voice, she said, ''He doesn't like me bothering him with questions of my own. Not anymore. He wants me to help other people.'' She winked at me, her eyelashes waving like a small black hand. ''But *you* could ask him, you see, and then we'd *both* know.''

I looked at my watch. A quarter to twelve.

I hadn't been to the office this morning. Rita and I had slept late at my house, and the only person I'd spoken to, besides her and Carol Masters, was Hector, who had told me that Paul Chang was doing well. I had tried to reach Peter Jones, but no one had answered.

Sooner or later today, I had to go to the office, to write up reports. But by now, the news that I'd shot Paul Chang would've gotten out, and I'd probably be spending most of my time dealing with messages on the answering machine. I might as well postpone all that for a while. And postpone checking the floor by the front door, to make sure that the service had cleaned away all of Paul Chang's blood.

Carol Masters said, ''It won't take long, you know. I promise.''

"Sure," I said. "Let's ask Araxys."

"Oh no, no. Not *us*. I won't be here. When he takes over, I get shuttled off to the side somewhere. Into the fourth dimension, he says, and I'm sure it's all very fascinating, but I can never remember what it's like, when I come back." She seemed a bit miffed by this. "But the point is, you see, you'll have to ask him yourself."

"Okay."

She smiled. "Oh *good*. It'll be such fun. You'll see. And I'm sure he'll be able to help. He just *loves* to help."

I nodded.

"Now you mustn't be frightened," she said, "by the way he sounds. He has a gruffish sort of voice and sometimes people get a little nervous. I've asked him if he can change it, but he says that's impossible."

I nodded again.

"Wonderful!" she said. "All right, then. I'll be back in a few minutes." She said this as though she were dashing off to the 7-Eleven to pick up a six-pack. And then she turned slightly on the sofa, settling her spine flat against its back and her feet flat against the floor. Closing her eyes, she placed one hand atop the other on her lap. Beneath their Nile green lids, her eyes quivered and twitched. She took a long, slow breath. For a moment, nothing else happened.

Then, abruptly, her head fell forward, dangling at the stem of neck, and her mouth opened and a man's voice came out, rough and raspy: *"You seek answers, my son?"*

I didn't believe that the voice belonged to a being from Alpha Centauri. But hearing it issue, so rough, so masculine, from the small fragile body of Carol Masters startled and unsettled me. Whether because of some racial memory of ancient terrors, witches and warlocks and vampires and shape-shifters, or simply because of the bogeyman tales of childhood, most of us carry around little pockets of atavistic fears. And when reality seems to shift slightly on its moorings and we grope for the reasons, sometimes we're tempted to admit into our conscious world precisely those things which are feared. Once, many years ago, I'd seen a

friend suffer an epileptic fit, and I'd felt the same thing then
that I did now: a cold uncanny shiver prickling down the
back of my neck.

"My son?"

Bowing her head like that, I realized, would allow Carol
Masters to deepen and roughen her voice. And she'd been
an actress. "Yeah," I said. By answering, which was kind
of a collaboration, I felt suddenly as embarrassed as if I'd
been the one who was making strange noises.

"There is no need to fear, my son."

"Right."

"What is it you wish you know?"

"Who killed Quentin Bouvier?" A consultation with a
phantom from Alpha Centauri. That would look great on
the résumé.

*"Death is an illusion, my son. And therefore, in the
strictest sense, there can be no killing. Bear in mind that the
bodily manifestations of you human beings are merely a
transitory concretization of eternal vibratory phenomena.
All your so-called physical characteristics—your size, your
shape, your palpable existence—are in essence unreal, as
fleeting as a ripple on a pond, or the path traced by a falling leaf through the autumn air. Even the sexuality of which
you make so much, your maleness and your femaleness, is
an illusion, as is, of course, your so-called ego, that false-
hood which so often troubles you. Bear in mind that the
underlying reality is nothing less than Love, Love dancing
with itself, Love in love with Love."*

I nodded, and then realized that neither Araxys nor Carol
Masters could see me. "Right," I said. "Do you think you
could be a little more specific?"

A low, raspy chuckle came from Carol Master's mouth.
*You are a Quester, my son, a seeker after Truth. Hearken to
my words and you shall discover the thing you ultimately
seek. I bid you farewell, now, and wish you a most fruitful
journey."*

Carol Masters's tiny frame gave a sudden start, her right
foot kicking out, and then she jerked her head upright. She
opened her eyes, blinking, and gasped in a breath. Leaning

forward, thick eyebrows raised, she looked over to me. "What did he say?"

Gibberish, I almost answered. But actually, I'd kind of liked the notion of Love dancing with itself. "Not much," I told her.

Still excited, the words rushing out: "Did he tell you who did it?"

"Not exactly."

"What did he *say*?"

"Something about vibratory phenomena. Love in love with Love."

She nodded quickly, waved a dismissive hand. "He always says that. But nothing about who killed Quentin and Leonard?"

"No."

She pounded her small fist against the sofa cushion. "Damn." Then, abruptly, she sat back. She frowned again, thoughtfully. "Well," she said. "Sometimes, you know, what he says only *sounds* mystical, but it has a simple, everyday meaning. Sometimes he tries to be deliberately cryptic." She bit thoughtfully at her lower lip.

"I'd say he succeeded."

"So what he said didn't mean anything to you." Some lipstick had come off onto her teeth.

"I'm afraid not," I said. I still felt a kind of residual unease. I had no idea whether I had just witnessed a nicely performed piece of theater, or a peek, provided without her conscious knowledge, into the subterranean mind of Carol Masters.

She nodded, and then leaned toward me. Lowering her voice, she said, "He's wonderful, but sometimes, honestly, he drives me absolutely crazy."

THE TOWER.

SPOTLESS.

Just inside the doorjamb, the bleached oak floor of the office was spotless. Not a single bloodstain, not even a darkening in the cracks between the waxed planks.

It was as though the cleaning service had provided me with magic as well as reliability, had wiped away not only the stains, but the past. For a moment, I found myself almost believing that nothing had happened yesterday. That Paul Chang had never come here, that I'd never fired two slugs into his body. That he wasn't lying in the hospital at the moment, attached to tubes and wires.

Life, unfortunately, doesn't clean up as easily as hardwood floors.

Forget the guilt, I told myself. You did what you had to. At least he's alive. Get to work.

I got to work. As I'd thought, there were messages waiting for me on the machine, including one from Rita. She was still in Albuquerque, and said that she'd call back. The rest, in the order in which they were recorded, were from a coy Justine Bouvier, Veronica Chang, a writer who worked for the Santa Fe *Reporter,* a patient Justine Bouvier, Eliza Remington, the writer again, a bored Justine Bouvier, and finally an irritated Justine Bouvier.

I took a deep breath and called Veronica Chang.

"This is Joshua Croft."

"Yes," she said flatly. "I'm glad you called. I wanted to tell you that I think you're despicable."

"Miss Chang—"

"Do you know that my brother almost *died?*" No flatness now in her voice. "If he hadn't gotten prompt medical attention, he'd be dead right now."

"He got prompt medical attention because I called for it."

Her brief laugh was shrill and humorless. "How *kind* of you. How very *thoughtful.* Do you always call for an ambulance when you shoot someone?"

"Miss Chang, your brother ran me off the road two nights ago. He—"

"*Liar!* You liar! That is *totally* untrue. He was here with me that night. He was *here* when you had your accident. With *me.* And then you sent that big idiot of a cop after him, asking questions, pestering us with his clumsy suspicions—can you blame Paul for getting upset?"

"I can blame him for coming into my office with a loaded pistol."

"All he wanted to do was *talk.*"

"I don't talk to people who point guns at me."

"No, you shoot them. You *bastard.*"

"Look, Miss Chang—"

"I just want you to know that you're going to be very, very sorry for what you did. You're going to regret it for the rest of your life."

"Telephone conversations can be recorded," I said. And so they can be; this one wasn't. She was beginning to annoy me. "You might want to be careful what sort of threats you make."

"I don't need to make threats. I'm telling you. You're going to be very sorry." And then she hung up.

I sat back. Almost immediately, the phone rang. I leaned forward, picked it up. "Hello."

Justine Bouvier's expansive voice came trilling down the line. "*Joshua!* What *is* this I hear about you shooting Paul Chang?" A small quick bark of delighted laughter. "You certainly know how to bring a little excitement into a dull old town, darling. A shootout at the O.K. Corral! I want to hear every single delicious detail."

"Sorry, Justine, I can't talk right now. I'm hemorrhaging." I hung up.

To prevent her getting through again, I lifted the phone once more and dialed Eliza Remington's number. No answer.

So far, I still hadn't been able to reach Peter Jones. I dialed his number.

This time, he answered.

"Peter, this is Joshua Croft."

"Good. I just called you, about five minutes ago."

"I've been trying to reach you for the past few days."

"Yeah, I haven't been answering my phone. Listen. Could you get out here? Out to my place?"

"Why?"

"I don't want to say over the telephone. But it's important. And I think it'll be helpful to you."

"I'll leave now."

THE WEATHER WAS still unseasonably warm as I drove north, out of Santa Fe, through the badlands. The snow had melted everywhere but in the mountains, where it lay bright blinding white against the powder blue backdrop of sky. A few big fluffy clouds hung up there, motionless, looking as though they'd always been hanging exactly there, would always be hanging there.

Despite the stiffness in my muscles and joints, my mood was better than it had been earlier. Partly, I suppose, because at some level, before I'd talked to her, I'd been concerned about dealing with Paul Chang's sister. I had known that I would have to, and hadn't known what I was going to say. As it turned out, she hadn't given me a chance to say much of anything. In a way, her anger and her refusal to listen had let me off the hook. I felt, if not absolved, then at least relieved.

If she wanted to lay some Saku double whammy on me, that was her business. I'd just have to potter along, regardless.

I was feeling expectant, as well. Maybe Peter Jones did have information that would be helpful, that would let me crack this case.

And it was a beautiful day, and this was the first fairly long trip I'd taken in the Jeep. The beast rode well, its big engine purring comfortably beneath the expanse of hood. I was perched higher than I'd been in the station wagon, which permitted me to look down, disdainfully, at the drivers of lower, less aggressive vehicles. The car and I spent some time developing an intangible bond between man and machine.

It was about two o'clock when I pulled into the long, straight driveway worn in the flat caliche. The narrow tower in which Peter Jones lived was still huddling at the base of the immense red column of rock that loomed behind it. But today, with the sun nearly overhead and its light rolling out across the high desert, the building seemed less bizarre, less forbidding. It looked merely quirky, like a playhouse erected out here in the emptiness by some goofy kid.

A second car was parked beside Peter Jones's ancient Karman Ghia. It was a Cadillac Seville, an old one, and I knew that I'd seen it before. After a moment, I remembered where. It had been parked outside Eliza Remington's mock Tudor home, on the hill overlooking Santa Fe.

I knocked on the door. Peter Jones opened it. He was wearing black again: denim shirt, denim slacks. Maybe, I told myself, he always wore black. Maybe he was an existentialist. Maybe he was Zorro.

I'd been spending too much time with these people. My thought processes were being addled.

His handsome Gothic face suddenly looked puzzled. "What happened to you?"

"Automobile accident."

He nodded. The puzzlement went away, but the face was still strained, the skin still tight, as though he were worried. "Come on in," he told me.

Eliza Remington sat at one end of the futon sofa. She wore black shoes, black stockings, a gray silk dress buttoned all the way up to the Peter Pan collar, and a matching jacket. At her neck was a black silk scarf. In her hand was a glass of something that looked like it might have been poured from the bottle of Jameson's Irish Whiskey that sat on the coffee table. She had told me, I remembered, that she never drank.

"You want a drink?" Peter Jones asked me. He seemed awkward, tentative. "Or some tea? Some coffee?"

"Nothing, thanks."

Peter looked at Eliza Remington, who said nothing, merely sat and stared bleakly at me. Peter turned to me. "Sorry," he said. "Have a seat." He sat down himself on the other end of the couch, glanced again at Eliza.

I sat in the black canvas director's chair.

Eliza suddenly spoke. "Did Paul Chang do that to you?" She nodded toward the foam collar at my neck.

"Probably?"

"And you shot him?"

"It's a bit more complicated than that."

"But you shot him. I heard about it this morning."

"I shot him."

She frowned, looked down, shook her head. She turned to Peter. She shrugged, quickly, almost bitterly. "You wanted to tell him. Tell him." She drank some whiskey and sat back, holding the glass on her lap. She stared at me.

Peter glanced at her, turned back to me. "I haven't been answering my phone," he said. "This whole thing, Quentin getting killed, then Leonard, I guess it's thrown me for a loop. So I've been hiding out. Meditating. Trying to make sense of it, I suppose. Anyway, Eliza's been trying to reach me since this morning. She knows that I can go for weeks at a time without paying any attention to the phone. And so finally, a couple of hours ago, she drove out to see me."

He hesitated, glanced again at Eliza, who continued to ignore him and stare at me. "Look," he said to me. "Can you make us a promise?"

"What promise?"

"Can you keep Eliza's name out of this?"

"Out of what?"

"I…" He looked at Eliza, looked back at me. "If we tell you something, can you promise us that you won't go to the police with it?"

"That's not a promise I can make. In order to keep my license, I'm required by law to report any felony I learn about. Are we talking felony here?"

Peter frowned. "What if we discuss this…hypothetically? What if we—"

"Oh, for God's sake, Peter," said Eliza. "Forget it. I told you he was a Boy Scout." She tossed back the rest of her drink, looked at me, her face set, her shrewd blue eyes steady behind her spectacles. "My Tarot card. The Death card. It was a forgery."

She leaned forward, loudly set the empty glass down on the coffee table, then sat back, her arms crossed, her head raised, defiant.

"A forgery," I said.

She nodded. "Counterfeit. Phony."

I nodded.

"Fake," she said.

"I get the idea. You forged it?"

She shook her head. "My great-grandfather."

"When?"

"When he was staying in Italy, with Crowley."

"And you've known all along that it was a forgery?"

"Of course I have."

I sat back in the director's chair and looked at Peter Jones.

"Look," he said earnestly, leaning forward with his elbows on his knees and holding out his hands. "Eliza never intended that any of this should happen. Quentin and Leonard getting killed. All the rest. The police can't blame her for that, can they?"

"Did you know about the card?" I asked him.

He sat back defensively. "Not until today," he said. "When Eliza came and told me."

I turned to Eliza. She hadn't moved. "Did anyone else know?" I asked her.

"Leonard."

She was having no problems with her hearing today, I noted. "Leonard Quarry? For how long?"

She frowned impatiently. "For God's sake," she said, "don't you get it? From the beginning. It was his goddamn idea."

A few things suddenly began to make sense. "Quarry was never bidding for a third party," I said. "The two of you were whipsawing Quentin Bouvier. Quarry was jacking up the price."

She nodded.

"How much did he get?"

"He was supposed to get a third. Sixty-six thousand. Sonovabitch wanted half. I didn't think he deserved more than a quarter. If that. We settled on a third." She frowned, quickly, bitterly. That still bothered her.

"Supposed to get?" I said.

"Never gave it to him. All the money's still in my account. After Quentin got killed, I was afraid to transfer the funds. Afraid the police might find out and think that it had something to do with Quentin's death."

"Maybe it did."

She scowled. "Horseshit. Giacomo killed Quentin. Still pissed off about that little hippie girl in Albuquerque."

"And who killed Leonard? Giacomo was in prison when that happened."

Her face was suddenly splotched with red. "I don't know, goddamn it."

Peter Jones leaned forward again, back into the conversation. "Eliza's been concerned," he said to me. "Quentin's death bothered her, of course. And so did Leonard's. And when she heard that you'd...that you and Paul Chang had been involved like that, him ending up in the hospital—"

"Don't be so mealy-mouthed, Peter," Eliza snapped. "I don't give a damn about Paul Chang. Sneaky little arrogant asshole. But too many people are getting hurt. Or killed. Maybe the card isn't responsible. Personally, I don't see how it could be. But if it is, I want all this stopped."

I said to her, "You left a message on my machine this morning."

"Before I came here. Yes. I wanted to find out what was happening."

Peter said, "Eliza's just trying to do the right thing."

"Horseshit," she said. "I want this nonsense to *stop*."

I nodded. "All right," I said to her. "Why don't you start at the beginning."

She frowned, leaned forward, opened the bottle of Jameson's, poured some of the whiskey into her glass. For a teetotaler, she poured a healthy shot. She capped the bottle, drank from the glass, and then sat back, once again holding it on her lap.

She said, "Everything I told you was the truth. About my great-grandparents and Crowley. They lived with him for almost a year, in Sicily. You know that Crowley designed a Tarot deck of his own?"

I shook my head.

"Well," she said, "he was working on that deck while my great-grandparents were there. Kirby—my great-grandfather—was an artist. A damn good one. He was helping Crowley doing drafts of the deck. He and Crowley went to Catania, to look at the Borgia deck—there's a museum in Catania, it's got ten of the cards. Then, one fine day, Crowley had an idea. He asked Kirby if he could make up a copy of the Death card. A copy that could fool people into thinking it was the real thing. Crowley owned a card, genuine, dating from about the same period. Valuable, but nowhere near as valuable as the Borgia card. Same size, same kind of pasteboard. He told Kirby he could paint the card on that."

I asked, "Why did Crowley want to forge the Death card?"

She shrugged. "Who knows? He was a fraud. Maybe he wanted to sell it. Maybe he wanted to brag that he had it."

She drank some more whiskey. "Anyway. Kirby agreed. There were enough descriptions of the card in the literature to make it feasible, and he knew Pinturicchio's style. He stripped the original oils from Crowley's card and painted the Death card onto it. He used the same oils, the same gilt. They baked it in an oven, he and Crowley, to age it." She shrugged. "It fooled people. Everyone who saw it."

"But there are tests now," I said. "Scientific tests. They'd prove that the card was a phony."

Again her frown was impatient. "Quentin was a believer. He'd never have the card tested. Give it up to someone else, maybe get it damaged. Get some idiot scientist's vibrations all over it?" Scornfully, she pressed her lips together and shook her head. "Never. Not Quentin."

I said, "But you must've had something that indicated the card was genuine." Even Quentin couldn't have been fool enough to buy it otherwise.

"Letters from Crowley to my great-grandfather," she said. "I told you, Kirby took the card with him when he left. Crowley was pissed off—the original card had been his, after all. Thing is, he never mentioned in the letters that the card was a fake, just said he wanted it back. Didn't say it was a fake, maybe because he'd already told everyone it was genuine. Afraid, maybe, that Kirby would come back at him with the letters."

She drank some whiskey. "The letters would've been enough, probably, for Quentin. But Leonard wanted the card, too, or said he did, and that was what carried the day."

"And jacked up the price."

She winced slightly. Stiffly, she nodded.

I said, "How did Leonard get involved?"

She sipped from her glass. "I'd told Leonard about the card years ago. Just mentioned it in passing. But Leonard had a memory like an elephant's, especially when it came to money. Last year, I had to sell him some of my things. Some gold, some jewelry. Trying to raise money for Adam, my cousin—that was true, what I told you about Adam. He was dying. And Leonard had the idea that I should get the card from Adam. Put it to good use."

"By scamming Quentin Bouvier."

Another scornful look. "Quentin had more money than he knew what to do with. Two hundred thousand dollars was peanuts to him. And my cousin was dying. He wasn't much, Adam. I used to say, if brains were dynamite, Adam couldn't blow his nose." Still another frown. "But he was family. He was all I had."

A touching moment, perhaps. And perhaps I spoiled it by saying, "But Adam died before Quentin bought the card."

"Too late by then," she snapped, her face red, her voice angry. "Quentin wanted the goddamn card." I suspected that there was some guilt in her anger, and possibly some shame.

I could've been wrong. But at least she hadn't tried to put all the blame on Leonard Quarry. Who was, at the moment, in no position to deny it, or anything else.

Peter Jones had been sitting off to the side, acting as audience to her story. Now he said to me, "What do you think we should do, Mr. Croft?"

To Eliza Remington, I said, "You're going to have to go to the police."

Peter Jones said, "Will it help them? Help them find out who killed Leonard?"

"I don't know. Have they talked with you about the man at Agua Caliente?"

"The thin man with the tan? Yes. They were here two days ago. They asked me if Leonard knew anyone involved in the theater. The only person I could think of was Carol Masters."

I asked Eliza, "Did they talk to you?"

She nodded bleakly. "Asked me the same question. Carol's the only one."

"Is going to the police absolutely necessary?" Peter asked me.

"I'm sorry, but yes, it is." To Eliza: "If you don't, I will. I have to. I told you, up front, what my situation is. And this is information that may be relevant to their investigation. They have to have it."

"How is it relevant?" Peter asked.

"I don't know yet. But if Eliza didn't think it might be relevant, she wouldn't have told you. Or told me."

Eliza frowned "I'd have to give back that damn money, won't I?"

I nodded.

"To Justine," she said.

"Legally, it belongs to her."

She sipped at her drink, frowned again, as though the whiskey had gone sour. "I can't think of anyone else in the world I'd *less* like to give two hundred thousand dollars."

"You're not giving it to her. You're returning it."

"Somehow that's not a hell of a lot of consolation."

Peter Jones asked me, "But the police? What do you think they'll do?"

"That's something else I don't know." I turned to Eliza. "Do you have a lawyer?"

She shook her head.

"I know one," I said. "Would you be able to see her today?"

"Her?" she said.

"Sally Durrell. She's one of the best in the state. She can go with you when you talk to the police."

Another sour frown. "And how much is she going to cost me?"

"You'll have to discuss that with her. But the police, the D.A.'s office, they're going to see this as major fraud. If I were you, I'd get the best lawyer I could afford."

She pursed her lips. "I have some money coming in. From England. From the sale of Adam's house."

I shrugged. "It's up to you."

She drank some whiskey. Frowned again. Nodded. "I'll talk to her."

"Does this help *you*, Mr. Croft?" Peter Jones asked me. "With Giacomo? Knowing about the card?"

"Maybe. No way to tell right now." I turned back to Eliza. "Did anyone else know that the card was a forgery?"

"No one."

"Not even Quarry's wife?"

"I told you. Sierra's an idiot. Leonard would've never told her what he was doing."

"So presumably, whoever has the card still thinks that it's genuine."

She nodded, sipped some whiskey. "Unless he's had it tested."

I doubted that he had, whoever he was. He couldn't have had it tested without his answering a lot of questions.

She cleared her throat. "Mr. Croft?" she said.

"Yeah?"

"Do you honestly believe that the card is the reason for all this? For Quentin's death? For Leonard's?" She was still sitting upright, her head raised, but there was a brittle note of tension in her voice, as though she were bracing herself for my answer, or daring me to give one.

I suppose I could have sugarcoated it for her. Even if the cops went lightly with her, she was in for a rough time. But if she and Leonard Quarry hadn't tried to con Quentin Bouvier out of two hundred thousand dollars, then maybe Quarry and Bouvier would still be alive.

"Yeah," I said. "I do."

USING PETER JONES'S telephone, I called Sally, told her what was going on. When I told her that the card was a forgery, she muttered another one of those technical legal terms. When I asked her about meeting with Eliza, she said that she'd be free at five that afternoon. Then she hung up. People keep doing that to me.

I said my goodbyes to Peter and Eliza. She was still sitting on the futon sofa, still sipping at her Irish whiskey, her face empty. Walking me out to the Jeep, Peter Jones assured me that he'd drive her into Santa Fe for the meeting with Sally.

I drove back to town, trying to think of a way that what I'd learned would help me prove that Giacomo Bernardi hadn't killed Quentin Bouvier. I couldn't.

At the office, there were three messages on the machine. One was from Hector, telling me that Paul Chang had been moved from Intensive Care. One was from Rita, saying she'd be late coming back tonight, asking me to come over to her house tomorrow morning. But the first message was from Justine Bouvier:

"Listen, Mr. Asshole Private Detective. How *dare* you hang up on me? No one treats me like that." Click.

I was putting myself in solid with the New Age community. Pretty soon, if I wasn't careful, evil spirits would start appearing in my refrigerator, hovering over the Cheez Whiz. Or one morning I'd roll out of bed and my arms and legs would fall off.

I finished my reports, thought about going to the pool, decided that my body was so stiff I'd probably sink like a stone. Went home, stir-fried some chicken, read for a while, went to bed. Lay there, trying to puzzle everything out. Didn't succeed. Felt as though I never would. Finally fell asleep.

Next day, it was all over.

THE SUN .

"IT DOESN'T MAKE any sense," I said. "I never really bought the idea that Leonard Quarry was killed by a hit man. Seems to me, a professional wouldn't have screwed around with an ice pick, especially not in a public place. He'd have shot Quarry in private, and then walked. And a hit man is even less likely now, when we know there was no third party involved in the bidding for the card. Quarry was only bidding to raise the price, and his own share."

Rita nodded. "Did Eliza Remington meet with Sally?"

With a temperature lazing in the upper fifties, the Sunday morning was warmer than any February morning in Santa Fe has a right to be. The air was clear and still and it smelled of pine. The sky was blue and cloudless. Rita was wearing dark brown boots with low heels, lightweight tan wool slacks, and a pale brown turtleneck sweater beneath her new leather jacket. The slacks and the sweater were also new, purchased yesterday, presumably, in Albuquerque. Her purse was slung over her left shoulder and she carried her cane in her right hand. So far, she hadn't really used it. But at the moment we were only a hundred yards or so down

.he Ski Basin Road from the entrance to her driveway. We were making the walk that Rita had promised herself, and promised me, when she had first been imprisoned in the wheelchair. I had told her what I'd learned yesterday, from Eliza Remington and from Carol Masters.

Today she had been dressed and ready, cane in hand, when I arrived. "Let's go," she had said as soon as she opened the door.

"Go where?"

She had smiled. "To the Plaza. I told you I'd walk down there today. Are you up to it?"

I had frowned. "Are you sure *you* are?"

"Positive." She had stepped out onto the front porch, shut the door behind her.

I had said, "It's almost two miles to the Plaza, Rita."

She had laughed. "Joshua, you've been trying to get me to walk down there for as long as I can remember. I must've walked twice that much in Albuquerque yesterday." Slipping her arm into mine, she had smiled up at me. "Come on."

When she saw the Cherokee parked big and bold in her driveway, she had concealed her enthusiasm for the machine, or possibly her envy, behind a merely casual comment: "It's a pretty car."

"Pretty?" I said. "It's beyond pretty, Rita."

She had smiled. "Are you going to give it a name? Ursula? Nellybelle?"

"No one likes sarcasm in a woman. It's a scientific fact."

She had grinned at me.

And now we were walking arm in arm along the side of the road, Rita on the outside. I was a bit worried. The surface here was uncertain—pebbles and grit, the occasional beer can—and the traffic was fairly heavy, locals and tourists driving up to the Basin so they could ride a pair of sticks down the sunlit slopes. We were walking on the left side of the road, just like they tell you to do in elementary school. Every time a car zoomed by, its slipstream slapped rude and cold against my face and whisked at Rita's long black hair.

"Yeah," I told her. "I talked to Sally this morning. Sh
called Herb Maslow at the D.A's office. She and Eliza me
with him last night and Eliza signed a statement. She'll b
charged on Monday. Sally convinced Maslow not to hol
her until then. Pointed out that Eliza had come in of he
own free will."

"Will the police be releasing any information about th
card?" Rita asked.

"Sally convinced Maslow not to. He's like everybody els
at the D.A.'s office—he thinks that Giacomo is guilty. Bu
Sally persuaded him that if he *is* guilty, releasing the infor
mation wouldn't make any difference. And if he isn't, an
it gets out that the card is worthless, then whoever has it wi
probably toss it. And then zap, no evidence."

"Maslow's being very cooperative."

"I think he's got the hots for Sally."

"Joshua." Mildly reproving. "What about bail for Eliza
Will that be a problem?"

"I doubt it. Sally says that Eliza can borrow money o
her house, if that's necessary. But she says she'll probabl
be released on her own recognizance."

"What sort of a sentence does she think Eliza will re
ceive?"

"Whatever it is, she thinks it'll be suspended. Eliza vol
unteered her confession, and on Monday she'll be return
ing the money to Justine Bouvier."

Rita smiled. "That must make Eliza happy."

"I think there's a part of her that would rather go to th
chair."

Her smile broadened. "At least it'll make Justine Bou
vier happy."

"Yeah. I'm sure it'll make Justine very happy."

She squeezed my arm. "You don't like these people ver
much, do you?"

A Porsche ripped by us, upshifting theatrically. Porsche
tend to do that.

"Some of them I don't like at all," I said. "Justine. Ve
ronica Chang. Did I tell you that Veronica's going to pu

some weird kind of hoodoo on me? Turn me into a snail. Or a cockroach."

"Or a grown-up," she smiled. "Yes, you did. What about the others?"

"Well, Carl Buffalo's a moron. What's his name, the writer, he's a jerk."

"Bennett Hadley. You're sounding a little bitter, Joshua."

"Yeah. Did you ever get Hadley's medical records off the computer?"

"No. I didn't think it was necessary. It's not likely, I think, that he killed Quentin Bouvier. And obviously he didn't kill Leonard Quarry. So his headaches aren't really any of our business."

"Obviously *none* of them killed Leonard Quarry. The guy with the ice pick must be a figment of the imagination. Quarry must not be dead."

The gravel crunched and clicked beneath our feet.

"What do you think about Brad Freefall and Sylvia Morningstar?" she asked me.

"As killers?"

"As people."

"I don't know. I suppose their intentions are good. I think they're sincere about what they're doing. But I don't know. I wonder whether it's not basically dangerous. Sylvia might be using her crystals to treat someone who really requires traditional medicine."

"Perhaps," she said. "But on the other hand, perhaps there are people whom she genuinely helps."

I frowned. "By giving them some kind of hope, you mean."

"At least that, yes. But you know about the work that's been done on the psychological side of healing. Imagining. Visualization. It's possible that Sylvia is providing a belief system that these people can accept. And possible that the beliefs actually enable them to heal themselves."

"Or maybe her crystals have some real mojo working."

She smiled. "Or maybe that."

"I think I'll stick with penicillin."

Another smile. "What about Sierra Quarry?"

"Kind of a space cadet, I thought."

"And Peter Jones? You liked him, you said."

"I did. I do. And I like Carol Masters, too. She's what I've been searching for all my life. A happy medium."

Rita's elbow thumped into my side. I laughed. I said, "I'm not so sure about her friend Araxys, though."

"He said some interesting things, from what you tell me."

"Love dancing with Love? Yeah. I liked that."

"I was thinking about something else he said."

"What?"

She said nothing. When I turned, I saw that she was smiling one of her small secret smiles.

I stopped walking. Rita stopped beside me. "Shit," I said.

She looked up at me innocently. "What?"

"You know something, don't you, Rita? You only smile like that when you know something that I don't. What is it?"

Rita laughed and tugged at my arm. "Come on. Let's keep walking."

A Ford station wagon whooshed by, skis tethered to the rack on its roof. We had stopped at a spot where the road dipped abruptly, rolling down into the city. All of downtown Santa Fe was spread out below us—the trees, the adobe walls, the tin roofs of the homes and shops, the mismatched towers of the cathedral. Far off to the west, the purple-gray slopes of the Jemez Mountains rimmed the horizon. I may complain about the tourists and the sharks who feed on them, but all I need is a walk like this to remind me that I probably wouldn't be happy living anywhere else.

We walked. "So what is it?" I asked her.

She smiled. "Let's go back to the beginning," she said. "What was the first assumption we made about the killer?"

"The killer of Quentin Bouvier? That he was probably one of the people who was at the party that night, down in La Cienega."

She nodded. "And when did we put that assumption aside?"

"I love it when you do this. The Socratic method. They killed Socrates, you know."

"When?" she asked me again.

"Jeez, I dunno. The fifth century before Christ, I think." Her elbow thumped me again. Harder.

"Why did we drop the assumption?" she asked.

"I haven't really dropped it. I just don't see how I can justify it."

"Why?"

"Because someone stuck an ice pick into Leonard Quarry."

"And from his description, that person wasn't one of the people in La Cienega."

"Right."

"And you want to believe that Bouvier and Quarry were both killed by the same person."

"Yeah. The two of them die within a week of each other. They're both involved with the Tarot card. It seems to me that the deaths have to be connected. But the guy with the ice pick—I don't know who he is, or how he fits in. Like I said, he doesn't make any sense."

She nodded. "Have you checked with Motor Vehicles about the truck that ran you off the road?"

I turned to her, frowning. "What's that got to do with anything?"

"Have you?"

I sighed. "Hector told me it didn't belong to Paul Chang. It must've belonged to someone he knew. But I've been a little busy lately."

"I checked. There are quite a few ten-year-old Chevrolet pickups in the state of New Mexico."

"Yeah?"

"To be on the safe side, I asked for a list of all the Chevy pickups that were between twelve and eight years old. Would you hold this for a minute?" She handed me her cane, swung her purse around, opened it, pulled out a folded sheet of paper.

She offered me the paper. I traded her the cane, opened the paper. Not surprisingly, it was a list of Chevrolet trucks, with the owners' names and addresses.

"That's only one sheet," she said. "There were four of them."

I was studying the paper. No names leaped out at me. I looked at Rita. "So?"

"The fifth listing from the top."

I looked at the paper. "Fred Richards?" I looked at Rita. "Who's he?"

"I'm fairly certain that he's the owner of the truck that ran you down."

I frowned. "Who the hell is he, Rita? Why would he run me down?"

"What I said was that his truck ran you down. I didn't say that *he* ran you down. According to Motor Vehicle records, he's in his late seventies. He lives with his son. I can't really see him racing up and down the mountain."

"What are you talking about?"

"Joshua, look at the address."

I did. I looked at Rita. "But..."

"Think back to the day you were run off the road," she said. "Before you left for your appointment with Veronica Chang, who did you talk to? What did you say?"

I thought about it for a moment. I mentioned some names. At one of them, Rita nodded.

"No," I said. "But... wait a minute." I frowned again. She smiled.

"Rita," I said.

Her smile grew wider.

WE TALKED ABOUT Rita's theory, and what we should do about it, and what we could do, all the way into town, down the Ski Basin Road, and then along Washington Street, where the thin shade beneath the leaf-striped trees chilled the air. Back in the sunshine, we passed the public library, and then the Burrito Factory. We crossed Washington, dodged through the mob that milled at the entrance to the portico of the Governor's Palace. We crossed Palace Avenue, and finally we were on the Plaza.

It was crowded, as bustling in the warm winter sunlight as if this were a day in summer. Mothers strolled with their children. Couples ambled. Businessmen marched. Cowboys and pigeons strutted. Nearly all of them, it seemed to me, eyed the foam collar around my neck. Near the Memorial, some teenage boys lightly kicked and lightly tapped with sneakered feet at a frayed rubber ball. More teenagers, boys and girls, most of them sporting punk haircuts and army surplus clothes, sat in small clusters on the yellowed grass. The grass looked cold to me, but I hadn't been a teenager for a very long time now. And hadn't been one for very long, when I was. None of these people would be, either, but I didn't plan to tell them that. They wouldn't have believed me anyway.

At the northeast corner, just at the entrance, I stopped and looked at Rita. The olive skin of her face was slightly flushed and her eyes were shining.

It had been almost three years since she told me she would make this walk. I smiled. "So," I said. "You did it."

She grinned. Rita has an extensive repertoire of expressions—grimaces, frowns, smiles that range from thoughtful to amused to ecstatic. This was definitely a grin, big and bright and delighted. "I did," she said, "didn't I?"

I bent down to kiss her and her arms came around me. For a moment, the Plaza vanished.

It, and the rest of the world, reappeared suddenly when someone tapped me on the shoulder.

I released Rita, turned.

A big broad-shouldered man wearing boots, jeans, a zippered fawn jacket, a tattersall shirt, and a wide, pleased smile. "May I have this dance?" he asked Rita.

She laughed and stepped forward to take his arms and to kiss, and get kissed on the cheek.

"Hector," I said. I looked at Rita. "Is this a coincidence?"

She laughed again. Eyes gleaming, face alight, she looked as young as the children scattered about the grass. "I asked Hector to meet us."

"Does he know about . . . ?"

"Not yet."

"About what?" Hector asked.

"Rita has an idea," I said.

He smiled. "Great. Rita's ideas are always nasty. But let's not talk here. I've got us a table at the Ore House. Oh, Josh?"

"Yeah?"

"Love the collar. It's really you."

THE TABLE WAS out on the Ore House's open balcony, beneath a radiant heater affixed to the ceiling. Hector ordered a beer, Rita and I ordered hot spiced cider laced with Applejack. Sitting beside the white wooden railing, we could look down on the people thronging the Plaza. We did more talking than looking down.

When Rita had finished explaining, Hector sat back and sipped at his beer. He looked at me. "So it wasn't Paul Chang."

"Who ran me down? No, not if Rita's right."

He nodded. Then he smiled, shook his head. "Well, it probably won't take much to tie this guy to Quarry's death. The attendant at the pool—what was his name?"

"Paco," I said.

Hector nodded. "He should be able to make an identification. But that's not going to help you with Bouvier. And that's what you're supposed to be working on."

I said, "That Tarot card is probably there. At the house."

"You'd need a warrant." He frowned. "Maybe you could work something with Paco. Have him make his identification from a distance. Take his deposition. A judge might buy that." He shrugged. "But I can't help you. It's out of my jurisdiction."

"You can talk to Hernandez," Rita said.

Hector smiled. "I was beginning to wonder where I fit in."

"And I don't think we'll need Paco," she said.

"This is the good part," I told Hector.

He smiled.

"I think," Rita said, "that we can get a confession."

JUDGEMENT.

THE BLEACHED SKULL that hovered over the doorway had stopped dripping. The snow that had covered the lawn was gone. An old Volvo sedan, its fading black paint streaked and dusty, had beached itself in the driveway. Presumably, it had belonged to the owner of the house.

I knocked on the door and waited. After a few moments, Sierra Quarry opened it, pale and beautiful and tentative.

"Oh," she said, and put a slender hand to her breast. Today she was wearing an opened gray cardigan, several sizes too large, over a loosely fitting cotton granny dress, black with white polka dots. Her feet were still bare.

"Hello, Mrs. Quarry," I said. "I was in the neighborhood and I wondered if I could talk to you for a few moments."

"Oh my," she said in her soft solemn voice. "But I've already told you everything I know. And the police."

"I realize that. But I think we may be close to the man who killed your husband. I just need to ask you a few questions. It won't take long, I promise."

"Oh," she said. "Oh. Well."

She stood back and I stepped in. She closed the door and I followed her into the small living room with its fragile embroidered chair and its smell of wood smoke. Sierra Quarry indicated one of the chairs and said, "Please."

She circled around the heavy cherrywood table and lightly sat down on the floral sofa. I lowered myself into the chair. She picked up a blue bundle of knitting from the sofa and placed it in her lap. She smiled at me, tentatively. "I haven't knitted for years. I only just started again. It helps me to relax now. And concentrate. Is it all right? Do you mind?"

"No, of course not."

"Is there something wrong with your neck?"

"I had an accident. I'm supposed to wear this for a while."

"Oh. I'm sorry."

"No need. I'm fine."

She nodded, and tendrils of her long Pre-Raphaelite black hair grazed her shoulders. "It's a sweater," she said, as she arranged the ball of yarn on the sofa. "I made this one"—lightly she touched the sweater she wore—"for Leonard. Years ago. It was too small for him. And now it's too big for me." She smiled sadly.

"I apologize for having to bother you again."

"Oh no," she said. "You have a job to do. I understand." She began to knit, the needles delicately clicking.

"Mrs. Quarry, you have a neighbor. A Fred Richards. Up the road about a quarter of a mile."

She looked up, smiled. "Fred, yes. A sweet old man. His wife died a few years ago."

"Yeah, I just talked to him. He seems very kind. He's very fond of you."

Click, click went the needles. She looked up. "How is Fred? I haven't seen him for a while."

"He's just fine. You haven't seen him for three days, not since you borrowed his pickup truck."

She nodded over her knitting, then looked up. She smiled. "Leonard's car, the Volvo, it has one of those stick shifts."

She shrugged lightly, helplessly. "I've never learned to drive one."

"You can drive a pickup truck, though."

"Well, yes. That one. It's an automatic."

"I was pretty impressed with the way you handled it last Thursday night, on the Ski Basin Road."

She was good. She rested her hands on her lap and she produced a completely convincing frown of puzzlement. But I'd known, before I started talking to her, that she was good. "I'm sorry?" she said. "The Ski Basin Road? In Santa Fe? But I haven't been there for years. What on earth are you talking about, Mr. Croft?"

"Mrs. Quarry, I spoke with you on Thursday at about two in the afternoon. You borrowed Fred Richards's pickup at two-thirty. You told him you were driving into Espanola to see a friend. It's only about thirty miles from here to Espanola. You're probably not aware of this, but Mr. Richards keeps track of his odometer. Neither he nor his son has driven the truck since you returned it, early on Friday morning. The odometer says that you traveled over a hundred and sixty miles. That's more like the distance from here to Santa Fe and back."

For the first time, she laughed. Lightly, easily, totally unconcerned. "Is all this because of some silly odometer? Mr. Croft, I went for a long drive before I went to Espanola. I was unhappy. Depressed. This has been a terrible time for me. I wanted to get away from myself for a while. Whenever I feel that way, I like to take a long drive in the country."

She was so convincing that for a moment I wondered whether Rita had gotten it all wrong. "I didn't leave my office," I said, "until five o'clock that afternoon. You had plenty of time to get down there, wait outside until I left, then follow me home. You knew what my car looked like. You'd seen it here, when I came to talk to your husband. You waited outside my house, then followed me again when I drove up to the Ski Basin. I'm not sure why you didn't try anything on the way up—maybe you thought that pushing

me into the side of the mountain wouldn't be lethal enough.
But pushing me over it, that was fine with you. And so you
drove past the Big Trees Lodge when I parked, turned
around, and waited again. When I drove out, you picked me
up, followed me, and tried to run me off the road. You tried
twice. It worked the second time.''

Her mouth was open in surprise. "But Mr. Croft,
that's... that's *ridiculous*. That's *crazy*. Why would I do
something like that?''

"Because when I talked to you that afternoon, I made
you nervous. I told you that I was going to learn who killed
your husband. That I was determined to learn. The police
wanted to learn, too, but I was the one who believed his
death was connected to Quentin Bouvier's. The police didn't
believe that. And I mentioned Starbright, Giacomo Bernardi's friend in Albuquerque, the young woman who killed
herself. The police knew about her, but they never mentioned her to you. I know they didn't. I asked Hernandez.
But I mentioned her. And you decided that I was getting too
dangerous. It was time to get rid of me.''

Looking confused, baffled, she shook her head. "But I
told you, I never even heard of that Starbright person.''

"I think you did. I don't know who told you, or when.
Probably your husband. But it was because you knew about
her, knew about Giacomo's involvement with a woman who
hanged herself, that you tried to frame him for Quentin
Bouvier's murder. When you stole the Tarot card.''

"The *Tarot* card! My God, Mr. Croft, you are completely insane.''

"It's a fake," I said.

She blinked. "I'm sorry? What?''

"The card. The Death card. It's a fake. A forgery. It was
done by Eliza Remington's great-grandfather. It may have
some value as a curio, but otherwise it's worthless. Your
husband and Eliza Remington were conning Quentin Bouvier. The only reason your husband was bidding on the card
was to raise its price. Sweeten the deal that Eliza made with
Bouvier.''

She shook her head. "No. No. Leonard would've..." Her voice trailed off.

I think she'd been about to say that Leonard would have told her. And then she'd realized, of course, that he wouldn't have. He never talked with her about business.

Just then, and only for an instant, I caught my first brief glimpse of the real person who hid behind the role she played. Her eyes darted to the left, desperate.

Looking for help? Looking for the card?

And then, effortlessly, she slipped back into her part. Her level glance met mine and she shook her head. "No. You're lying, Mr. Croft. I don't know why you're lying, or why you're saying all these terrible things. But I do know you're lying about the card."

"I'm not lying. It's worthless. It's just an old piece of pasteboard with some paint on it. And you killed Quentin Bouvier to get it. And you killed your husband."

Rita's plan had been for me to keep impersonating William Powell until my suave exposition convinced Sierra that I knew everything. At that point, according to the script, I would offer to keep silent about my knowledge, in exchange for a large fee. When Sierra agreed, we would have our confession. It was a swell plan. It always worked for William Powell.

Unfortunately, Sierra and I never reached that point.

She came over the coffee table in a leap, more quickly than I would've believed possible. Her mouth in a rictus, both hands wrapped around one of her knitting needles, its point lunging for my heart, she dived at me.

I caught her forearms in my hands but our combined weight was too much for the antique chair. It toppled backward, legs shattering as it went. I landed with a thump on the floor and she landed with a thump on me, slamming my breath away. Her teeth were bared, her eyes narrowed. Fury and desperation gave her an impossible strength—her arms were trembling, tendons taut, as she tried to drive the needle into my chest. The needle's point twitched in the air, only inches above me.

I rolled into my side, pulling her with me, away from the wreck of the chair, and she started using her knee, ramming it at me, going for my crotch. I swiveled atop her, pinning her legs beneath mine. Her head darted forward like a cobra's and she sank her teeth into the fingers of my left hand.

I may have squealed. I do know that the pain suddenly energized me. I slipped my right hand loose from her forearm and I popped her, as hard as I could, on the point of the chin. Her head banged back against the floor and bounced once.

Her eyes lost their focus. Her arms lost their strength and the knitting needle fell harmlessly away, onto the floor. I rolled off her and sat up, panting.

Dimly I heard a door crash open. The cavalry had arrived. Hernandez and Green rushed into the room, waving guns. Green, I noticed, was still wearing his earphones. I wondered what the struggle with Sierra had sounded like, broadcast from the concealed mike I wore.

"You okay?" Hernandez snapped at me.

I nodded.

Someone else came rushing into the room. Rita. "Joshua!" She ran to me, and I saw that she was limping. *She shouldn't be running,* I thought. "Are you all right?" she said as she knelt down beside me.

I nodded some more. "Yeah. Fine."

"What happened to your hand?"

I looked. Blood was streaming from my fingers, pattering against the wooden floor, pooling there. "She bit me."

"Probably need a rabies shot," Hernandez said. He had moved around the unconscious Sierra. To Green, he said, "This guy's good, huh? He gets the suspect to eat right out of his hand." And then, bending down onto one knee, holding the gun on her with his right hand, he reached forward with his left and twined his fingers in her long, black, Pre-Raphaelite hair. He tugged, and her wig came free.

He stood up, holding it away from him as though it were a dead raccoon. "Shit," he said.

"Sierra?" Giacomo Bernardi said. "She is a man?"

I nodded. "Yeah."

Monday morning. He and I were back in the Interview Room. In his droopy T-shirt and orange pants, Bernardi looked exactly the same. Since I'd last seen him, however, I myself had been somewhat modified. Bruises, a foam collar, bulky bandages on the first two fingers of my left hand.

"But how?" he asked me.

"How what?"

"How could she..." He frowned, blinked. "He? How could he do such a thing? To be living as a wife? And no one knows?"

I didn't blame him for his confusion about the pronoun. I'd been a bit confused myself. But Sierra had lived most of her life as a woman, thought of herself as a woman, and if that was what she wanted, that was fine with me. So long as she didn't try to stab me with a knitting needle again.

"It was easy enough," I said. "When she and Quarry got married, no one in San Francisco knew she was a man. She had false papers saying that she was Maria Sorenson. She changed her name to Sierra when the two of them came to Santa Fe. She never went out as a man in San Francisco, and she never did here."

"So the marriage was legal?"

"No. It was invalid. But no one knew that until now."

He thought for a moment, brow furrowed, his hand rubbing at his salt and pepper stubble. He looked at me. "And he steals the card for the money?"

"Yeah. She didn't plan to kill Bouvier, she says. She planned to slip into his room, grab the card, and slip away. But Bouvier woke up and saw her. She hit him with the piece of quartz , but she realized that that was just a temporary solution to her problem. Bouvier had seen her. She'd never be able to keep the card and, worse, she'd be arrested. Her real identity—who she was, what she was—would be revealed. She knew about you and Starbright, knew about the fight you'd had with Bouvier that night, and decided that you'd make a nice patsy. She went to the closet in your

room, got your scarf, came back and hanged Bouvier. You
were still asleep in the library.''

"She could do that? Lift him up to the ceiling?''

"She's strong when she wants to be.'' As I could attest.
"After she killed him, she ran back to the guest house,
where she was staying with Quarry. He was still asleep in the
next room. The guest house is connected to the main house,
and from the window, she was able to watch the corridor.
She saw you go into Bouvier's room, saw you run out again.
She saw you leave the house. When you did, she ran back to
your room, burned the card's leather folder in your fireplace. There was some blood on her arms, from Bouvier,
and she rinsed it off in your shower. She knew about foren-
sic evidence. She was clever.

"Clever, yes, but stupid also. Someone could see her
when she was running. Someone could wake up and come
into the hallway and see her.''

"Yeah. She was improvising. But she didn't do too badly.
She managed to get you locked up in here.''

Giacomo frowned. "And she kills, *he* kills his—'' He
frowned again, blinked. "He kills Leonard Quarry?''

"She thought, she says, that Leonard had figured out
she'd stolen the card. Probably he hadn't. Probably, if he
had, he would've told her it was a fake. And from what she
says about Leonard, he would've laughed about it. The two
of them had been having a rough time for the past couple of
years. She wanted out of the relationship. Leonard wouldn't
let her go. She had no money, nothing of her own. Everything was in Leonard's name. She couldn't divorce him,
because they weren't legally married. She was trapped, she
says. And Leonard made a point of reminding her that she
was trapped. The card, and the money it represented,
would've been her way out. But then, according to her,
Leonard was beginning to suspect that she'd stolen it.
They'd had a big fight just before he left the house that day.
She was still simmering. When I showed up, asking about
the card, she was afraid Leonard would tell me his suspicions. Or so she says.''

"But the police, they talk to her too. She did not kill him then. And you say he did not know."

"She was ready to dump Leonard. And she'd learned how easily murder could solve her problems. By then, I think, she was turned on by the idea of killing. Turned on by actually doing it, the danger, the role-playing, and then turned on by getting away with it. I think it appealed to her actress instincts."

Rita, who tends in general to be more compassionate than I, had a different notion. She believed that Sierra had been demonstrating the self-destructiveness that murderers sometimes show—unconscious guilt driving them to increasingly more dangerous behavior. Maybe. But Sierra hadn't seemed to be displaying much unconscious guilt when she was trying to turn my heart into a shish kebab.

"So she improvised again," I said. "She had some dark body makeup—she owned just about every kind of cosmetic that exists. She slapped it on, dressed up in a pair of jeans, a shirt, and running shoes, got an ice pick from the kitchen, and then walked along the river to the springs."

"But this, this was stupid too, no?"

"Yeah. But she got away with it again. Stabbed Leonard, dressed, left the springs, walked back to her house. Wiped off the makeup, burned the towels and the clothes in the wood stove. By the time the police arrived, she was ready to play the bereaved widow. She played it well. But she was a natural actress. She'd been playing a part for most of her adult life."

Giacomo shook his head. "Amazing, eh?"

"Yeah."

"Amazing," he said, looking off. He turned to me and his face brightened. "But now it is all over, eh? Soon I can leave this place."

"Well, no," I said. "Not exactly, Giacomo."

He frowned again, confused. "No? Why? It is all over now."

I reached into my jacket pocket. The movement wa
painful. Falling backward in Sierra's chair had done some
thing to my back. I was getting too old for all this.

I took out the Polaroid, handed it to him. It showed
medallion, a small ebony ankh enclosed in a delicatel
molded circlet of gold.

"You recognize that?" I asked him.

He shook his head. "No." He looked up at me.

"The police found it on the floor of Starbright's house
the day she died."

He looked at the photo again, shook his head. "I neve
see it."

"That's funny," I said. "There's a guy down in Albu
querque who claims that Starbright gave it to you."

"No," he said. He shook his head. "Never. I never se
this thing." He put the Polaroid on the table.

"He's the same guy who claims he saw you leave Sta
bright's house on the morning she died."

"No." He shook his head. "I never see her that day."

"The guy's name is Brody. William Brody. He was Sta
bright's next-door neighbor. He was moving, leaving th
state, on the same day Starbright was killed. He moved t
California, never even knew that she'd died. The Albu
querque cops tried to track him down, but they never foun
him. After the suicide verdict was handed down, the
stopped trying."

Giacomo shook his head again. "I never see her tha
day."

"My partner doesn't like loose ends. She was down i
Albuquerque this week, and one of the things she did dow
there was talk to the police about Starbright's death. Sh
learned about Brody and she decided to find him. She'
good at that. Finding people. Uses a computer. Turns ou
that Brody had moved back to New Mexico. Back to A
buquerque, as a matter of fact. She talked to him."

"He is lying."

"By now, naturally, he'd learned that Starbright wa
dead. That she committed suicide. Supposedly. But he'

married now. Whatever interest he had in Starbright is gone. He never bothered to find out exactly when she died.''

Giacomo shook his head. "No."

"He's a jeweler. He made the ankh, gave it to Starbright. When he asked her about it, a few months later, she told him he'd given it to you."

"No, never. I never see it."

"He remembers because he was pissed off. He'd made it for her, not for you. So how did the ankh get back to Starbright's house, Giacomo?"

"I *tell* you, I never see this thing." Beneath his stubble, the pale skin of his face was growing pink.

"The ankh," I said, "all by itself, doesn't prove much. But his testimony that he saw you leaving her house at ten o'clock that morning—well, Giacomo, that doesn't look good. According to the medical examiner, ten o'clock is about the time she died."

"Lies," he said stubbornly. "All lies."

"Maybe. Anyway, you'll only be here for a little while longer. The Albuquerque cops are sending someone up to get you. Probably today."

I stood. Giacomo looked up at me, his face red now, his features sullen.

"See you," I said. "You can keep the Polaroid."

OUTSIDE IN THE parking lot, I unlocked the Cherokee and climbed in. The sky was gray now. Overnight, the temperature had dropped nearly thirty degrees. A storm was due today.

I drove out onto Airport Road and headed east.

I kept seeing Giacomo, his sullen face staring up at me.

Sierra Quarry had been sullen, too. Sitting there in her living room, shoulders slumped, she had pouted and sulked as she confessed to two murders. When she talked about killing Quarry, she had begun to cry.

"It was all his fault," she'd said. "I never wanted to kill him. It was all his fault." Tears had rolled down her face and fallen to her lap.

In the end, we all cry for ourselves.

As I drove past Villa Linda Mall, the snow began. A few gray flakes went sliding past the windshield.

I wondered if it snowed in Cancun.

XXI

THE WORLD.

SIERRA QUARRY, whose real name was Robert Eastlake, was tried on two counts of first-degree murder. She dressed as a man in court, in a conservative three-piece suit, very nicely cut, I thought. She repudiated the confession she'd made that day in Agua Caliente and had later signed in Santa Fe. She was acquitted on the first count, the death of Quentin Bouvier. Despite her being in possession of the stolen Tarot card—she claimed that Leonard Quarry had stolen it—the jury felt that reasonable doubt existed. But primarily because of the testimony of Paco Murales, the attendant at the hot springs, she was convicted on the second, the death of Leonard Quarry, and sent to the state penitentiary. I hear she's doing well there.

Giacomo Bernardi copped a plea and was convicted of manslaughter. He, too, is currently a guest of the state.

For a while there, it looked as though I'd be having some legal problems of my own. Veronica Chang apparently decided to opt for litigation over voodoo. I received a notice from a local lawyer which said that Paul Chang planned to sue me for violating his civil rights, and would be asking for enough money in punitive damages to bankroll a small country. Sally Durrell talked to the lawyer. The case never came to court. A few weeks later, Veronica and Paul Chang left Santa Fe.

Rita and I didn't get to Cancun. She had programmed one of her databases to report on the appearance, in any newspaper, of the name Ralph Bonner, that being the alias adopted by Frederick Pressman, a gentleman who had stolen two million dollars from the company for which he worked. About a week before we were due to leave for Mexico, a bank was robbed in Golfito, Costa Rica. The robbers were shot by the police, and turned out to be two American thugs wanted by the F.B.I. One of the witnesses quoted in the A.P. article was a Mr. Ralph Bonner, who had watched the excitement from the window of his new, and apparently flourishing, boutique. The database electronically clipped the article and delivered it to Rita.

She made some phone calls. Four days later, at the expense of Mr. Pressman's former employers, we flew to Costa Rica. Mr. Pressman had been arrested. Rita identified him. The American and Costa Rican authorities arranged his extradition.

Rita and I spent the rest of the month there, nearly two weeks. It didn't snow the entire time.

THREE BEDROOMS, ONE CORPSE
Charlaine Harris
An Aurora Teagarden Mystery

First Time In Paperback

A KILLING IN REAL ESTATE

Armed with a hefty inheritance, Aurora "Roe"
Teagarden is embarking on a new career in real estate.
But her first showing is, well, murder…
when the elegant master bedroom reveals the
body of a real-estate broker.

The house was all wrong for Roe's client, anyway. But
the client is definitely right for her. Tall, sexy
and rich, he's just what a thirtyish ex-librarian needs.

But when a second corpse appears at another showing,
it's clear that a killer is on the loose in this cozy
Atlanta suburb. And that Roe's new career may
suddenly come to a dead end.

"[A] high-spirited Southern cozy."—*Publishers Weekly*

Available in September at your favorite retail stores.

Take 3 books and a surprise gift FREE

SPECIAL LIMITED-TIME OFFER

Mail to: **The Mystery Library™**
3010 Walden Ave.
P.O. Box 1867
Buffalo, N.Y. 14269-1867

YES! Please send me 3 free books from the Mystery Library™ and my free surprise gift. Then send me 3 mystery books, first time in paperback, every month. Bill me only $3.69 per book plus 25¢ delivery and applicable sales tax, if any*. There is no minimum number of books I must purchase. I can always return a shipment at your expense and cancel my subscription. Even if I never buy another book from the Mystery Library™, the 3 free books and surprise gift are mine to keep forever.   415 BPY ANQ2

Name	(PLEASE PRINT)	

Address		Apt. No.

City	State	Zip

* Terms and prices subject to change without notice. N.Y. residents add applicable sales tax. This offer is limited to one order per household and not valid to present subscribers.

© 1990 Wolrdwide Library.

EMMA CHIZZIT AND THE
MOTHER LODE MARAUDER

MARY BOWEN HALL
An Emma Chizzit Mystery

First
Time in
Paperback

DEATH PROSPECTS

Emma Chizzit, sixty-something owner of A-1
Salvage, is hired to help with plans to preserve the
historic gold mining town of Buckeye, California.

The savvy sleuth soon discovers that she's not
welcome, as rattlesnakes in picnic baskets and
threatening notes reveal. But the plucky Emma
is not fazed—until murder takes the spotlight.
She must expose dirty town secrets before a rush
of killing strikes the mother lode.

"Good mystery!"   —*Rendezvous*

Available in September at your favorite retail stores.

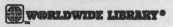

A SAFE PLACE TO DIE
Janice Law

First Time in Paperback

An Anna Peters Mystery

A DANGEROUS PLACE TO LIVE

For the rich and security conscious, Branch Hill offers the posh Estates—an exclusive community of impressive homes and a state-of-the-art security system.

Anna Peters and her artist husband arrive there for his gallery exhibit—but murder steals the show. The victim is a fourteen-year-old girl found bludgeoned near her home.

Anna quickly discovers the gilded Estates are a little tarnished around the polished edges. And when another death occurs, she begins to put together a complicated puzzle as tragic as it is terrifying.

"A sharp-eyed pleasant guide...along dark, peculiar paths."
—*Publishers Weekly*

Available in October at your favorite retail stores.

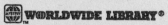
WORLDWIDE LIBRARY ®

PLACE

Live To Regret
Terence Faherty

First Time in Paperback

An Owen Keane Mystery

LOST...AND FOUND

Ex-seminarian turned sleuth Owen Keane has been hired to look into the strange behavior of his friend Harry Ohlman, whose wife, Mary, was tragically killed.

While observing Harry during his retreat in a small seashore town, Owen can't resist the allure of Diana Lord, an enigmatic beauty obsessed by a death that had occurred there many years before.

But as Owen gets closer to the truth about Harry, he is forced to confront his own feelings for Mary and his unsettled score with his friend—as crimes of the heart, past and present, unfold in Spring Lake and a town gives up its secrets.

Available in October at your favorite retail stores.

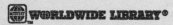

MURDER AT THE CLASS REUNION
TRISS STEIN

A Kay Engels Mystery

First Time In Paperback

CLASS KILLER

After making it "big" as a New York journalist, Kay Engels returns to her twentieth high school reunion, hoping to find a good human interest story.

So when Terry Campbell, voted Best Looking in Her Class, is found strangled in her hotel bed while her classmates danced nearby, Kay's got her story. Terry had always been poison, and age had not impoved her.

As Kay puts her reporter's instincts into police business, she finds romance with the former class bad boy and uncovers a shocking secret in her own past. Then another murder brings her closer to a killer who will give her the story of a lifetime...but she may be too dead to write it.

Available in October at your favorite retail stores.

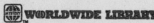

WORLDWIDE LIBRARY®

REUNION